LUCIDITY

LUCIDITY

DAVID CARNOY

THE OVERLOOK PRESS
NEW YORK, NY

This edition first published in hardcover in the United States in 2017
The Overlook Press, Peter Mayer Publishers, Inc.

NEW YORK
141 Wooster Street
New York, NY 10012
www.overlookpress.com
For bulk and special sales, please contact sales@overlookny.com,
or write us at the above address.

Cataloging-in-Publication Data is available from the Library of Congress

Book design and typeformatting by Bernard Schleifer
Manufactured in the United States of America
FIRST EDITION
ISBN 978-1-4683-1087-0
2 4 6 8 10 9 7 5 3 1

For the fantastic four: Natalie, William, Andrew, and Catherine

LUCIDITY

0/ Prologue

THE FIRST CALL CAME IN AT 6:08 AM.

"Send an ambulance to Central Park West and 75th," a male caller said in an eerily measured voice, as if arranging a ride to the airport. "Someone just got hit by a car. There's a body in the middle of the street. I can see it from my window."

"OK, sir," the 911 dispatcher responded. "Let me make sure I heard you correctly. You said someone was hit by a car?"

"Yes."

"How long ago did this happen?"

"Like fifteen seconds ago."

"Did you see it happen?"

"No, I heard it. Get some paramedics here quick."

The line went silent.

"An ambulance and the police are on the way," the dispatcher said after a moment. "Can you tell me what you heard, sir?"

"I heard a screech of tires and a kind of thud. Now this woman is standing outside her car screaming. It's a BMW 3-series."

"You hear screaming now?"

"The woman who hit the person is screaming. I can see the whole thing. I'm on the third floor. Hold on, I'm going to take some pictures."

Another short silence.

"Sir, are you still there?"

"Yeah. She's totally freaking out. You've gotta have more calls coming in."

They did. Another dispatcher was speaking to a woman who lived on the eighth floor of the same apartment building. And a third caller, who identified himself as a doorman, sounded distressed.

"It looks bad, man," he said. "Tell them to hurry."

The first calls came mostly from the north tower of the fabled San Remo, a hulking twin-steepled architectural gem that dominated the western skyline over Central Park. The San Remo was one among many grand pre-war co-ops along Central Park West, the West Side's so-called "gold coast." But it was also grander than most. It even had its own Wikipedia page that included a list of celebrities—past and present—that owned apartments there.

The only eyewitness to the accident, a runner on her way into the park, reached a 911 operator a full five minutes after the first caller. A little breathlessly she explained that she'd just seen a woman get pushed in front of a car.

"I'm sorry I didn't call sooner but I didn't have my phone with me. I had to borrow someone's."

"That's OK," the dispatcher said. "Have you spoken to any police officers yet?"

"No, they're trying to keep everyone away from her. The ambulance just got here. The paramedics are working on her. There's a lot of blood. My God, I hope she isn't dead."

"OK, I need you to stay there and give a statement to a police officer. They need to know what you saw. But I also want you to tell me what you saw and I'll make sure they get it."

The NYPD had a smattering of high-resolution cameras in and around Central Park, but none near the intersections of 74th or 75th and Central Park West; the closest was a block south at 73rd. The San Remo, however, had its own security cameras and one of them did record the accident. The grainy video would support what the jogger told the dispatcher:

"This guy, he looked like a homeless guy, came up to her while she was in the crosswalk," she said. "She was walking her dog. He was slightly behind her to her right. She looked over at him. I don't know if she said anything or not. But suddenly he lunged forward and pushed her into the street just as a car was coming."

The vehicle's front bumper struck the woman just below the knees, taking her legs out from under her. She rolled up onto the hood, ricocheted off the edge of the windshield and corkscrewed gymnasti-cally in the air. Her right hand hit the pavement, followed by her hip and torso, and then her head, face-first. One of her shoes came off and her cell phone skittered across the street, all the way to the other side, where it was found resting next to the back tire of a parked car, the screen cracked but otherwise operational.

"I went over to help," the jogger said, her voice wavering. "I didn't know what to do. I'd never seen anything like that. There was so much blood. It was coming out of her ears."

PART 1

1/ Readers Love Ballsy Women

"MY PROTAGONIST IS THE PROBLEM," THE PROSPECT SAID. "The rest is good."

The rest wasn't good, Fremmer thought. But at least it was bad in a good way. A campy way.

"She use the U word?" he asked the prospect.

"The U word?"

"Unsympathetic."

The prospect's eyes flashed a glint of pain. His name was Brian. Brian Tynan. Compliance officer by day, aspiring novelist by commute, he'd written a zombie techno thriller while riding on Metro North. Croton Falls to Grand Central and back. The first draft took a year. The rewrites another eight months, maybe longer.

"I made the changes she suggested," Brian said, referring to his agent. "I made him more sympathetic. But she won't send it out anymore. Look, the guy, the protagonist, is a tech entrepreneur. He's a little bit of a douchebag. They all are. It's part of their DNA."

Fremmer nodded. They were seated near the front window of the Starbucks on Columbus Avenue and 81st Street. Fremmer had scootered there fifteen minutes earlier from his apartment a few blocks away. Brian was already at a table, waiting for him, not exactly what Fremmer expected. When a guy tells you he's a compliance officer for a bank, you think little bald guy with spectacles. But Brian was tall.

Maybe six-three, a little overweight, big head and features and wavy salt and pepper hair parted neatly to the left. In his late forties, he was wearing a standard-issue gray suit and blue striped tie. Physically, he was imposing. But as soon as he started talking he shrunk. Not timid exactly. Just unsure of himself, not comfortable in his skin. He had a tic, too. The right eye, it fluttered now and then.

"I'm more partial to penis," Fremmer said. "Or prick. Douchebag is overused at this point. So much so that you sound like a douchebag for using it."

"Oh, sorry," Brian said.

"Don't be sorry. The point is he's not douchey enough."

"Not enough?"

"Not even close."

"But how would that make him more sympathetic?"

"It wouldn't. But it would make him more likeable. You're looking for likeable, Brian, not sympathetic."

"Aren't they the same—or at least similar?"

"You said your wife left you for your contractor."

"He wasn't *my* contractor. He was just *a* contractor. He has a masonry business. What's that got to do with anything?"

Fremmer leaned forward, lowered his voice. "It's a crappy situation. Wife leaves you. Custody battle. Now you get your kids every other weekend. Bummer. I feel bad for you. But then I hear you've got a little bit of a temper. You lose it from time to time. Go off. Some might call it an abusive streak."

"I told you she only said that because she was trying to get full custody. Believe me, she was far more abusive than I ever was. She called me names. Demeaning names."

"You're the victim, Brian. I get that. But see how easily I've made you unlikeable. Just from the guilty look in your eyes right now I can totally understand why your wife left you for your contractor."

"He wasn't my contractor."

"I know. The point is your agent who's not really your agent because she only took you on because your older, more successful brother asked her to, isn't going to give it to you straight because she doesn't want to harsh on someone who's in such a fragile state of mind."

"Younger brother," Brian said. "He's my *younger* brother."

"Whatever. Just understand that I don't have a problem telling it like it is. I'm not going to toss off some dismissive comment about your protagonist not being sympathetic enough. He's actually pathetic, if you want to know the truth. He's completely overshadowed by the villain, the Evil Steve Jobs character."

The antagonist had a real name, but skimming the book while sitting on the toilet that morning, Fremmer noticed a line about how the bad guy—the diabolical venture capitalist using the protagonist's social-media start-up to turn everyone into zombies—reminded people of "an evil Steve Jobs." The description stuck.

The prospect slumped in his chair. He was crestfallen. Mission accomplished. Teardown complete.

"So you don't think I should publish it?" he asked.

"No, by all you means you should publish it."

A woman at a nearby table glanced up from her laptop. Fremmer often raised his voice when uttering the "p" word in Starbucks. He likened it to a duck call—but for writers. These places were teeming with potential clients.

"I should?"

"Absolutely," Fremmer said. "But not for the bullshit reason you gave me. Sure, in your present financial condition, it'd be nice to make some extra money. But we know the real dream is to show your ex-wife that you aren't the putz she thinks you are. That instead of forever talking about writing that novel, you went ahead and did it."

"So you think it's publishable?"

"Anything's publishable, Brian."

"What I mean is, you think there's enough here…you think it's good?"

"With a little work, I can make people think it's good. And I can also make you feel like you accomplished something."

"How much will that cost? To do that?"

"About nine grand," Fremmer replied without hesitation. "And that's only if we do the e-book."

Brian blanched. "That seems a little steep."

"Very. So here's what I'm going to do. Normally you'd have to pay a professional editor at least $3,000 to go through your book and give you a detailed critique. And that doesn't include line editing or copyediting."

"I thought that's what you did. You're a book doctor."

"No, that's just my Google title. For SEO. Think of me more as a book expediter, a shepherd if you will. I've spent years vetting the right cover designers, formatters, copy editors, and the people you're going to pay to review your book, etcetera, etcetera."

Brian laughed, but he clearly didn't find the remark funny. In fact, he was offended. "So you have people create fake reviews for my book? That's what I'm hiring you to do?"

"First of all, I don't work for you, you work for me. You're hiring me to work for me. Secondly, they're not fake reviews. They're real reviews written by fake people. That's different from fake reviews written by real people. Those are the ones you get from friends and relatives. You'll need some of those, too."

Another laugh, this one more incredulous than the last. "You're a piece of work, Fremmer. The scooter, the T-shirt, all part of the act, right?"

"Max," Fremmer said, not taking offense. "Call me Max."

Fremmer leaned down to fish out a small pad of paper from a backpack sitting on the floor next to a folded-up Xootr kick scooter. Judging from his attire, that scooter could easily have been mistaken for a fashion accessory—or, as Brian had put it, "part of the act"—for Fremmer looked like an over-the-hill skateboarder or former Internet executive who'd gotten his big exit and decided to check out of the rat race for a while. He was wearing jeans, vintage Fred Perry tennis shoes, and a white long-sleeve shirt layered under a green Mohegan Sun casino resort T-shirt that he'd picked up at a thrift shop. It had the words "Double Down" written on the front in cartoonish letters. A sporadic shaver since college, Fremmer's face showed five or six days of stubble speckled with gray. His short hair was stylishly unkempt. His nose, prominent but straight, was juxtaposed against a set of bright blue eyes. The eyes won. They stood out.

He wrote some numbers on the pad along with their correspon-ding services. Then he turned the pad around and slid it across the small table toward Brian.

"I've read your manuscript, and except for the protagonist problem, it's pretty polished," he said. "So here's what I'm going to do. I'm going to tell you how to fix that problem so we can knock out that editor's fee." He then did just that, drew a line through the first number, $3,000. "And to be clear, what I'm about to tell you is worth far more than three grand. It will completely transform your book."

Brian crossed his arms and smiled.

"Wait, don't tell me, the catch is I've got to pay for all the other stuff to get this incredibly valuable piece of advice."

"Nope. This is a freebie, my gift to you for schlepping up to the Upper West Side and buying me my third chai latte of the day. Walk away with it. It's yours to keep."

"I'm listening," Brian said.

"You turn him into a her. You make your protagonist a woman."

Another laugh. However, this time he seemed genuinely amused—at least until he realized Fremmer wasn't kidding.

"You're serious?"

"Think about. It's an easier fix than you think. And as soon as you do it, you'll realize how much more sympathetic your character will become. The dynamics will totally change."

"I thought you said I wanted him to be likeable."

"They're pretty much the same thing, Brian. You said so yourself."

"But what about the guy's wife?"

"Husband. She's a man now. Same scenario only he's now the not-by-choice stay-at-home-dad who's developed the drinking problem and is banging the neighbor's wife down the street. See how much better that plays?"

Brian looked away for a moment, trying to wrap his mind around the sex-change operation.

"I know it's a lot to process right now," Fremmer went on. "But take a few days to go through the manuscript. You'll see what I mean. Yeah, you'll have to redo some descriptions, but most of the time you'll just be looking at a pronoun change."

Just then a buff-looking Asian guy wearing a Philadelphia Eagles jersey and gold chain around his neck looked at Fremmer. Fremmer had noticed him scanning the place for a spot to sit down. Or so

Fremmer thought. Their eyes locked, but instead of turning away, the guy kept staring.

"You know, you may be right," Brian said. His thoughts churning, he failed to notice that the Eagles fan had approached their table and unfolded a sheet of paper, which he then held up for Fremmer to inspect.

Fremmer was looking at himself.

"This you?" asked his new friend, who upon closer inspection had a boyish face but strands of gray in his hair.

It was his Facebook profile picture, blown up to headshot size. Fremmer noticed that he was wearing the same T-shirt in the picture that he was wearing now, which was sort of embarrassing.

"Yeah, what's going on?" he asked.

The paper went away and was replaced by a gold-colored police shield. He introduced himself as Thomas Chu, a detective with the NYPD. "We've been looking for you," he said. "There was an accident. I need you to come with me to the station house."

Fremmer's stomach dropped. His whole body tensed, bracing for the worst. *Jamie*, he thought.

"Who, my kid?"

"No, not your kid. A woman."

The weight on his chest lifted, but only temporarily.

"What woman?"

"Candace Epstein. She was hit by a car this morning."

Fremmer noticed that the detective observed him carefully, studying his reaction as he spoke. Fremmer couldn't hold back the shock—and perhaps a little alarm—from showing in his eyes.

"Christ. How bad?"

The detective didn't respond right away. So Fremmer asked again: "How bad?"

"Bad. She isn't expected to survive."

Fremmer sat there, dumbfounded. *Hit by a car? Not expected to survive?* He had a vision of her hooked up to life support in the ICU, tubes jutting out of her, a heart-rate monitor beeping rhythmically. With each imagined beep, he felt his own pulse speed up. He'd exchanged text messages with her only yesterday. In the last month, she'd made more than a few cryptic comments about a soured relationship that had turned threatening. He pressed her about it, but she would only say was that she knew something bad about someone. The kind of bad that lands you in prison for a long time.

He didn't know what to believe. Part of him thought she was taking him for a ride to avoid paying him. He'd taken precautions to avoid being stiffed, but she was one of a few clients with whom he shared royalties instead of accepting a larger, upfront payment.

Now he was terrified he'd completely misread her. He'd been dismissive of her fears—and it was all going to come out that he was a callous son-of-bitch who just wanted to get paid. Or worse. Maybe they thought he had something to do with it.

"Where did it happen?" he asked.

The detective nodded to his left, in the direction of the park. West. "On CPW."

"Did someone run a light or something?"

"I can't discuss that. We have an active investigation. Which is why we need you to come in. We need you to provide us with some background info."

Yeah, right, Fremmer thought. *Background info.*

"Now?"

"Sounds good to me," the detective said, flashing a charming smile. "You need a minute to conclude your business?"

Fremmer looked over at Brian, who seemed both stunned and perplexed. The poor guy had gone from despair to hope to *what the fuck?*

Fremmer leaned over and picked up his backpack and scooter, then stood up, one in each hand.

"I was serious about what I said, Brian," he announced. "You're a pair of tits and a vagina away from fulfilling your destiny. Readers love ballsy women. The detective here loves ballsy women."

Fremmer glanced over at the detective, who, judging from the expression on his face, clearly didn't love ballsy women—or more probably thought Fremmer was a lunatic.

"OK, maybe not," Fremmer said. "But the readers do. And I do. So make the change. And do it with conviction. Do whatever you do with conviction. Always."

2/ The Best Thing in the World

FOUR MONTHS BEFORE NYPD DETECTIVE THOMAS CHU ABRUPTLY ended Fremmer's meeting with aspiring author Brian Tynan at the Starbucks on Columbus, another aspiring author on the other side of the country, one Detective Hank Madden, Menlo Park PD, Retired, was debating the future of his book project.

His problem was more acute than Tynan's, for he'd lately come to the conclusion that he really couldn't write. He never thought it would be easy. But he didn't think it would be that hard. After all, he was telling his own story, he wasn't using his imagination, and everybody said he had a compelling story to tell. Not only had he led two sensational murder investigations in a span of just a few years, he also had his own well-documented narrative of overcoming childhood sexual abuse. So many people insisted the book would write itself.

It didn't. Madden spent days sitting at his desk, staring at the screen, trying to decide where to begin. He began many beginnings but never finished any. The more he examined his life, the more he didn't like what he saw, although he had much to be proud of. The evidence was right at his fingertips. All he had to do was type his name into a Google search bar. Or "handicapped detective." That worked, too.

The links went on for pages. TV reports and newspaper articles repeating themselves as smaller newspapers and blogs reposted them with clever headlines or some unique insight. Some of these reports were word-for-word copies of the original news stories while others adopted a more narrative or opinionated tone, with a couple of highfalutin think-pieces thrown in for good measure. When he'd still been on the job, Madden mostly ignored the posts. But now he couldn't resist clicking.

He clicked on the *People* magazine profile entitled "Handicapped Detective Makes His Big Exit." He clicked on articles in *Variety* and *The Hollywood Reporter* about a film that was in early development based on the *People* profile. He smiled rereading about the actor Kevin Spacey's interest in playing him, the handicapped detective, in "The Big Exit," the working title for the elusive movie.

As a child Madden had one of the last cases of polio in the U.S. The disease left him with a drop foot and a limp. According to the articles in the trade magazines, Spacey, adept at playing physically challenged characters—he did a bang-up Richard III and won an Oscar for his portrayal of the palsied con man Roger "Verbal" Kint in *The Usual Suspects*—was perfect for the role. Madden clicked on all the photos comparing the actor's receding hairline to his own.

They were hardly dead ringers, Madden thought. His face was longer and narrower than Spacey's; his hair, the little that ringed his head, was grayer, and he wore a neatly trimmed moustache. But he had nothing against Spacey playing him.

In the two years since he'd retired, he'd become even slimmer. Now sixty-six, he looked truly slight, and he'd recently traded a pair of half-rimmed glasses for thicker tortoise-shell Ray-Ban frames that had come to define his face and make him look hip in a throwback, old-school way. Or so several people had told him.

After the *People* article first appeared a couple of years earlier, his agent in Los Angeles kept him apprised of the developments. Until there were no more. She mentioned something about ageism in Hollywood and that was the last he heard from her until one day she called him about a potential book deal. *Could he write a synopsis? An outline with a sample chapter?*

He said he could, then never did. No one asked him for them again, so he assumed no one wanted them. But the book idea stuck. He believed he could do it, wanted to do it, if only because he wasn't really doing anything else. Also, he'd told a few people that he was working on a book outline for his agent and they kept asking him about it.

"How's the book coming?" his friend, Nick Page, the owner of the Ace Hardware on Santa Cruz Avenue in downtown Menlo Park, asked him every Tuesday and Thursday when Madden turned up there to work.

"Slowly," Madden sometimes replied. Or: "It's coming."

At his wife and kids' urging he'd completed all the coursework and passed all the exams to get his private investigator's license. But six months later he still hadn't taken the next step to set up his business and acquire the liability insurance for a firearm. He needed an open schedule to write the book, he told himself, but the resulting lack of structure and schedule started to weigh on him. When Nick offered him a part-time job at the hardware store, he decided to take it.

He didn't need the money. Under the state and city's "3 at 50" pension formula for public safety employees, cops who were hired before 2010 could retire as early as age fifty and receive three percent of their highest annual salary for each year they'd worked for the city, up to thirty years. Madden had put in thirty-two years, and was now receiving 90 percent of his highest salary for the rest of his life, a sweetheart deal if there ever was one. But sometimes he felt bad that he didn't feel better about his situation. His friends thought he was the luckiest guy in the world. But he didn't. Far from it.

The hardware store job mainly entailed helping people find what they were looking for in the relatively small retail space. Even though it was an Ace franchise, it was pretty mom-and-pop, so it didn't seem unusual for a senior citizen to work there, especially one who looked pretty fit for sixty-six, despite his pronounced limp.

He and Nick put sale items in front of the store in an effort to capture some of the limited foot traffic on Santa Cruz. Technically, Santa Cruz Avenue was the main drag in downtown Menlo Park, but it wasn't a shopping destination like Stanford Shopping Center and University Avenue in Palo Alto were. No one came to spend the afternoon on Santa Cruz; people went to a shop or two, maybe a restaurant, then got back in their cars and drove away.

One day—or more precisely, one hundred thirty days before a car mowed down Candace Epstein in New York City—a man came into the store. Late thirties, medium height and build, a little preppy, with a full head of dark curly hair. He walked past Madden to the back of the store. Madden looked down an aisle and saw that the guy had stopped in the tool section and was examining a shovel. After giving him a minute or two, Madden set off down the aisle, his awkward gait making him look like he was in the process of rehabbing a knee after surgery.

"Can I help you find anything?" he asked.

The customer looked at him and smiled. He seemed familiar for some reason, but Madden couldn't place him.

"I hope so," the customer said. "I want to dig a hole. A pretty big hole. Say at least six feet deep, but maybe deeper. Pretty wide, too. Which one of these shovels would you recommend?"

When a guy said he wanted to dig a hole six feet deep, a salesman didn't have to be a former detective to get a little suspicious. But former detectives didn't come right out and show their suspicion. Instead, Madden said:

"That would take a long time to do by hand. You looking to do this by yourself?"

He didn't look like the type of guy who'd dig a hole by himself. He was dressed in a tight, long-sleeve navy polo shirt, chino pants, and a pair of fancy sneakers that were meant to pass for casual dress shoes. Madden noticed a large, well-worn gold class ring on his right hand. From which university Madden couldn't tell, but it seemed oddly out of place and made his hand seem small.

"Yeah," the guy said. "The ground's really hard, too. Drought's a bitch. How long you think it would take to dig?"

"Alone? It could take you a couple of days. And your back might go out. What are you looking to put into this hole?"

"Let's say for argument's sake, a body."

Madden smiled. "What kind of body?"

"You know, a dead one. A corpse."

"Why would you want to do that?"

"I killed my wife."

Madden tried his best to look amused but he wasn't. "For argument's sake?"

"Well, if I'm dumping her in a hole, I think we can assume she lost the argument." He erupted into hearty laughter. "Am I right?"

Madden gave him a hard look. He didn't like this guy. Not one bit. But he was also pretty sure someone was trying to put one over on him.

"That one you were holding is a good choice," he said, continuing to play along. "You might call it the Mercedes of grave-digging shovels."

The would-be wife-killer looked at the shovel, which was made of high-grade steel and had a polished, gleaming look. "Mercedes, huh?" he said with a straight face, picking it up again. "I'm more of a Tesla guy. You got one of those? Anything I can plug in?"

He started laughing again, but then stopped abruptly.

"Sorry, man," he said. "I'm just kidding around. Hal Shelby. It's an honor to meet you, Detective. A real honor."

Hal Shelby extended a hand. Madden let it hang there a few seconds, then shook it reluctantly.

"Do I know you, Mr. Shelby?"

"A mutual acquaintance told me you were working here. Tom Bender. He suggested I speak with you. Says you're writing a book but that it isn't going too well and that you're in a bit of a funk."

"That so?" Madden replied, a little perturbed yet not surprised Bender was broadcasting his personal life. Bender had made a career out of saying whatever he wanted to whomever he wanted whenever he wanted. He was a narcissistic tech blogger whom Madden, for better or worse, had gotten to know through his last case, the murder of a Silicon Valley executive.

"I have a proposition for you, Detective."

"I don't need help writing this book, Mr. Shelby."

"Hal," Shelby said. "No one calls me Mr. Shelby."

"OK. Hal. I don't need any help. I'm doing just fine, thanks. Now if you don't mind, I'm going to see if that customer who just came in needs any assistance."

A woman in workout gear had walked into the store and was chatting with Nick, who was behind the counter. Madden took a step away, but Shelby wasn't ready to let him go.

"I'm going to tell you something that I don't tell a lot of people," he said.

Madden looked at him. He couldn't help it. But he also doubted Shelby was about to tell him anything proprietary.

"When I was a kid, I wanted to be a cop," Shelby said. "I was in a Police Explorer Unit when I was a teenager. Right around here. When they had the old station house."

Madden was a bit taken aback. "That so?"

"You know that unit?"

"Sure."

A lot of police departments around the country had Explorer programs. The one in the Menlo Park Police Department had been organized through the Explorer program of the Pacific Skyline Council of Boy Scouts of America.

"I enjoyed it," Shelby went on. "They used to call us in whenever they had any sort of tedious project. You know, we'd have to walk along the side of the freeway and try to find evidence people had chucked out the windows of their cars. I loved doing it, even though we almost never found anything. They made you feel part of the team. And they'd teach you stuff as you were doing it."

"It's a good program," Madden said, still unsure why Shelby was bringing it up.

"You remember Stacey Walker?"

At first, Madden thought he was asking about an old colleague of his. But then he realized the name was familiar for another reason. The Walkers. Stacey and Ross. She didn't come home one night. Four months later, as the DA was preparing to file charges, Ross split the country and never came back. They'd never found her body. Or him.

"Of course I do," Madden said. "I was a patrol officer at the time. I went to the house a few times."

"That article, the one that was in *The Merc* a couple of weeks ago, the one about the twentieth anniversary? That got me thinking. I've thought about it a lot over the years, but I didn't have time to *really* think about it, you know, to really do something about it."

Do something about it? What was he going to do?

"They had us down there on the husband's land in Saratoga," Shelby went on. "When I was in the Explorers. We had those metal rods and we went around for hours, poking the ground, looking for soft patches." He raised his right fist up and down, performing an imaginary thrust into the earth. "I was on the property on and off for a week, maybe longer. I was sixteen."

"I remember you guys doing that," Madden said. "And all the other volunteers."

"For years afterwards I had dreams about her. Weird ones. Sometimes I'd be looking for her in my own backyard."

The case had haunted a few people, Madden thought. Not only did he know the detectives who'd worked it, he was also friendly with Carolyn Dupuy, who'd been an ADA in the San Mateo County District Attorney's office at the time and was now in private practice.

Shelby took the shovel off the rack again. He examined the shiny head for a moment, then extended it to Madden and said:

"Hold onto that. You're going to need it."

He then reached into his back pocket and pulled out a blank white envelope that was folded in half. He handed it to Madden.

"There's a simple contract in there along with a check for $10,000 to get you started," he started. "If you cash the check and sign the document, I'll send you over a check for another $10,000. I'll pay expenses, too. Whatever you want. An assistant. A slush fund to bribe people. Whatever."

Madden looked at him, dumbfounded.

"What do you want me to do?"

"I want you to do some digging. Literally."

"So this isn't about the book?"

"Screw the book. You're not a writer, are you?"

No, Madden admitted, he wasn't.

"I'm not either," Shelby said, "which is why I didn't write my book. And I'm not a detective either. Which is why I want you to find that woman's body. And while you're at it, I want you to find her husband. You'll be well compensated if you succeed at one or both. The terms are in your hand."

Madden looked at the envelope, which he didn't quite remember accepting, then back up at Shelby.

"Look, I don't know who you are, but a lot of people—smart people —have already spent a lot of time trying to do both of those things. Most of them think Ross Walker isn't alive anymore. I'm sure you're quite aware that the DNA tests on those remains came back a match."

"*Remains*?" Shelby scoffed. "You call one arm remains? Where was the rest of him?"

Madden smiled. "So you're in *that* camp."

"You're damn right I'm in that camp."

That camp was the Ross-Walker-had-sacrificed-an-arm-to-fake-his-own-death camp. Madden found its hypothesis rather far-fetched, but plenty of people were sure Walker was still very much alive. They pointed to the fact that it was only the lower portion of his left arm, everything below the elbow. That wasn't so bad, their reasoning went, especially given the quality of available prosthetics. And besides, it was possible that he'd developed some sort of infection and had to have it amputated anyway.

Madden didn't buy it. "It seems like there are better ways to fake your death than chop off your arm," he told Shelby.

"Well, you need to open your mind, Detective. And I think those figures in that envelope might help you do that."

Madden glanced one more time at that envelope, which suddenly felt a little heavier in his hand. Then he said to Shelby:

"Even if I open my mind, what makes you think I'm the one who can find him? Why me?"

Shelby smiled. "I'm going to let you in on another little secret, Detective." This time, he leaned a little closer and lowered his voice: "You know the reason I wanted to make all the money I've made?"

Madden slowly shook his head. He had no idea.

"So I could afford to make mistakes," Shelby whispered.

"That must be nice."

"It is," he continued in a low voice. "It's the best thing in the world. And I don't mean that in an arrogant way."

"You didn't answer my question."

"Oh, I think I did, Detective. I think I did."

3/ iPhones for Guns

FREMMER WAS LED INTO THE 20TH PRECINCT STATION HOUSE ON West 82nd Street, his collapsed scooter in his left hand, dangling by his side.

He'd walked or ridden past the cold, three-story bunker-like building and its utilitarian gray cement façade dozens of times, but he'd never been inside or given it much thought. According to an engraving in the stone on the front of the building, it was erected in "AD 1972," during the dark ages of New York City architecture. It didn't fit in with the block's more charming, renovated brownstones. Instead, its gloomy presence reflected a bygone era of high crime rates and bankrupt city government.

Much had changed since Fremmer came to Manhattan over twenty years ago. It wasn't something he often thought about, but he thought about it walking into the station house.

Entering the building was a somewhat startling experience, like entering a time capsule. The interior couldn't have been renovated since the building went up. Just around the corner on Columbus the street was lined with ritzy little coffee shops, restaurants, and boutiques, along with a stray bodega or two, faint reminders of the neighborhood's less gentrified, more immigrant past. Inside the 2-0 he was transported back to the Nixon era. He felt like he could've been on the set of *Serpico*.

Fiberglass bucket seats, the type that once graced airline terminals at JFK, served as chairs in the entrance area. Past the chairs was a metal police barricade, the kind that contained the crowds at the Macy's Thanksgiving Parade. A traffic sign had been affixed to it with wire, a bright red directive for civilians to stay away from the door that led to the bullpen, which Fremmer could see through a glass window to the left of the barricade.

Chu stopped to talk to a Hispanic guy wearing a suit.

"Looking spiffy, man," Chu said, the two of them shaking hands and doing a one-shoulder bro hug. "Looks like retirement's treating you right."

As the two caught up, Fremmer's eyes came to rest on a big sign stuck to one wall near the ceiling: "Cash for Guns." According to the smaller print, you could trade any gun for $100, no questions asked. Fremmer lifted his phone and took a picture of the sign.

"Sorry about that," Chu said, leading him past the stop sign and to the bullpen door. "Old friend. What were you taking a picture of?"

"iPhones would be better," Fremmer said.

"What?"

"The sign back there should read 'iPhones for Guns.' You could sell that, get some real publicity."

Chu laughed. "That's above my pay grade."

"I didn't mean *you* you," Fremmer explained. "I meant the collective you. Who's behind the program, the police commissioner? Or the mayor?"

Chu didn't know or seem to care. Following him into the bullpen Fremmer called up the photo he'd just taken and selected it. He then hit the Twitter icon and quickly tapped: *Wouldn't trade a gun for $100. But maybe for iPhone or Android. You? @apple @att @nycgov Get creative. Get #gunsoffourstreets.*

As the tweet was sent out to his 78,383 followers, Chu introduced him to Detective Jason Gray, white, around forty, with a tight buzz-cut and receding hairline both in front and on top. Inside the bullpen the furniture was less dated but still seemed tired. Gray did, too. Sitting at his desk in an L-shaped cubicle, dark circles under his eyes, he looked a little weary. But when he stood up to greet Fremmer his demeanor changed. He was lively and congenial. His deep, booming voice reminded Fremmer of his high-school basketball coach.

"My brother's got one of those," Gray said, referring to the scooter. "Xootr," he said, pronouncing it correctly—*zooter*. "That's not the electric one?"

"No."

Fremmer explained to them that he'd originally bought a scooter years ago because he got tired of chasing after his son, who'd become dangerously proficient on his scooter. At the age of four the kid would zip ahead down the sidewalk and turn the corner, causing Fremmer to lose sight of him. Now Jamie was twelve and Fremmer's scooter, upgraded to a more deluxe model, had evolved into a day-to-day transportation vehicle.

"You look like you've put some miles on that one."

"A few," Fremmer said.

They were acting very chummy, which worried Fremmer. There was an awkward silence before Gray half-sat down on the edge of his desk and, motioning to a simple "guest" chair, said:

"Well, have a seat. We've been trying to track you down to get some info on the pedestrian who was hit this morning. Your super said you were probably at one of the Starbucks in the area. You're a book doctor? What's that? Like a freelance editor?"

"Something like that," Fremmer said, hesitantly taking a seat.

"My wife wants me to write a book," Gray said. "She's always telling me I've got some good stories I should get down. You know, if nothing else, for the kids. But she's my wife, right? She's biased."

"At least she doesn't hate your guts," Fremmer said.

That got a laugh out of them.

"You divorced?" Chu asked.

"Never married," Fremmer said.

"But you got a kid?"

"I do."

His curt response was met with silence. They were clearly waiting for him to say more, but he didn't. So Gray finally just came right out and asked him.

"What's the backstory on that?"

"Backstory?"

"On the kid. He's got a mother, right? She live with you?"

"What's that have to do with Candace? Look, I don't want to tell you how to conduct your investigation, but could we stick to the pertinent questions? I actually need to pick my kid up from soccer practice in a little while, so I don't want to waste your time. The bus leaves him up the street, in front of the soccer shop on Amsterdam."

The two detectives looked at each other. There seemed to be some sort of acknowledgment in their glance, as if they were on the same page, though it was unclear what that page was.

"Fair enough," Gray said. He picked up a notepad on his desk and opened it to a blank page and set it back down. "We're trying to get some background on the victim, who we understand is a client of yours. How long have you known her?"

"Candace?" Fremmer paused to consider exactly when they'd met, but his thoughts were disrupted by the way Gray had said the word "victim." For some reason, perhaps his own paranoia, Gray's inflection suggested *crime* not *accident*. "I guess I've known her about two and a half years but she's been a client for about eighteen months. I'd have to check my records to give you a specific date."

"We tracked down a daughter but no significant other. She got a husband somewhere? Or an ex?"

"I think he died five, six years ago," Fremmer said. "He was older. Had some money. I saw some photos. I know he was in his late sixties when she met him. I don't think the daughter was his, though. Candace mentioned something to me about a sperm bank and being able to pick out her ideal male. The main character in her stories had been married to kind of a sugar daddy. After he died, she'd turned to online dating sites. The guys she met never matched their profiles. So she ended up fantasizing about their profiles and never going out on the actual dates. When you know the author, it's sometimes hard to know what's fiction and what isn't."

"You helped her write a book?"

"Books, actually. I helped her self-publish a series of e-books."

"Under her own name?"

"No, she writes under a pseudonym. Lexi Hart."

Gray asked him to spell that for him. As he transcribed the name, Chu pulled out his phone and did a search. Fremmer watched his face take on a perplexed look that quickly transitioned to amusement.

"Check this out, man," Chu said, holding the phone up to his partner. "It's porn."

"No," Fremmer interjected, "it's erotica. And a sub-genre of that."

"What sub-genre?" Gray asked, making a notation on his notepad.

"I like to call it corporate fetishism."

Gray's pen stopped moving. He looked up at Fremmer. "Corporate what?"

"Well, according to this," Chu spoke for him, "it's a story about a woman who gives handjobs to guys in Apple Stores." He giggled a little as he read the book description from its Amazon product page. "I might have to buy this. It's only two-ninety-nine."

"You are correct," Fremmer said. "My client, your victim, has written three books in which the main character surreptitiously jacks off men in Apple Stores. There's a bit more to it than that, including a Craigslist component, but that, shall we say, is the hook. Sadly, she is my most successful client."

"And she owes you money?"

"Yes."

"How much exactly?"

Fremmer had a strong suspicion they already knew exactly how much she owed him because he'd texted her the amount on more than one occasion.

"About fifteen thousand dollars."

"And you were actively trying to retrieve this sum from her?"

He nodded. "Look, fellas, I wanna help you out here, but can you tell me what's going on? Honestly, I'm in shock about the whole thing. Before I go any further, I really need to know what happened. Was this an accident or something else? Because the way you just said victim, it didn't sound like an accident."

The detectives looked at each other again. After a moment, Gray said:

"We have reason to believe it was not an accident."

"And what reason would that be?" Fremmer asked.

"We have a witness who says she was pushed in front of the vehicle."

"Pushed? By whom?"

"We're not at liberty to say right now," Gray said. "But her cell phone was found near the scene and we're obviously interested in speaking to the people she'd most recently been in contact with."

"Look," Fremmer said. "If you guys think I had anything to do with this, you're crazy. She kept making excuses why she couldn't pay me. I pressed her on it. She seemed stressed about something, and I was like 'Come on, Candace, what's wrong here? What's going on?' She mentioned something about knowing someone who'd done something bad. Really bad, apparently. I didn't know what to believe. She owed me money. People make up all kinds of shit when they owe you money and can't pay. I didn't think it would be a problem with her. She lives in a good apartment. She said her husband left her some money when he died."

Gray looked at him calmly. "We didn't say you had anything to do with it, Mr. Fremmer. We're just trying to get some background info."

"Max," Fremmer said. "Everybody calls me Max. How is she by the way? Are there any updates?"

Chu shook his head. "As I said, it doesn't look good. She's had severe trauma. Her heart stopped once in the ambulance. They had to resuscitate her."

"Christ," Fremmer said. He put his hand on his forehead, partially covering his face. "Her kid. I feel so bad for her. She's a nice kid."

He pictured Candace's eleven-year-old daughter Mia getting pulled out of class and being told what had happened. Thinking about it made him nauseous. It also reminded him that he had his own class to teach.

"I gotta go," he murmured in a bit of haze. "I can come back later. But I've really gotta go."

"Where do you have to go?" Gray asked.

Fremmer looked up. "I teach a spinning class at the Equinox on 92nd and Broadway. But beforehand I pick my kid up from soccer practice on Amsterdam and 94th. Tuesdays are tight for me. And I don't have my stuff with me."

Gray: "Can you arrange for someone else to pick him up?"

"Another parent from the team?" Chu suggested. "Gotta be someone."

They were right, of course. There were people he could call. And while he might be able to get a last-minute teaching sub, he'd already done it several times, and the fitness manager had warned him that other instructors were available to take his slot, he didn't care that Fremmer was one of the gym's most popular spinning instructors.

"How do I know you guys aren't fucking with me?" he asked. "How do I know what you're saying to me is true?"

"I assure you we aren't fucking with you," Gray said. He then turned over what looked like a standard piece of paper on his desk but was really a piece of thicker, photographic paper that had a photo on the front. "You ever seen this guy? The one on the left?"

Fremmer leaned forward and peered more closely at a photo of two guys in their early sixties, both dressed formally in coats and ties. Fremmer recognized them immediately, but wasn't sure how he knew them until he saw the prosthetic hand sticking out of the guy on the left's coat sleeve.

"Yeah, they're the lucid dreaming guys. They have that place, a center or institute or something, uptown. You know, you try to take control of your dreams. Candace is into that stuff. She does some bookkeeping for them and some other stuff. I'm not sure if she gets paid for it or not. I met the guy on the left once. The one with the fake arm. Braden, I think his name is. I Googled him at some point. The other guy is a former Columbia professor, I think. There was some talk of doing a book. She wanted to do one."

"Did she show you anything she'd written about him?" Gray asked. "Or the institute?"

Fremmer shook his head. "Not that I remember. Why?"

"We're just checking up on some people she's been in contact with recently. Like you."

"You think she had some dirt on him?"

"We're still trying to determine what exactly their relationship was."

"So someone pushed her? You know that for a fact?"

"We have a witness," Chu reiterated.

"And some video," Gray revealed.

"Video, huh?" Fremmer said. "Well, seems to me like you're looking at least at murder two and possibly murder one."

"Maybe," Gray acknowledged. "Maybe not."

"No offense, fellas, but I have a law degree from an accredited university. I even passed the bar. And that's some serious shit. I wouldn't tread lightly around that, would you?"

The detectives looked at each other again. They didn't seem to know quite how to respond. So Fremmer went on:

"As I said, I want to cooperate, but I've got some things to do. And I don't think there's anything to stop me from getting out of here. I can come back after the class or first thing in the morning."

That didn't seem to sit so well with Gray. He glanced at Chu one more time, then said:

"What if I told you there actually was something stopping you from getting out of here?"

"What would that be?" Fremmer asked.

"A warrant out for your arrest."

Fremmer's eyes opened wide. "A warrant? For what?"

"A parking ticket."

"A parking ticket?" Fremmer laughed. "Are you kidding me? I don't own a car. When's it from?"

"1998."

"1998? Are you serious? That's almost twenty years ago."

"Well, you should have paid it," Gray said.

4/ Embrace the Hate

MADDEN DIDN'T OPEN THE ENVELOPE RIGHT AWAY ONCE SHELBY left. The customer in the gym outfit needed help picking out a bungee cord to secure a couple of bikes to the rack on the back of her car. He suggested she buy a combo pack with some shorter and longer cords, then went outside and attached them to her bikes for her.

A few other customers came in, not exactly a steady stream, but enough to keep him occupied. He broke for lunch forty-five minutes later, the envelope still sealed in the back pocket of his jeans, walked up the street to Cafe Barrone and settled in at an outdoor table.

Shelby's contract was a single page. Madden felt his heart race as he read through the terms. The whole thing was crazy. Was he reading the zeroes correctly? There were six, weren't there? He counted again, just to make sure. He was still staring at the contract when his phone rang. He looked at the Caller ID and saw it was Tom Bender. His first impulse was to decline the call, but after letting the ringer cycle twice, he decided he needed to speak to the guy sooner rather than later.

"Madden," he said.

"Bender," Bender said. "What's up, dog?"

"I think you know what's up."

"I'm always trying to make the world a better place. And that includes your little world, Detective. How does it feel to be back in business? You stoked or what?"

"Who's Hal Shelby?"

"Ever heard of Google? Use it much?"

"I was about to. Then you called."

"Well, I'll give you a hint. He had one dumb idea. Crowdfunding. We take it for granted now, but who'd have thought that you could stick your inane concept up on the Web and people, perfect strangers, would give you money for it?"

Bender's site was called OneDumbIdea.com—or ODi, as the site's prominent red logo read. It covered start-ups and personalities of Silicon Valley. Its tagline, attributable to no one, was "Most smart ideas seem dumb at first. Just like this website."

Shelby was the guy behind an operation called Gushr, Bender explained. He'd sold it to Facebook about nine months ago and walked away with something in the neighborhood of four hundred million in cash and stock. Madden vaguely remembered reading about it in the papers.

"How did it come up?" Madden asked.

"What?"

"This whole thing with me."

"I don't know. I think he sent me a text. Or maybe it was an email. He only sends one-sentence emails, so they seem like texts."

The fact that Shelby had some sort of email brevity rule didn't surprise Madden.

"Sometimes you don't even get a full sentence," Bender went on. "A lot of the time it's one word or even just a piece of punctuation or an emoticon. I think he just said, 'What's Detective Madden doing?' That's pretty verbose for him. He once told me that his dream was to be quoted in the press with a period, but the press refuses to quote just a period. They always say he had no comment. And he always calls up the editor of the publication and says that he had a comment. A period. 'What's that mean?' the editor asks. It means whatever you want to it to mean, but it's a comment, he says. I actually did a story about it. It was called, 'Hal Shelby's having a period.' I thought he would hate it, but he loved it. He sent me three exclamation points. We've been friends ever since."

"Well, he certainly conducts himself a little oddly."

"It's about gaining a psychological advantage," Bender said. And then Madden heard him say it again. There was an echo on the phone. "That's the way it is with these guys." Again, the echo. And suddenly he realized Bender was there in the flesh, standing just behind him to the left, his phone in one hand, a dog leash in the other, his pug attached to it. He had sort of an Indiana Jones–style distressed leather man purse strapped across his chest, resting against his right hip.

Bender was one of those guys who looked clean and well coiffed yet tired at the same time, his white pasty face framing the dark bags under his eyes while small clusters of spider veins nestled high on both cheeks. He'd put on weight since the last time Madden had seen him. He was a little more corpulent, and his usually spiky, gelled hair, was longer and slicked back. He stared straight ahead for a moment, gazing in the general direction of the El Camino, its lanes thick with traffic, before sitting across the table from Madden.

"How much is Shelby's deal worth?" Bender asked. He folded his hands on the table expectantly.

"One million for finding the body," Madden volunteered. "Another for finding the husband. And a million bonus if I do both."

Bender let a low whistle. "Not bad," he said.

"I'm telling you because you'll find out anyway."

"That's a given," Bender said.

"But if those numbers leave this table, there will be repercussions."

"Is that a threat, Hank? Because you know I don't do well with threats."

"I don't either," Madden said. "And I bite. A lot harder than that mutt of yours."

"That's low, Hank. Insulting the dog."

Madden looked down at Beezo, named after Amazon's CEO Jeff Bezos, one of the few people Bender seemed to truly respect. Beezo didn't look insulted. Quite the opposite. Madden reached down and gave him a pat.

"How'd you know I'd be here?" Madden asked.

"Because you're a creature of habit, Detective. You come here every Tuesday and Thursday at almost exactly one o'clock. You're an easy mark. You're lucky no one's out to get you. Myself, I keep moving. I mix it up. I take precautions."

"Since when?"

"It's toxic out there. There were always haters. But now they're bolder, more vicious. They actually want to harm you. And not only mentally. I'm talking physically. It's the jihadification of the Internet. Extremism rules."

"I hope you didn't write that anywhere."

"Of course I did. And I may have inadvertently disparaged several religions and the State of Israel in the process. There is no equivocation in provocation, my friend. Which is why I'm now wearing this bulletproof vest."

Madden looked at him more closely and realized that Bender really wasn't heavier but was simply wearing something underneath his clothing, apparently the aforementioned vest.

"Pretty good, huh?" Bender said. "You can barely tell, right?"

Madden nodded his approval. It was better than the one he used to wear.

"The truth is it wasn't my idea," Bender said. "I made some crack on Twitter about needing a flak jacket, and I got contacted by this company. Now they're paying me twenty grand to wear this thing around for a couple of months and write about it. Which got me thinking about the whole self-defense market. You know, embrace the hate. We do a contest. Have someone win the chance to taze me. And we video the whole thing and give any money we make to charity. You know, little kids with polio in Cameroon or wherever the fuck that outbreak is. You can emcee the ceremony. Talk about your own bout with polio. Hank Madden, one of the last cases in the U.S. That's real, man. Living proof. You can even throw a line or two in about overcoming your childhood sexual abuse at the hands of your pediatrician. What do you think?"

Madden looked at him with a mixture of disbelief and horror.

"Are you serious?"

"By definition."

Madden shook his head. Alas, the rest of Silicon Valley wasn't as colorful as Bender. In fact, it was pretty mundane, which Madden had been struggling with in his writing. He was OK laying out the bones of his story, but the flesh, the descriptions of people and places, that part always fell flat. He'd been having a hard time bringing the milieu to life. The generic niceness of the place, its pervasive pleasantness. The weather, the outdoorsy-ness, the proximity to so much natural beauty; the beach, mountains, Napa, Sonoma, Tahoe, Yosemite. That proximity was important. It was what California dreams were made of. But it also created pressure. If you weren't taking advantage of it, there was something wrong with you. You weren't living. How did you write about that? For Madden it wasn't really sweetness but a concept of sweetness. Like Splenda. A yellow packet of Splenda. Healthy yet unhealthy.

He'd thought about that one day walking up to The Dish, the radio telescope set in the foothills right off Stanford campus, one of those points of interests on the long list of points of interest. A series of paved paths snaked up into hills, and at the top—or even near the top—you could look down into the valley and see all the way to the bay. The first thing that caught your eye was the Hoover Tower, home of the conservative Hoover Institute (Herbert Hoover was literally the university's first student), because it was the tallest building for miles, a monument amongst the sprawl.

Staring out at that view, Madden could see something majestic about the place, the grandeur of man's control of the land, almost every acre of which had been carved up and developed. But inevitably he'd find himself imagining it long ago, in its nature-wrought state. The bucolic early days. The haciendas. The beginnings of towns. No cars. The real El Camino Real, when it was a dirt road, with no pavement, no cars. And instead of a university, he saw the farm where Leland Stanford bred his racehorses.

Madden wished he could have been there. Strange, he thought, that as he got older he looked back—way back—instead of looking to the future. He didn't care about the future. Didn't care about the spectacular advances in technology, the ones he'd never see. Those were the things Bender cared about. Boldly declaring the next big thing before it was the next big thing—or as Bender once told him, "People don't remember when you're wrong. They just remember when you're the first to be right."

"So that's it?" Madden asked. "The next big thing—embrace the hate?"

"You gotta zag when the world zigs," Bender said.

Just then the waitress came by with Madden's salad and set it down in front of him. Noticing he had company, she asked Bender whether he wanted a menu.

"It's all right," Bender said. "I'm not staying. I want to give this man his privacy."

He said it pretty loudly, so it came off sounding like he actually didn't want to give him his privacy.

Once the waitress left, Madden said, "Look, I'm not sure I'm going to take Shelby up on this offer. Unlike you, I don't like to rip people off, even billionaires."

"I don't think he's a billionaire, Hank."

"Whatever. Two, three months from now, he's going to ask me what progress I've made, and I'm going to say none. And he's going to say why did you take this on if you knew you couldn't do it. I know how these guys work. They may not seem like they expect results, but they do. And they get nasty when they don't get them."

"Who cares," Bender said. "And who says you won't get results."

"I just wanted to write a book. You said it would write it itself, Tom. You encouraged me. You were one of the ones."

"This is the book, Hank. Write this. You're having trouble because you aren't a guy who lives in the past. So live in the present and write about the past while you're at it."

That made some sense, even though it was completely contrary to his own thinking as of late.

"I'd need to get a look at the case file. Refresh myself. There's politics. I can't just walk in and announce I'm working this case. It's still active. It would rub people the wrong way, especially if they knew what I was getting paid on top of what I'm already getting paid from my pension."

"You're looking at it wrong," Bender said. "Start with the guy who's already done the research."

"Who? Pastorini?"

Pastorini was the detective who'd worked most closely on the case before he ascended to the job of Menlo Park Police Chief. He was Madden's friend and former boss.

"The guy had a stroke," he reminded Bender. "He's learning to walk and talk again."

"Nah. Not the detective. The guy who wrote that book about it.

Frank Marcus. He did a lot better job investigating the case than you guys did."

Oh, Christ, Madden thought. *The book.* Madden remembered the bold red letters of its title all too well: *Never Found Never Dead.* And all of a sudden there it was in front of him. Bender had reached into his man purse, pulled out a hardcover edition and set it down on the table.

Madden had read the book years ago, when it first came out. He even attended an author event at the old Kepler's Books bookstore, which had since moved to the building right next door to where they were now sitting.

"He'd be the first one I'd talk to," Bender said. "He says people still come to him with tips."

Madden wasn't sure whether Bender was ignorant or whether Bender was just being Bender. Possibly a combination of the two.

"I don't know if you know, but there's some bad blood there. Some things he wrote didn't sit too well with the guys working the case."

"Of course they didn't. Which is why you should go talk to him. You're not a cop anymore, Detective. You're a mercenary."

"He embarrassed the MPPD."

"I embarrassed you," Bender said. "You got over it."

"Not really," Madden said.

5/ Suspect in Custody

FREMMER KNEW ATTORNEYS, PLENTY OF THEM, THOUGH ONLY A handful of criminal attorneys, two of whom he considered friends. He'd never given much thought as to who would do the better job representing him or who would charge less, but he had asked both whether he could count on them if he ever got into trouble.

"You remember when I asked you whether I could count on you if I ever got in trouble?" he now reminded Carlos Morton, reaching him on his cell phone.

"Who's this?"

"Max."

"Oh, hey, Max. How are you?"

"Not well," Fremmer said. "I'm being held at the 20th Precinct station house on 82nd."

"For what?"

"I'm not exactly sure. But you gotta get me out of here. The little patience I have left is about to expire. A client of mine was apparently pushed in front of a car this morning while she was walking her dog. They called me in for questioning."

"Was she killed?" Morton asked.

"No. But she's in bad shape. They don't think she'll survive."

"And they think you had something to do with it?"

"I don't know. I exchanged texts with her last night. They're questioning people who've been in contact with her recently. For background info, they said. But I wasn't so sure about that. Then I got antsy, partly because I got a little concerned with the tone of their interrogation, partly because I have to pick up Jamie from soccer practice. And I have a spinning class to teach. But when I told the cops I'd come back later, they suddenly pulled this crap about me having an outstanding parking ticket and that there's a warrant out for my arrest. Apparently, I've been driving around with a suspended New York license, which seems odd since I have a Connecticut license. They read me my rights and everything. Is that bullshit or what?"

"When you have an outstanding parking ticket they issue you a virtual New York license if you don't have a New York license," Morton explained. "They suspend the virtual license. Look, be very careful what you say over the phone. They're probably listening. You get someone to pick Jamie up?"

Morton knew the soccer-practice drill. Both of their kids played for the same club, though not the same team anymore. They practiced on Randall's Island in the middle of the East River and the club provided bus service to and from practice—for an extra fee, of course.

"No," Fremmer said. "You're the first call I made."

"They take away your phone? This isn't your number."

"No. But I can't get a signal in here. I wanted to live-tweet the whole thing. They handed me this cordless phone. I asked them to call the Equinox at 92nd for me, but I don't know if they did."

"Hold on a sec, I'm in my car. Let me pull over. I'm just getting back into the city, just drove over the 59th Street Bridge."

The line went silent.

"Where'd she get hit?" Morton asked after a moment.

"Central Park West," Fremmer said. "I don't know what cross street."

"OK, I got something here. There are a few stories up already. No name released. But it says an unidentified woman was pushed into the path of an oncoming car this morning at CPW and 75th Street. Police are treating it as an attempted murder. Oh, and they've got a suspect in custody."

"In custody?"

"That's what this article on the *Post* site says. Timestamp on it is thirty minutes ago. How long you been there?"

"I don't know. An hour?"

"Well, sit tight. I'll call the Equinox and grab Jamie. He's on that 6:30 bus, right? I'll drop him off at your place and then come over there."

He said something else, but Fremmer didn't hear him. He was too busy trying to figure out whether what he was doing—or rather where he was—meant that he was in custody. He was in a holding cell with bars on it. If that didn't mean he was in custody, what did?

"Max, you still live on 77th, right?"

"Yeah. Sorry. Thanks. And thanks for getting him. Just don't freak him out. Tell him I've got an old parking ticket I'm trying to clear up, which is true."

"I got you covered."

"Carlos?"

"What?"

"I just want you to know I called you first. I had other options, but I called you first."

"Of course you did," Morton said. "Why would you call any-body else?"

6/ Killing It, Frankly

W HEN HE WAS ON THE POLICE FORCE AND INVESTIGATING A CRIME, Madden would often show up at a person's home or place of business without warning. In most cases it was best to retain an element of surprise and not leave a potential witness or suspect time to prepare.

In his new role he wasn't quite sure what the protocol was, but he decided to stick with his old script. So two days later, his bank account flush with the $20,000 from Shelby, he showed up unannounced at Marcus's small office on Hamilton Avenue, a tree-lined street a few blocks over and parallel to University Avenue, the Main Street of downtown Palo Alto.

The author of *Never Found Never Dead* was no longer a writer. Several years ago he'd joined his wife in the real-estate business. She'd left a larger firm to start her own boutique operation that, if the press clips were to be believed, had prospered mightily by catering to newly-minted millionaires of the tech boom and foreign clients, mostly Chinese.

The office looked more like a furniture store or art gallery than a realty office, with wide-plank white wood floors and white walls. On one side of the room there was a pewter-colored modern leather couch facing two matching leather lounge chairs, a glass table sitting on a carbon-colored shag rug between them. A large-screen TV was mounted on the wall behind the couch, showing CNBC with the sound muted.

In the back were two small desks and a table with a fancy cappuccino machine sitting on top of it. A young woman with blond hair pulled back in a ponytail sat at one of the desks, working on an iMac. She poked her head around the computer when Madden walked in but didn't get up.

"Can I help you?" she asked.

"I'm looking for Frank Marcus."

"He just went to get a scone," she said. "He should be back soon. Do you have an appointment?"

"No. If you don't mind, I'll just wait."

She didn't seem opposed to that. "Can I get you some coffee?" she asked cheerily. "We also have cold drinks."

"No, thanks. I'll just wait over here if that's OK."

Madden sat down on the couch, which was firm yet comfortable. Nevertheless he felt uncomfortable sitting there. Or perhaps awkward was the better word. He checked email on his phone and then turned to the various shelter magazines fanned out neatly on the coffee table. *Architectural Digest, Dwell, Atomic Ranch, Elle Decor.* He'd seen them before but never opened any of them. Never had any interest.

He lived in a ranch-style house in West Menlo Park that he'd bought for $65,000 in 1975. It was worth well over a million today, maybe two. Most of the current MPPD cops couldn't afford to live in the area. Several commuted across the Bay from Fremont and other towns just over the Dumbarton Bridge. Or even further out. He'd been one of the few locals, a graduate of Woodside High, which, in his day, during the Vietnam years, had earned the nickname Weedside.

His wife had consulted some of these magazines when she'd remodeled their home. He remembered her chattering away in rapid-fire Spanish with their Mexican contractor, discussing the pages she'd torn out and collected in a folder.

His wife was from Nicaragua, the former housekeeper of his former boss, Pastorini. Now, twenty-one years and two kids later (their daughter was in high school, their son a freshman at UC San Diego), except for the color of her skin and her charmingly accented English, she was hard to distinguish from the rest of the suburban moms. Her bourgeois transformation was both a source of pride and consternation, for he could have done without some of the things she wanted. But he also knew he couldn't have it both ways.

"Hello, how can I help you?"

Madden looked up and there he was, Frank Marcus, standing toward the back of the room, looking much older but still dapper in jeans and a well-pressed, untucked white dress shirt with two buttons open at the top. In his hand he held a scone wrapped in thin wax paper. He hadn't come in through the front door, but a back entrance that wasn't immediately visible.

"Oh, wow," Marcus said before Madden could speak. "It's you, Detective, isn't it? Charlotte, do you know who this is?"

Charlotte, the young woman at the iMac, looked at Madden, then at her boss. She had no clue who he was.

"This is Detective Madden," Marcus said. "He was involved in that whole Sinatra impersonator case. And the one with the doctor. What was his name? Cogan, right?"

Neither registered with Charlotte.

"He was in *People* magazine," Marcus tried again. "Like a four-page spread."

"Oh, wow," Charlotte said.

Marcus came over to the table, and transferring his scone to his left hand, went to shake Madden's hand with his right. His hair was thinning and flecked with gray, but he looked tan and healthy. The former bartender had done alright for himself.

"She's not from around here," Marcus explained. "She doesn't know. When did you move here, Charlotte?"

"A little over a year ago."

"Fresh off the boat," Marcus said. "Connecticut."

"Massachusetts," Charlotte corrected him. "I went to school in Connecticut."

Marcus didn't seem to hear her. He was truly beaming, which seemed weird to Madden. At his book-signing event years ago, Marcus had been quite frosty, though, looking back, it might have been a wee bit intimidating to have six pissed-off cops standing in the back of the room, staring daggers.

"I'd heard they were making a movie out of your story," he said. "Kevin Spacey, right? How's that going?"

"It's not," Madden said, standing. "There was some interest but they haven't moved forward."

"Yeah, it can take years. My book got optioned. Got picked up twice by two different production companies, but they never did anything with it. But I did get well compensated."

"Actually, that's what I'm here for," Madden said.

"What, to get compensated?"

"No, for your book. I wanted to talk to you about it. And the case in general."

Marcus looked a little surprised.

"Oh," he said, "I thought you wanted to sell your house. It's a good time to sell."

"I know," Madden said. "My wife wants to upgrade. Get a bigger place. But we'll have both kids in college soon, so that seems stupid."

"Upgrades can save marriages, Detective."

"I'll stick to cars and jewelry," Madden said. "They're cheaper."

"To each his own," Marcus said. "So, why the interest in my book? You back on the case?"

"I was never really on the case. It was always Pastorini's. And, as you know, Burns worked it, too."

"Yeah, I'm sorry to hear about Chief Pastorini. I read that he had a stroke and had to step down. How's he doing? He was always a big guy. And he almost chain-drank coffee. Or was it Diet Cokes? Frankly, I'm surprised he didn't have a heart attack."

Pastorini had lost some weight but was still big. Opera singer big. Some of the guys used to refer to him as Luciano, which he didn't take too kindly to, though he did like Pavarotti.

"He's still got some paralysis on his left side," Madden said. "But his speech has gotten better."

"Well, send him my regards."

"He might have another stroke if I do that," Madden joked.

"You guys were way too sensitive," Marcus said. "I was respectful. I know how much effort was made. I wasn't out to make you guys look bad. I worked my ass off to put that thing together. I worked almost four years on it."

"Right now that's neither here nor there," Madden said. "You knew some things, but not everything."

"I knew more than you did."

"I know. And that's why I'm here. I'd like to use you as a re-source."

"So you are working on the case then?"

Madden nodded. "I have a private party who's interested in solv-ing it once and for all."

"Who?"

"I can't reveal that right now."

"The family?" Marcus prodded. "Which side? His brother's still got some money. But he never hired someone before so why hire someone now? So hers?"

Madden maintained his best poker face. "My client would like to remain anonymous."

Marcus smiled. "That makes you what, a PI? PI Madden?"

"Something like that."

"Well, I want to help. People contact me all the time. A lot of them are nutjobs but sometimes I get what seems like a credible tip. And I do an update on my website each year. As you know, the whole ex-perience transformed my life. I wanted to do another book, but then I got involved in all this real-estate stuff with my wife, and it's a hell of a lot more lucrative—we're just killing it, frankly—so I put the writing on the back burner. I do a fantastic company newsletter each month, though. Have you seen it?"

He turned to Charlotte. "You looking at porn again, Charlotte?"

"I'm updating that Atherton listing with some new photos," she said.

"You got a copy of this month's newsletter?"

She slid open a filing cabinet and after rummaging around, emerged with a single sheet of paper with printed material on the front and back. She set it on the edge of the table but didn't get up to give it to Marcus. He had to come over and get it.

"It's data heavy but I keep it entertaining and also throw in a lit-tle gossip," he said, handing it to Madden. "Most people read it dig-itally, of course. But it's got a bit of a following. A couple thousand people read it each month. I even have an advertiser now. We're mon-etizing it."

"That's great," Madden said, doing a poor job of feigning inter-est. He scanned the first page of the newsletter, then said:

"So you think our old friend Ross is dead? Or is he walking around somewhere with one arm shorter than the other?"

Marcus smiled. "Cutting right to the chase, Detective. Literally. I like that."

"When you were promoting the book, you seemed to be of two minds. Was that just for publicity sake? You know, to get people talking and stoke the debate?"

"That's a good way to put it. I mean, it's weird, right? You find part of the guy, but not the whole guy. And then there's his wallet and passport. I've said this many times before. From what I could tell— and I was there in Vietnam—the whole thing seemed a little staged. And look, the F.B.I. was in there and they said some things just didn't check out. Say what you want about the F.B.I.—I know some law enforcement in this country isn't all that impressed with them sometimes—but let me tell you, the two guys I dealt with were thorough. I was personally grilled for two days. They spoke to a lot of people in and around those villages. And by the way, the only reason I went there was because you guys gave me the tip that he'd been sighted in that area."

"Well, maybe you understand why people felt the way they did when your book came out. They felt betrayed."

"I blame my editor for that. She wanted to play up the tension between my investigation and yours. And at least they didn't get in any trouble for leaking information they shouldn't have."

"We publicly said we had information that led us to believe he was in Vietnam. We wanted people to know that."

"But you didn't say exactly where. And I got some other tips. I purposely didn't say how I got some of the information I got. They should have been happy about that."

Madden sighed. This is exactly what he thought would happen if he went to see Marcus. Old wounds would open. They'd argue. And nothing but anger and frustration would come out of the meeting. He'd hoped he'd be able to overcome his allegiances and take a more measured, calculated approach. But he was stupid for thinking he could.

"Look," he said, "this was probably a bad idea coming here. If I ever want to sell my house, I'll have my wife contact you. It'll make a good starter home for a junior Facebook manager."

He turned and started to walk towards the door but Marcus stopped him with what he said next.

"I think he's in the States."

"Who? Ross?"

"Yeah. And he may have been here for years. I think he came back pre-9/11."

"Where?"

"I don't know. But I'm pretty sure he's had some contact with his family. I know you guys were monitoring them for years."

More than monitoring, Madden thought. Pastorini used to stake out family members' houses at Thanksgiving and Christmas, hoping he'd show up. He claimed he just missed Ross a couple of times.

"I just haven't had the time or inclination to follow up on some of the leads I've gotten," Marcus said. "I just pass them on to my contact at the F.B.I. Life's too copacetic now to get sucked down that rabbit hole again."

"But you said you wanted to help."

"I did, didn't I? Well, you got me inspired there for a minute, Detective. I was idealistic once. Stacey was my friend. Every fiber in my body wanted to bring that bastard husband of hers to justice. But the book, going through that, brought some closure for me. I'd always wanted to write a book. I didn't know what it would be about, but I knew I would do it. And after I finished, it was weird, but I knew I wasn't a writer. I knew I wanted to do something else."

"It looks like you made the right decision," Madden said.

"I will help you, though. Give me a few days and I'll gather up what I have."

"I have a list of people I'd like to re-interview from your book," Madden explained. "I'd like to go over them with you. With these types of cases, enough time passes, and people start to talk more. Ross was an intimidating guy. People were scared of him. All these years later, they're more likely to say something, especially now that a lot of people think he's dead."

"I thought that, too," Marcus said. "I thought that someone would come out of the woodwork. But no one has. So far."

7/ Mr. Plant

NOT LONG AFTER FREMMER CALLED MORTON, HE HAD A VISITOR. Two uniformed officers escorted what looked like a homeless person over to the holding cell, but didn't put him inside the room with Fremmer. Instead, they handcuffed him to one of the cell's bars and left him outside, sitting on a bench.

The guy had many of the attributes you'd expect from someone who lived his life on the streets. Long hair. Body odor. A layer or two of extra clothing. Bushy beard. Fremmer could barely see his face. What stood out was a red bandana he was wearing around his head and a pair of brand new high-top basketball shoes. His right wrist was ringed with a variety of colored rubber bracelets. Judging from the white in his beard he appeared to be in his late fifties or early sixties, though Fremmer suspected that if they cleaned him up, he might drop ten years.

"How long I gotta stay here?" he called after the two cops as they walked away. When they ignored him, he turned his attention to Fremmer. He spoke through the bars, which also had a layer of thick mesh wiring covering them, so there was no way to throw anything or poke anybody through them.

"Who are you?"

"The book doctor," Fremmer replied. "Who are you?"

"I am the prophet who could not convince anybody of anything."

Fremmer let out a laugh.

"You think that's funny?" the prophet asked, leaning up against the bars with his shoulder.

"No. Well, yeah. In a way."

"You think it's funny to have eyes that see into the world when no one listens? You think it's funny because you rely on the media and the government for the purpose of deciding the truth. Well, they deceive you. They spread falsehoods."

Fremmer nodded in agreement. He wasn't about to dispute that.

"So, why are you in here?" the prophet asked, suddenly sounding quite coherent. "What'd you get pinched for?"

"Didn't pay a parking ticket."

The prophet lifted an eyebrow. He wasn't buying it.

"If you don't want to tell me, don't tell me," he said. "But don't lie to me. I don't like to be lied to."

"I'm not," Fremmer said, suddenly thankful for the bars between them.

"Yeah, OK. Fuck you and your fucking parking ticket, you double-down dick."

Fremmer didn't get the double-down reference immediately, but then realized it had been lifted from his T-shirt. Duh.

He braced himself for the tirade to continue, but it didn't. The prophet turned away aloofly, which Fremmer found interesting. He wondered what his story was. His speech pattern seemed educated. So what had derailed him? Garden-variety mental illness? Probably, but maybe there was a Hollywood hook to his life's arc. Perhaps a plunge from great heights. It was worth a check.

"How 'bout you?" Fremmer ventured after moment. "What they have you in for?"

"They say I pushed a lady in front of a car."

Fremmer felt his back straighten. *Holy shit. It's him. They got him.*

"Did you say 'push'?"

"They say they have a video of me pushing a lady in front of a car and that it will be in the media soon. It will become a virus. It will be everywhere."

"Viral," Fremmer corrected him. "It will go viral is what I think they meant."

The prophet gave him a hard look. "The media is a virus."

Fremmer weighed a response to that, but didn't think anything constructive would come out of it.

"So many people want to tell others how to live," the prophet went on. "They make a profession out of it. Nobody came to the planet to hate, to be angry and be miserable. Why bother to incarnate if your motivations are hate and anger?"

"Did you push her?" Fremmer asked.

"Why would I do that?"

"I don't know. Maybe you didn't mean to."

"Because someone offered me money? Hah. Money is a prison."

"So, someone offered you money to push her? Who?"

No response. Instead, the prophet looked upward into Fremmer's cell, peering up at the ceiling, scanning the corners of the little room. Fremmer wasn't sure at first what he was looking for, but then he figured it out: a camera.

"They said you were him," the prophet said. "But you're not him, are you? You're a plant. Well, Mr. Plant, I didn't push anyone."

Fremmer stood up and moved closer to the bars. "I'm not a plant. Or at least no one told me I was. Who's him? Who'd they say I was?"

"The Oracle."

"What are you talking about?"

"The man who took my picture. He said he was The Oracle. And that I was going to become famous. It was my destiny. He saw it. It was foretold."

"He offered you money to take your picture?" Fremmer imagined a tourist asking him for a picture, then offering him money.

"Listen," the prophet said. "Hear me as I'm intended to be heard."

"I'm listening. But I don't know what you're talking about."

"What are *you* talking about? A parking ticket. Hah. Who do you take me for?"

Christ, Fremmer thought. *We're back to that.*

"Look," he said, "I'm not a plant, and you're in a shitload of trouble. There's a woman in intensive care right now. I know her. She's my client. And if she dies, you're going to be up for murder. And you're going to find out real fast that money isn't a prison. Prison is a prison."

The prophet stared at him blankly. It took him a few seconds to absorb what Fremmer had said, but he did seem to absorb it, for all of a sudden he seemed quite distraught.

"I didn't push her," he said. "They just want to put me away again. They always have. It's OK, though. You know why it's OK?"

Fremmer didn't know.

"Because we're all best when we are challenged. Look at disabled people. They are bound and determined to face their challenge. It's part of the human instinct. When you face a challenge, you face something you really don't like. You get points for trying. We all get points for trying."

"What's your name?" Fremmer asked.

"Ronald."

"Ronald, you sure you didn't do this? Because if it was an accident, if you did something by accident, you need to tell them. They will give you some points for that."

"If there was an accident, I would have said there was an accident. I did that once. I saw an accident. I gave a statement. I'm an incredible witness."

"Credible," Fremmer corrected him.

"Yeah, that, too," Ronald said.

8/ She Doesn't Come Cheap

"THE TRUTH IS THAT AT THE TIME IT HAPPENED I DOWNPLAYED OUR relationship a little. I was worried people would view her in a bad light, that she was this, you know, adulterous ho and she had it coming to her. Because that's how people think. I told you guys we hooked up a few times. But it was more than a few. It was probably like once a week for six months. You do the math on that."

Sitting across from Madden was Vladimir Bronsky, Stacey Walker's former lover. Bronsky resembled the man Pastorini questioned at the old Menlo Park police station twenty years ago. Only he seemed far removed from his younger, more strapping self. The long dark hair he once wore in a ponytail was now gray and replaced by a crew cut that helped to camouflage a bald spot on the crown of his head. The shorter hair brought out his features more, and his prominent nose and high cheekbones were more pronounced than Madden remembered them. And while he remained slim, he looked unhealthy. Madden had never seen him smoke, but he looked like a guy who had a pack-a-day smoking habit.

"I guess it worked because you guys did a good job keeping it out of the papers," Bronsky went on. "It just kind of got slipped into the press that she even had a lover. And it was framed in a good way. It said that detectives had confirmed with a former boyfriend that Stacey was planning on leaving her husband and that she'd set up a secret bank account with some money so she'd have something to live on when she left. But that bank account was never touched after she disappeared. And her credit cards never used."

Madden remembered the article. It was in *The Almanac*, a small weekly newspaper, which had done the most in-depth piece on Stacey's disappearance. Not the *Chronicle*. Not the *Mercury*. *The Almanac*. And he also remembered they'd kept a lid on the boyfriend angle for the very reasons Bronsky cited: They didn't want the public to develop an unsympathetic view of Stacey.

"It sounds like you regret downplaying your relationship," Madden remarked.

"Look, I was a suspect," Bronsky said. "I knew you guys were pretty sure the husband had done it, but you couldn't overlook the other possibilities. And that woman from the DA's office went all pitbull on me."

Pitbull, huh. Madden smiled. He had a little surprise for Bronsky.

"But you had nothing to hide," he said.

"Subconsciously, I guess I was trying to protect her."

Madden nodded. He looked down at his phone to make sure it was recording. They were seated at one of the umbrella-covered outdoor tables in front of the Starbucks in Sharon Heights Shopping Center, one of Madden's favorite spots for coffee in the morning. The shopping center was just off Sand Hill Road, which served as one of the main outlets to the 280 freeway but was better known as a roosting spot for major venture capital firms. Their arrival decades earlier had changed the tenor of the area and Rosewood had built a high-end, pretentiously casual hotel with Napa Valley overtones on sixteen acres by the freeway. It catered to high-tech professionals and executives from around the world as well as the wealthy parents of Stanford students—or aspiring Stanford students, most of whom would never get in.

In contrast, Sharon Heights Shopping Center was decidedly more low-key and lower-rent, harking back to more middle-class days, which suited Madden just fine. A series of mostly simple one-story structures with flat, shingled roofs, it was anchored by a Safeway grocery store and hadn't changed much in the fifty years since it opened. Its name and the neighborhood's had been inherited from the former estate of Frederick Sharon, the son of Senator William Sharon, who, in the 1880s, was the largest single taxpayer in the state of California and had his own 55,000-square-foot estate up the road in Belmont when Menlo Park had only 250 residents.

Not that anybody cared about history, Madden thought. Or history pre-dating the founding of Hewlett-Packard in a garage on 367 Addison Avenue in Palo Alto in the late 1930s. *That* they cared about. That was sacred ground. The place where time began. The birthplace of Silicon Valley.

"What about the book?" he asked Bronsky.

"What about it?"

"I didn't see you say anywhere in there that you downplayed the relationship. As far as I could tell, you told Marcus the exact same thing you told us. You stuck to your story."

Bronsky gave a little shrug of his shoulders and Madden watched as a smile crept across his face. "Why shouldn't I? I mean, I didn't want to talk to the guy in the first place. I trust a writer less than I trust the police, especially an amateur like him. I didn't know what he was going to do with what I said. It's not like *The New York Times* is coming to talk to you, where they have fact checkers and all that. He was this guy who knew Stacey a little in high school then served her drinks for a few months and suddenly decided he wanted to write a book. He didn't even have a contract."

"But he was on a personal mission to solve a mystery."

"It wasn't a mystery to me. After all, she told me her husband threatened to kill her if she left him. He said he was going to kill her and bury her where no one would find her."

"But that's hearsay."

Madden may have been thinking the same thing, but he wasn't the one who said it. Rather, the objection came from Carolyn Dupuy, who was standing behind him with a Baby Bjorn strapped to her chest, a small head covered in dark peach fuzz peeking out from the top of it. She'd just emerged from the parking lot right in front of the Starbucks.

"Mr. Bronsky," Madden said, standing up. "Ms. Dupuy. You two know each other, I believe."

Bronsky stared at her, not knowing quite what to say. They were both in their early forties, but she looked younger than he did. With her olive skin and dark straight hair and brown eyes, she always came across as mildly exotic. However, depending on how much make-up she wore and her clothing selection, she was capable of raising and lowering the volume of exoticism. Today, it was more muted. She was dressed casually in jeans and a light blue blouse, with a short strand of white pearls around her neck. Despite the simplicity of her outfit, she wasn't a woman who just threw stuff on. She worked at looking good. She had a regime. She exercised. She didn't eat red meat. And despite the crow's feet and half-moons around and under her eyes, she was in such good shape that if she didn't have the kid strapped to her chest, Madden would've never guessed she was a new mom.

"Hello, Vlad," Dupuy said. "Thanks for meeting with us today."

"You're the bitch from the DA's office," Bronsky said.

"Well, I'm in private practice now, but yes, I'm still a bitch. And maybe bitch squared, if you count this little screaming terror attached to me. Man, she can cry when she's hungry."

Madden pulled out the empty chair next to him so she could sit down more easily.

"Ms. Dupuy's working with me on this," Madden explained. "She actually knows more about the case than I do, so I thought I should bring her on while she's still on maternity leave."

"Sorry I'm late," she said. "Please, go on. I didn't mean to interrupt."

"We were just talking about the Marcus book and how Mr. Bronsky came across in it," Madden recapped.

"I came across better than she did," Bronsky said.

"Well, that wasn't a high bar to get over," Dupuy replied. "Everything he got about me was filtered through people who had an ax to grind or didn't like me, which doesn't leave much room for a positive assessment. Even you had some choice words for me, Vlad."

"You said horrible things to me. You called me devious and a liar."

"I made you cry, Vlad."

"Yeah, you made me cry."

"And I'm sorry about that," Dupuy said. "I was young and insecure and perhaps a touch overzealous. But on a more positive note, we didn't charge you with anything and we publicly announced that we didn't find anything to implicate you in Stacey's disappearance."

"*Couldn't*," Bronsky shot back angrily. "You should have said *didn't*. But you said you *couldn't* find anything to implicate me. There's a big difference. You purposely left a little room for doubt. And that's part of the reason I spoke to Marcus. Because if I hadn't, he would have cast suspicions on me for not talking. If you don't fill the void, someone else will."

"So true," Dupuy said. Then to Madden in a quieter voice: "Behind you at three o'clock. Slow turn. That the car you were talking about?"

Madden waited a moment, then peeked over his right shoulder. The Audi sedan he'd seen the other day was parked over by the liquor store adjacent to Safeway.

"Think so," Madden said. "Same color anyway."

"I took a picture of the plate," she said.

"Woah," Bronsky said, suddenly alarmed. "What's going on?"

"Someone's following me," Madden said. "Or at least we think so."

"Who?" Bronsky asked.

"Probably my client. He likes to keep tabs even though he says he's hands-off."

"Who is he?"

"Can't say," Madden said.

"Would I know him?"

"You might. You might not."

"He must be paying you well," Bronsky said.

"Why do you say that?" Madden asked.

"Because she doesn't come cheap," he said, motioning toward Dupuy. "I know what lawyers cost. They sucked me dry in my divorce."

"Maybe she's working pro-bono."

Bronsky laughed. "Her? No way. She's in it for the dough. You are, too, Detective. What's this guy paying you?"

"Why do you care?" Dupuy asked. Maybe it was the shift to a more aggressive tone or that she leaned forward a little when she spoke, but the baby stirred, making a sound that was part cry, part cough. She looked down and stroked the baby's head for a moment, comforting her, then went back at Bronsky. "What do you want, Vlad? You want to know what's in it for you?"

"Back in the day there was a $75,000 reward for information that would help lead the police to finding Stacey," Bronsky replied coolly. "What's it up to now?"

Dupuy glanced over at Madden, their eyes locking for a moment.

"Do you have information, Mr. Bronsky?" Madden asked.

Bronsky looked down at the half-eaten blueberry muffin on his plate. He stared at it a moment, then broke a small piece off and tossed it in the direction of a couple of small blackbirds that had been patrolling the area, noisily scavenging for crumbs.

"That recorder still on?" he asked.

"Yeah," Madden said.

"Turn it off for a minute."

Madden heeded his request.

"Look," Bronsky said. "I've been doing OK lately. It's been good. I've had a lot of ups and downs. People think everybody here with an engineering degree from Stanford is raking it in. Well, that's not the case."

Madden was about to say something, but then he felt Dupuy's hand on his leg. She gave it a little squeeze, signaling him not to interrupt.

Bronsky looked down at his muffin again, picked another piece off, and threw it at the birds, only harder this time.

"You make a couple of bad decisions," he went on, "you go for the equity and get with a company you think has potential but turns out is run by a bunch of idiots who thought they were smarter than they really were, and things can go south. Fast. There's a lot of mediocrity in this valley. It's a goddamn mecca of mediocrity. And it's easy to become part of it. Easier than you think. And frankly the whole Stacey thing set me back. I needed to be at the top of my game and I wasn't. I drank. I did drugs. And I fucked some things up, including my marriage."

"But you're doing OK now," Madden said.

"Yeah. I'm doing well now and I don't want to screw that up. I've got my own business. I've got a good relationship with my kids. My ex talks to me like a human being again. I can't afford to be accused of something I didn't do. You understand? I can't afford to hire a lawyer."

"We're not accusing you of anything," Madden offered.

"I want her to be found as much as anybody," he said. "That's why I came today."

"But you want to be compensated in some way if you tell us something that helps her to be found," Dupuy guessed.

"I was thinking something along those lines," he said. "Until you showed up."

Dupuy pointed at her own face. "Me?"

"Yeah. I may have something. It also may be nothing. But if it is something, it's going to be a problem for me. I'm going to need a lawyer. I was thinking I could use the reward, if there still is one, to help pay for that. But now that you showed up, I'm thinking why not eliminate the uncertainty. I should just take you. Right now."

Dupuy recoiled a little.

"As my attorney," Bronsky clarified. "Pro-bono."

"Oh," Dupuy said. "I get it."

Madden smiled. It always amused him how people could go from making derogatory comments about Dupuy to wanting her to represent them. They didn't like a pitbull attacking them. But protection was another story.

Bronsky had other demands. "I want full service. Real representation. And before I say anything, I want it in writing. So you guys go ahead and talk it over and get back to me—"

"No, it's OK," she said, cutting him off. "I'll do it. I'll draw something up right now. Let me get my legal pad out of the car."

And she did. Within twenty minutes they had an agreement in place that seemed satisfactory. Then, at Bronsky's request, all three of them turned their phones into voice recorders and Dupuy read the agreement aloud to get it "on record."

When she finished it was Bronsky's turn to talk.

"I don't know if you know this," he began, "but on the two-year anniversary of Stacey going missing I got a call from Ross. I told the police about it. And they got the F.B.I. involved. They traced the call and found it came from a payphone in Washington State."

"What'd he say?" Madden asked.

"He just said, 'Hey, you know who this is? Well, I know what you did to my wife, you loser. And someday they're going to find out. They're going to find out and you're going to San Quentin.' And that was it. He hung up."

"And you were sure it was Ross?"

"I never met the guy. But I saw him interviewed on TV. And it sounded like him."

"And that's the only time you heard from him?" Dupuy asked.

"The only time I told the police about," he said.

They waited for him to say more, but he didn't. Instead, he looked away, in the direction of the Safeway, and ran his palm across his forehead up along the top of his scalp, as if he was pulling his hair back—as if he had hair to pull back.

He took a deep breath, then said: "About two years later I got another call. Sounded like the same guy. He said the same thing. 'You know who this is?' And then he said something again about knowing what I did to his wife and that I was going to pay for it. But then I realized he wasn't talking about me killing her, he was talking about me having sex with her, because he then said something about where he'd buried her. He said, 'They all think I buried her on my own property, but why would I do that? Wouldn't it be a whole lot smarter to bury her on the real killer's property?'"

"The real killer," Madden said. "Meaning you?"

"Meaning my property. He said, and I'll never forget this. He said, 'Why don't you look in your own backyard, lover?' And then he started laughing and hung up."

Both Madden and Dupuy sat there speechless for a moment. Finally, Madden said, "And you've never told this to anybody before?"

"No."

"And he never called back?" Dupuy asked.

Bronsky shook his head. "That was it. And then about a year after that the book came out. And there was the whole thing about finding his arm and the passport in Vietnam. And I was just hoping he was dead."

"So when you didn't hear anything, you assumed he was."

"I didn't assume anything. The truth is whenever I see a Caller ID number I don't recognize, a little part of me thinks it's going to be him."

"Did you do what he said?" Dupuy asked. "Did you look for her?"

Bronsky smiled. "I thought about it. I went onto my little patio and smoked a joint and tried, you know, to get my Zen powers going.

I got it in my mind that she was there, in this one spot in the corner of the yard by the fence."

"Did you dig there?" Madden asked.

"No. I did what I thought was the best thing for my sanity."

"What was that?" Dupuy asked.

"I moved the hell out."

9/ Best I Can Do

THEY MUST HAVE BEEN WATCHING OR LISTENING BECAUSE NOT LONG after Ronald told Fremmer his name and Fremmer gave Ronald his business card, Detective Gray came back and informed Fremmer he'd be leaving soon, they were just finishing up the paperwork and he'd be free to go. He sounded almost apologetic.

"As I said earlier, there's a protocol to this," he explained, standing a couple of arms lengths away from Ronald, who'd now taken a seat on the bench outside the cage. "We're just following it."

"I'm sure you are," Fremmer said.

"After he leaves, I want my call," Ronald announced.

"We gave you the phone," Gray said. "You didn't call anybody. Who do you want to call?"

"Him," he said, pointing at Fremmer.

Gray looked at Fremmer, who couldn't help cracking a smile, then back at Ronald. Gray wasn't happy.

"Why do you want to call him?"

"I have his phone number," Ronald said. "He said to call him. Happy New Year."

Gray shook his head, flummoxed. It was September.

"Is my lawyer here yet?" Fremmer asked.

Gray didn't answer. He just walked out. Then he came back a minute later with two uniformed officers, one of which produced the keys to the cell while the other kept his eye on Ronald. After they let Fremmer out Ronald took his place inside the cell.

"I want my call," he called as Gray led Fremmer back toward the bullpen area.

Gray took Fremmer to his desk, told him to sit tight, then left. On the other side of the room Fremmer saw a couple of cops looking at a TV screen mounted up near the ceiling. A few other TVs, tuned to the same channel, showed a woman news reporter talking to the camera. He couldn't quite hear what she was saying but he noticed a familiar-looking building in the background behind her: The station house they were in.

One of the cops turned up the volume and Fremmer heard the reporter say, "Police have yet to make an arrest, but they say they have a suspect in custody. My sources are telling me it's a person . . . a person who lives on the streets," she said, struggling to categorize Ronald in a politically correct way. "Someone we typically describe as a homeless person. That's what I'm being told."

The camera cut to the anchorman. "And has your source said anything about a motive, why he would do something like this?"

"No, no motive, Brad. But hopefully we'll get more information soon."

"OK, thank you, Ellen," the anchor said. "That's Ellen Park, live at the 20th Precinct on the Upper West Side. We'll check back in a little while to see if she has any more information about this terrible incident. A woman was pushed in front of a car this morning on Central Park West while walking her dog."

He then began chatting with his co-anchor. Like many visitors and transplants to the city, she'd long harbored fears of being pushed in front of a subway.

"On the platform, I always stand well back from the yellow line," she said. "You just don't know who's out there, who's standing next to you. You just don't know."

"No, you don't," the male anchor concurred, and they moved on to the next story.

The cop lowered the volume and shortly thereafter Gray returned. He handed Fremmer a piece of paper that Fremmer thought was a ticket of some sort. But it wasn't a ticket exactly, it was instructions for how to pay the license suspension termination fee.

"It's fifty bucks," Gray said. "You can pay online."

"So this is to reinstate my suspended virtual license, which automatically disappears once I pay the fee?"

"Best I can do," Gray said. "But the good news is you don't have to pay for the parking ticket. Too much time has passed."

Fremmer laughed. "Fantastic. You held me for not paying a parking ticket I now don't have to pay."

"Best I can do," Gray repeated. "Exit's this way," he said, motioning for him to get up and follow him. "Your lawyer's out in the waiting room with your belongings. You're free to go. However, we will want to talk to you in the future. Maybe as soon as tomorrow. We'll be in touch." He took a card out of his shirt pocket. "Call me anytime. My cell is on there," he told Fremmer, handing him the card.

Fremmer stopped at the exit door, looked at the card, then back up at Gray.

"So, that's it?"

"You're free to go, Mr. Fremmer."

"But you got him? That guy in there did it? He pushed her?"

"We have evidence that suggests he's the perpetrator. That's all I can say at this time."

"You arrested him already? You read him his rights and all that?"

Gray offered a faint nod. He barely moved his head, but the acknowledgment was there.

"But what about this oracle?"

"What about him?"

"Who is he?"

"You tell me," Gray said.

"I would if I could."

"I'm sure you would."

With that, Gray pushed the bar on the door, which automatically locked shut from the inside, and stood aside to let him pass. When the door opened, Fremmer saw Carlos Morton standing there. Fremmer's scooter and backpack were on the floor next to him.

He went out and shook Morton's hand. His friend smiled and said:

"I show up and magic happens."

"You do anything?" Fremmer asked.

"Not really."

"You talk to the detectives?"

"We had a quick chat. Let's just say I made my presence felt. Sometimes that's all that's necessary."

It wasn't hard for Morton to make his presence felt. He was six-four, and, while he seemed to have lost a little weight since Fremmer last saw him, was still heavy, well over two-hundred-fifty pounds. His head was completely shaved and he wore a set of gold wireframe glasses that gave him sort of a bookish appearance, though at first sight he gave the impression he'd played the line for his high school football team. In fact, he hadn't, and claimed he wasn't athletic. Neither were his two kids, which was a shame considering both were considerably bigger than the other kids in their age groups.

It was hard to tell whether Morton was black, Hispanic, or Pacific Islander. When you asked him what his family background was, he always said, "I check all the boxes, brochacho. I'm the united colors of Benetton. Got a bit of everything." He liked to think he had chameleon-like qualities, especially when it came to getting a jury to like him. He could tweak his personality a little one way or another to curry favor with certain jurors. Or so he claimed.

"Everybody's racist," he once explained. "People are so busy accusing white people of being racist they sometimes forget that black people are, too. You can play to that. I go Asian, too. You don't think I can, but I can. I'm a man of the streets. People like me. They think I'm a mensch, especially you Jewboys."

"I think they used me as a plant," Fremmer told him. "They were trying to get a guy back there in the cage to make incriminating statements."

"Did he?"

Distracted, Fremmer didn't answer. He was looking behind Morton, where a uniformed cop was standing, chatting to a guy in plainclothes, probably also from the police department. They were talking about the television crew outside but Fremmer couldn't tell exactly what they were saying. In contrast to when he first arrived, the room was now bustling with activity. People were moving in and out. The only stationary person was an older guy sitting in one of the fiberglass bucket seats, just sitting there holding his phone in front him, typing something. After he finished typing, he turned and looked in Fremmer's direction. Their eyes locked and Fremmer realized he knew him. It was Braden, the guy from the Lucidity Center. The guy with the prosthetic hand.

"They pulled you in here, too, huh?" Fremmer said to him.

Braden looked momentarily discombobulated. He seemed to recognize Fremmer but didn't know from where, so Fremmer clued him in:

"Max Fremmer," he said. "I met you with Candace at an event. You're the guy from the lucid dreaming center, right?"

Braden stood up. "Oh, yes. It's terrible what happened. I just heard they caught the guy. Why would he do such a thing?"

Braden's good hand was his right hand, so the handshake ritual wasn't awkward. When Morton introduced himself he probably didn't even notice the guy had one hand.

"Lucid dreaming," Morton said, "that's that thing where you realize you're dreaming and are able control what's going on?"

"That's one way to describe it," Braden said.

"And there's an institute for it in the city?"

"Yes, a center. We teach techniques and have nutritional supplements that enhance the probability of achieving such a state. And we have a research wing as well."

"I'll be damned," Morton said.

As the two continued to speak, Fremmer thought there was something a little off about Braden's face. His nose seemed a little too perfectly constructed, his cheekbones a little too high and angular, his neck a little too smooth. Fremmer was no plastic surgery expert, but it looked like the guy had a little work done. The odd thing was that both the hair on his head and his neatly trimmed goatee were distinctly gray. Someone who really wanted to look younger would also have dyed his hair, Fremmer thought.

"Remind me again how you know Candace?"

It took a moment for Fremmer to realize the question was directed at him. "I'm her editor," he said.

"I thought so," Braden replied. "We need to talk. You have something of ours."

"I do?"

"A manuscript she wrote. She told us you were working on it."

Fremmer thought about it before he shook his head. "Not that I'm aware of."

"We hired her to write it. We advanced her money."

"You, too, huh? That's why they had me in here. Because they thought I had something to do with pushing her. Fifteen grand she owed me. I wouldn't push someone over fifteen grand. So, who pulled you in? The guy with the Eagles jersey, Chu? Mr. Undercover Cop?"

He felt a tap on his shoulder. It was Mr. Undercover Cop himself, Detective Chu, standing right next to him.

"Don't you have a spinning class to teach?" Chu said.

"Thanks to you, probably not anymore. But hey, if they put me back on the schedule, I'll get you a pass and you can come take it as my guest. I'll put together a special playlist of cop-show theme songs. There are some good ones."

"You do that," Chu said. Then, moving past him, he extended a hand to Braden and thanked him for coming in. "I've been reading about what you do. Interesting stuff. I'm just going to have you come to my desk where we can speak privately. It shouldn't take long."

After they left, Morton lowered his voice and said, "You know, Max, you can't play around with these guys like that. This is a no bullshit situation you're involved in here. You can't mess around."

"What the hell was that about?" Fremmer said.

"What?"

"She told them I had their manuscript. Why would she do that?"

"Let's get out of here," Morton said.

"You get Jamie?"

"Yeah, I dropped him off at home."

"Well, hang out for a minute. We gotta wait for a call."

"From who?"

"The son of a bitch they say pushed my client in front of that car."

"Why are we doing that?"

Fremmer pulled his cell phone out of his pocket to check whether he was getting a signal. The indicator showed four dots out of five. *Good.* Back at full strength. Or close enough.

He went to put the phone away, but just as he did, a caller ID number he didn't recognize flashed across the screen and he felt the phone vibrate in his hand. He slid open the virtual lock and handed the phone to Morton.

"Meet Ronald," Fremmer said. "He needs a lawyer."

10/ A Strange Request

T HE QUADCOPTER TOOK OFF FROM WERRY PARK, WHICH REALLY
wasn't much of a park, more like a small grassy area with a jungle
gym surrounded by trees just south of Stanford Avenue on Dartmouth.
It ascended straight up to about sixty feet, hovered there, then slowly
began to make its way in an east, passing over Harvard, Princeton,
and Oberlin, before turning south at Cornell.

The area was made up of smaller houses, fairly densely packed,
many of them cottages or bungalows on quarter-acre lots. Back in the
day the houses were cheap; two- and three-bedrooms had cost a couple hundred thousand. Now sellers were getting two million for an
800-square-foot cottage that might very well be demolished and replaced by a much larger home.

"We started doing this a couple years ago," Marcus said as the reconnaissance video played on the large-screen TV in the same spartan
white office Madden had visited a few weeks earlier. "Right now we
only do it for our trophy properties, but it's a great marketing tool,
especially for folks who are newer to the area. You get a real sense of
the neighborhood and it really captures the grandeur of it all. We even
do some stuff where we walk a drone through the house. It creates a
Steadicam effect for a fraction of the cost. Looks great. You can get
some really cool shots. I've also got a guy working on some VR stuff
for me."

The drone came to a stop over a particular house and hovered
there for a moment.

"That's it alright," Bronsky said.

He, Madden, Dupuy, and Marcus comprised the small audience gathered in front of the television screen. Marcus's wife, Kendra Hargrove, a tall woman with very short blond hair sculpted in such a way that made you think she'd just come off a runway in Paris or Milan or the set of a science-fiction movie, had welcomed them warmly when they first arrived. Now she sat at a desk in the back of the room, working quietly on the computer. Somehow her presence hovered over the proceedings like her husband's drone. She had neither the time nor the interest to spend on her husband's high-tech presentation.

Madden had met her a few times. His early impressions were that she shared some of Dupuy's no-bullshit, cut-to-chase qualities. But he knew Dupuy well enough to understand that some of her boldness emanated from her insecurities. He'd seen her vulnerable side over the years. Hargrove seemed more emotionally detached, and Madden thought both she and Marcus had played against their personality types in forging their relationship. Marcus was the better looking of the two, she the more charismatic. The result was that when the two were in each other's company she came across more shallow while he gained some depth.

"It's changed a little," Bronsky observed of his old residence, "though not that much. They redid the deck."

The small redwood-colored deck had what looked like a hot tub, kidney shaped, with a dark brown cover over it, built in at one end. The deck overlooked a small lawn—probably no more than twenty-five feet squared—that was surrounded by shrubs, flowering plants and some trees. They could see some brown patches of grass, a byproduct of the drought and city-enforced water rationing, but it wasn't totally dead like some of the lawns the drone had flown over.

"As you can see, there's some landscaping," Marcus said, pausing the video. "It's not a big space, but you're still probably looking at five to ten grand at least to really rip everything up and put it back exactly as it was or make it better."

They'd assembled to discuss strategies for approaching the owners about excavating their backyard. Over the years Madden had searched homes and yards for evidence, but in those instances he'd been issued a search warrant that gave him the authority to go traipsing about private property. But here he had no authority, and despite being a mostly by-the-book guy during his career, for purely selfish reasons he wasn't ready call the Palo Alto PD or his old pals at the MPPD and encourage them to investigate. For starters, he wanted to preserve a clear path to Shelby's reward, but just as importantly he didn't want to look foolish if they didn't find anything. So he'd asked Marcus, the real-estate expert, what tactics they might employ to gain access discreetly. Marcus came up with the idea of a reconnaissance video.

"You don't have to do the lawn," Bronsky said. "I would have known if someone had buried her there. I would have seen that the ground was disturbed."

"You sure about that?" Dupuy asked.

"I went out there pretty regularly," he said. "You can't dig a grave in the middle of a lawn and not notice it."

They considered that for a moment, but before anybody could comment, Bronsky got up and went to the screen.

"I think you're just looking at the plant beds here," he said, running his finger around the perimeter of the lawn. "You could come into the lawn a little."

"If we're going to go to the trouble of doing it," Madden interjected, "we might as well do the whole thing. It's a small area. We could go over the place with a ground radar machine first, but it may not show anything."

Dupuy agreed. "Let's not leave any doubt."

"I would like to bring your attention to one small detail," Marcus said.

Now it was his turn to approach the screen. He hit a button on the remote to restart the video. After a few seconds the drone gradually began to descend. It hovered over the middle of the lawn at about ten to fifteen feet then made a slow right turn. Marcus hit the pause button.

He went to the screen and drew an imaginary circle around a set of plants on one side of the garden. "You see that," he said. "Our occupants are cultivating a little patch of cannabis."

Marcus was right. A set of five or six plants clustered together each bore the distinct leaf pattern of marijuana.

"How's that help us?" Dupuy asked.

"I was thinking the opposite," Marcus said. "It may actually hurt. These people may not want anybody near their backyard, especially anybody remotely associated with law enforcement."

"Who are they anyway?" Dupuy asked.

"Young couple," Kendra Hargrove interjected from the back of the room in a commanding voice. "The guy works at IDEO, the design company. The woman does PR for some sort of Kickstarter-backed fitness-tracking device and a couple of other start-ups. She's got a gmail address on this press release so I'd bet this phone number is for her cell. I'll call her right now. You guys need to stop over-thinking this. Just give me a budget, Mr. Madden. What are you comfortable with?"

That morning he'd spoken to Shelby, who'd been emailing him sporadically with the same question in the subject line and no text in the body.

How goes the fight, Detective?

Normal people would have asked how the investigation was going. Or if there was any progress. But *how goes the fight?* What was that?

Madden didn't want to have anything to do with Shelby's one-line email messages. They made him queasy. Whenever he received one he got an urge to refund Shelby and walk away. The only problem was he'd already spent a good chunk of the initial payment. Five thousand went to Dupuy as a retainer fee, eight he'd put aside for taxes, and his wife got the rest. She was always asking him for money to send to her relatives in Nicaragua and was usually happy to get five hundred here or a thousand there. But a check for seven thousand! Wow! She couldn't believe it. Her eyes welled up with tears. Actual tears. When he got the key to the city, she'd never showed that kind of emotion. But one fat check for her extended family and he was suddenly a hero.

"No major breakthroughs," he wrote Shelby back each time. "As agreed upon, will have a full report at the end of the month."

Dupuy had counseled him to be very careful about what he put in writing. Which is why he'd chosen to call Shelby that morning instead of email him. It didn't take long for his new boss to approve funding the excavation—and even provide his own landscaper—but he wanted the cost of the project to come out of Madden's reward money should they find Stacey. He wasn't being petty, he explained, he just wanted Madden to think like a guy who was spending his own money, not someone else's.

"My client gave me a $25,000 cap," Madden now told Hargrove. "I'm not saying he won't go higher, but that's the number he gave me."

"Got it," Hargrove said, then picked up the office phone and dialed a number.

"Wait," Madden said, moving toward her, semi-panicked. "What are you going to say?"

Marcus grabbed him by the arm, stopping him.

"Chill," he said. "Let her do her thing."

Hargrove held up a hand, indicating she wanted silence in the room.

"Veronica," she said. "Is this Veronica McCarthy?" A pause, then: "Hi, this is Kendra Hargrove from Hargrove Realty in Palo Alto. Sorry to bother you, but I have a little bit of a strange request from a client that I think will interest you. Regarding your property."

Another pause.

"I'm glad you've heard of us," she said after a moment. "And no, this isn't a mistake, someone didn't list your home on Airbnb. Hear me out if you don't mind. I have a client who lived in your house way back when. Or he had a girlfriend who did. I don't know the full story. But he apparently got the idea for his company while he was living there with a couple of other people. And somehow he got it into his head that instead of going on some fancy retreat, he wanted to take a few of his top executives and hang out there in his old house for the week and you know, kind of relive their youth, get inspired and all that stuff. I think he's crazy, but he's bent on doing this and is willing to pay well above market and put you up in a nice hotel for the week. We could do the Four Seasons or Rosewood. Or whatever you want."

They all sat there, staring, as she waited for a response.

"Ideally in the next couple of weeks," she went on. "He's offering eight thousand for the week but I may be able to get him to go a little higher. And we could talk about some sweeteners. I think he'll work with you to make this happen."

Hargrove glanced over at Madden and flashed a confident smile. She made some faces as Veronica spoke.

"No, I'm sorry, I can't give you his name. He doesn't want this getting out. I mean, if this got out, social media would have a field day. I see the tweets now. 'Wealthy tech entrepreneur goes back to his roots, slumming it in tiny $2 million Palo Alto home.' In some ways it's worse than him throwing one of these ridiculously lavish parties."

Another pause, this one longer.

"Of course you need to speak to your husband about it. Just get back to me soon. I'll be in the office 'til six today and you're welcome to come by at any time, just let me know."

She said goodbye, hung up the phone, then stood up and assumed a self-satisfied victory pose, her hands on her hips. She was Wonder Woman in a different costume. Everybody except her husband was slightly awed.

"Now we just have to wait for the husband to sign off," she said. "But she seems on board, which means we're ninety-eight percent of the way home. I tell you, if it were me, I'd take that deal in a heartbeat. Wouldn't you?"

11 / First Mover

"I CAN'T DO THIS," MORTON WHISPERED.

"Sure you can," Fremmer said. "You have to."

Morton had just gotten off the phone with Ronald and they were still standing in the waiting room of the police station. Now Morton was visibly upset.

"I don't think you understand something, Max," he said, loosely covering his mouth with his right hand to muffle his voice. "I have two kids. I have an ex-wife. I have to pay child support. And if I don't pay it, I become a deadbeat dad. I don't want to become a deadbeat dad. So, you know what that means?"

"I do," Fremmer replied, also covering his mouth.

They looked like a pitcher and catcher conversing on the mound, hiding their lip movements with their gloves, except they had no gloves, just hands.

"That means I have to make money," Morton said. "And in order to make money, I need clients who have money and are actually willing to pay me with money. The guy in there has no money and has no ability to pay me. And that is why he will get a fine public defender to defend him. I can't afford to do pro-bono work. Is that clear?"

"We're going to do this," Fremmer said. "Just hear me out."

"We? How did this become *we*?"

"I'm going to help you. I may not be a practicing lawyer, but I passed the bar in New York and I've kept up the CLE requirements and paid my bar dues every year. I'm fully accredited."

"OK, now I get it," Morton said. "This is really about you. You want to defend this guy. Well, you go right ahead."

"You know I can't do that. But I can help. And I can get you money."

That got Morton's attention.

"How are you going to do that?" he asked.

"I'll get it. Trust me. This is going to be good for you."

"You have no idea what's involved in a case like this, Max. The time. The cost. We'd have to hire expert witnesses to evaluate him. I've never done an insanity defense."

"So you're going to spend your whole life doing divorces, DUIs, and defending assorted other petty criminals?"

"You're one to talk. If we're talking barrel scrapings, I think you're the low man on the board. You make a living gussying up people's dreck and publishing it. I got news for you, it's still dreck."

"I'm more partial to drivel," Fremmer said. "But I like your use of 'gussy up.' It's an underused verb slash preposition."

"I'm serious, Max. I don't want to represent this guy."

"Yes, you do. I told you, he didn't do it."

"Come on. Stop it."

"Just think about this for a minute. My client told me she knew something real bad about someone and she feared for her safety. I didn't believe her at the time, but the fact is that's what she told me. And then a couple weeks later she gets pushed in front of a car by a homeless guy. Really? Does that make sense to you?"

"Coincidence," Morton said. "Negative attitude. People bring bad things upon themselves."

Fremmer cocked his head a little to the left, made a face.

"I'm telling you there's something very strange going on here," he went on. "You need to be a first mover on this. You need to get in there and help this guy. This is how you make a name for yourself. You get in front of the cameras, get some press. Yeah, I understand the concept of building a reputation gradually and with care. But you're what, forty-five, forty-six—"

"I just turned forty," Morton said.

"Well, you look like shit."

"I just went through a divorce."

"The client I met with a few hours ago did, too. And look at him. He wrote a novel. Just banged it out, the novel he's always wanted to write. Now it's your turn. This is your novel, Carlos. This is your game changer."

Morton pondered all that for a moment.

"They'll deny him bail," he said, thinking aloud. "Probably take him downtown. The Tombs."

"Well, you gotta get in there now and introduce yourself. He needs to see a face. Even if it's for a minute. I'll wait for you outside. I'm going to sell some books."

"Sell some books?" Morton said, suddenly alarmed.

"I gotta speak to the media. I've gotta let them know about Candace's books and frame them correctly. It's going to get out there eventually. We might as well own it."

"Do not do that, Max. As your counselor, I advise you not to speak to the press."

"I have to. Not for me. But for her kid. She's gonna need the money."

"That's a really bad idea. Now's the time to protect their privacy."

Just then a police official dressed in plainclothes, a community affairs officer, approached them. They were clearing the waiting room.

"Sir, I need you to leave," he said to Morton.

"I can't leave," Morton declared. "You're holding my client."

"Who's your client?" the officer asked.

"The guy everybody's outside for. Ronald Darby. I need to speak with him now. He's entitled to see his attorney."

"I thought you were *his* attorney," he said, motioning to Fremmer.

"I was. Now I'm Mr. Darby's. I spoke to him on the phone a few minutes ago. Go ask him. Morton's my name. Carlos Morton."

The officer clearly wasn't sold on Morton's story, but he also wasn't ready to dismiss it. In the end, he settled for removing just Fremmer, who gathered up his scooter and backpack and headed for the exit.

"Don't do it, Max," Morton said as he left.

"Thanks again for coming," Fremmer replied without looking back. "Despite what your ex-wife said in that deposition, you're a good man. Text me after you get out."

PART 2

12/ Lennon's Least Favorite Beatles Song

ONE NIGHT MADDEN HAD A DREAM THAT HE WAS IN THE BACKYARD of Bronsky's former home looking back at Hal Shelby standing on the deck behind him.

"Here?" Madden asked him.

"Is that what the map's telling you?" Shelby said.

Madden didn't realize he had a map. But there it was, in his hand. It looked like a pirate's map, the kind his grandfather drew up for him on his birthday when he was a little kid. His grandfather used to create elaborate treasure hunts that took several hours to set up. The treasure never amounted to much more than a small stack of silver dollars, which at the time seemed like a fortune to Madden.

He looked at the map, then at a spot in the plant bed in front of him. It looked right, so he started to dig.

The shovel went into the ground much easier than he thought it would, considering the drought. The earth was moist, dark and rich. An earthworm wriggled in the soil on his shovel. Madden dumped each shovelful onto the pile next to the deepening hole.

Then he hit something. Not a rock. But it was hard, maybe something wooden. A miniature treasure chest?

He probed around the object until first one corner was exposed, then the whole top. It was the chest. Had to be. He dug around it a little more, then dropped the shovel and got down on one knee to extract it. But when he went to lift it he noticed a hand was grasping it. Not a skeleton hand, a real hand, fleshy and undecayed. Was it alive? It seemed alive. Madden picked up the shovel and dug as fast as he could.

The hand became a full arm and then a shoulder and a flash of hair. Long golden hair mixed with dirt. He dropped to his knees again, cleared dirt away from the face, a female face, with his hands. But she wasn't Stacey Walker. No, the face was younger, that of a girl, and he realized she was Kristen Kroiter, the seventeen-year-old whose suicide he'd once investigated as a murder.

"Is it her?" Shelby called out.

He stared at Kristen's unblemished, serene face. "No," he said, dumbfounded. "It's someone else."

"Someone else?" Shelby said. "That's not in the contract. Who is it?"

"Kristen," Madden said. And as soon as he said her name, her eyes opened. Then he woke up.

A week later he found himself on the deck in the backyard of Bronsky's former home sitting at an umbrellaed table a few feet from where Shelby had been standing in the dream. Madden was watching a ground-radar technician push around a contraption that looked like a modified baby stroller.

The technician, a guy in his late twenties with a full beard, was wearing a pair of headphones and listening to music. He nudged the machine forward a few feet at a time then stopped to look at a monochrome screen that showed subtle variations or "disturbances" in the ground. There was nothing detailed about the images—they looked more like a series of disconnected, compressed lines—and the technician had warned him that while the technology was improving, it wouldn't show the outline of bones or specific shapes of objects.

On the table in front of Madden was a platter of lox and bagels and another with fruit on skewers. Dupuy had decided to cater their little expedition, make it a brunch-slash-dig, and was in the kitchen filling an ice bucket to hold the bottles of sparkling wine and fresh-squeezed orange juice she'd picked up at Draeger's in Menlo Park. She was making mimosas to celebrate the completion of breast-feeding her daughter, who was asleep in a baby carriage parked near the table.

Reaching for a fruit skewer, Madden heard a muffled scream from inside the house. He jumped up from his seat, knocked his leg against the underside of the table and nearly fell over. After regaining his balance he limped over to the open sliding glass door, pushed aside the sheer curtain, and entered the small living room, where, near the entrance to the kitchen, he saw Dupuy standing face-to-face with an intruder, a tall, sleepy-eyed, forty-something male wearing cutoff jeans, flip flops, and a navy blue T-shirt with the slogan "Where is your wall?" Instinctively, Madden reached across his chest to grasp the gun he quickly realized wasn't there.

"Hey," the intruder said cheerfully, "you guys are here early. What's that machine out there? It's like a grave finder machine, isn't it? It can see underground?"

"Who are you?" Madden asked.

"J.J."

"Do you live here, J.J?"

"Temporarily."

"Temporarily?"

"I'm here for the week," he explained. "Hal Shelby set me up. And from your reaction, I'm guessing he didn't tell you."

"You scared the shit out of me," Dupuy said. "No one's supposed to be here."

"What exactly are you doing here?" Madden asked, annoyed.

"Just chillin'. Clearing the mind. Getting back to my roots. It was Hal's idea. Get the creative juices flowing. I grew up in the area, in a house like this. Gunn High. Class of '85."

"You an entrepreneur?" Dupuy asked.

"No, musician."

It was if he'd uttered some magical word, for suddenly her eyes lit up, her jaw dropped a little.

"You're J.J. Carradine, aren't you?" she said.

The name didn't ring any bells for Madden. The only Carradine he knew was David, who played the Shaolin monk cum martial-arts expert Caine on *Kung Fu*, a TV show he'd watched religiously during his twenties.

"That's what they keep telling me," J.J. said.

"This guy's a rock star, Hank," Dupuy said. "Literally, a rock star."

Well, more of a has-been rock star, Madden soon learned. Which was why he was holed up in a small cottage in one of the more modest sections of Palo Alto, looking for inspiration. It wasn't for lack of money. He had plenty of that. Too much, in fact. In the '90s, his band, for which he was the focal and spiritual leader, had a string of hits and sold out Madison Square Garden in their last tour. Then nothing. They couldn't get their next album out.

J.J. took full blame for their demise. "I just started hating everything I was writing," he explained to Madden. "Everything seemed trite, shallow. And then I just got in a bad mood with everybody always asking where the new album was. Every person I met was like, 'Hey, love you guys, where's the new album?' And I'd be like 'Dude, it's coming.' And it just got oppressive. I felt fat, man," he said patting his flat stomach. "I felt like I was carrying around all this extra weight even though I was a stick. I wasn't eating."

He was still a stick. A good-looking one, too. Clean cut, he had a strange hairdo. His hair was cut very short on the sides but longer on top, with a stunted ponytail flaring out of the back of his head, cinched off with a hair tie. He looked more frat boy than rock star, with only a couple of small tattoos visible—a tiny bird on his left forearm and da Vinci's Vitruvian Man across his right shin; it was almost the size of a soccer shin pad.

J.J. said his band, now comprised of only two original members, didn't play stadiums anymore. They mainly played corporate gigs for a couple hundred thousand bucks a pop, sometimes more. Which was how he knew Shelby.

"Thank God for the tech boom," he went on. "All these overcompensated geeks are suddenly nostalgic for their youth. Fine by me. The way I look at it I'm in a cover band for my own music. That's all the Stones are, a cover band of The Stones. Hey, is that food out there? If you don't mind, I'm starving. I fasted yesterday."

Dupuy didn't mind at all. She happily led J.J. out to the deck, leaving Madden in the house to stew. A minute later he was on the phone with Shelby, expressing his dismay.

"Did you forget to tell me something, Hal?" he asked.

"What?"

"Let me give you a hint. He sold out the Garden back in '95."

"Oh, J.J." Shelby chuckled. "You've met?"

"What's he doing here, Hal? There isn't supposed to be anybody in the house. On the small chance this is a crime scene, I don't need any random over-the-hill rock stars roaming the property."

"Relax. I had to arbitrage the situation. I don't like dropping twenty grand and getting nothing in return. So you got J.J. I'm covered now."

"Covered for what?"

"He's playing my niece's wedding. Five songs. Acoustic set. There's a little club you don't know about. We barter. It's all about bartering these days. It's the new economy for rich people who have too much money to spend."

"And what's he get out of it?" Madden asked.

"A concept for his next album. The Walker case went down right when he was at his peak. We were talking the other day and when I brought it up, it hit a nerve. He said he once thought about writing a song about Stacey. And I said, 'Why not do a whole album?' He's got a bad case of writer's block. I'm sure you can commiserate."

"Fantastic."

"I'm a facilitator, Detective. I put people in a position to succeed. When they succeed, I succeed."

"What happens when they don't?"

"They fail. And I enjoy that, too. Sometimes more."

"So you win either way?"

"Who's keeping score? Like I said, relax. What are you doing there anyway? Sitting around? Now you get to party with a rock star."

"I thought the phrase was party *like* a rock star, not party *with* a rock star," Madden said.

"Got a call coming in, gotta jump," Shelby responded and the line went silent.

Madden walked back to the sliding glass door, pausing before the opening to look outside. *Oh, no,* he thought. J.J. had found a rapt audience in Dupuy, who'd entered a state that could only be described as fawning. Madden never would have guessed she had it in her.

He limped outside and fixed himself a mimosa, light on the orange juice. He never drank on the job when he was on the force, so it felt a little decadent to be drinking now, especially at ten in the morning. But he didn't care. This so-called investigation was turning into a joke. And thanks to slamming into the table, both his leg and foot were hurting. His back, too.

"He's going to write an album based on the Walker case," Dupuy said excitedly after he reclaimed his seat.

"So I hear," Madden said.

He noticed that J.J. only had lox on his plate and no bagel. *Low-carb diet? Probably.*

"You forget that at one point these people were in love," J.J. said. "I'm going to open with that. Ross had been married once, was in kind of a rough patch. Then he meets Stacey at a friend's barbecue. Twenty-two, right out of college. Tight body, totally fresh. And he just falls for her. Typical story. People warn her. He's got a mean streak. She doesn't listen, of course. I had a girlfriend like that. Everybody told her to be careful. And we were together for four years before the wheels came off. Which is what I'm thinking is the title for the opening track. *Before the wheels came off.* I thought of that this morning when I was lying in bed."

"What's 'Where's your wall?' stand for?" Madden asked, eyeing J.J.'s T-shirt.

J.J. turned around and showed him the back of the shirt, where there was a silkscreened image of a soccer ball and the name of a local store Madden recognized.

"My buddy has a soccer shop," J.J. said. "You know, if you're a kid and you're serious about playing, you gotta get out there and play by yourself sometimes and knock it against a wall to get better. You gotta find your wall. But I read it more metaphorically. *Where is your wall?* There's something mystical about that. It's all about finding that wall and using it to move forward."

"So, where's your wall?" Dupuy asked in a low, husky voice that induced in Madden flashbacks to Kathleen Turner in *Body Heat.* A little too seductive for his tastes.

J.J. smiled, leaned closer to her and looked into her eyes. "Maybe here," he said. "In this expensive little dump."

The two continued to stare at each other, which made Madden nervous.

"What about that for the name of a song?" he broke in. "Expensive little dump."

"I like it," J.J. declared.

Just then the baby stirred in the carriage, crying out for a few brief but jarring seconds before becoming silent again. J.J. looked over at the carriage as if seeing it for the first time.

"That belong to you?" he asked Dupuy.

"Uh, yeah," she said. "That's Chloe. She's five months old today."

"Adopted or biological?"

Dupuy was little taken aback by the question. "No, I birthed her," she said.

"Wow," J.J. said. "You look great. I'd never have guessed you just had a kid."

He held up his wine glass and made a toast.

"To hot moms who've had biological kids," he said.

Dupuy didn't quite know how to react to that either, but she clinked his glass anyway. Then it was Madden's turn. He got a clink from both of them. He was starting to enjoy this.

"Actually, this is good," J.J. said. "The baby's a good audience. Hold on a sec. I'll be back."

With that, he got up and left. Madden couldn't help but laugh.

"What's so funny?" Dupuy asked.

"Let me know when you regain control of your faculties."

"That bad, huh?"

He nodded.

"You don't understand," she whispered. "I had such a crush on that guy when I was in college. Or maybe it was law school. I can't believe he's here."

"I'm not your father or your boss," Madden said. "But I suggest you find your wall and put a moat around it."

Dupuy let out a little giggle. "Where'd he go?"

They soon found out. J.J. returned to the table with a friend, his beat-up guitar. Sitting back down, he rested it on his thigh and said:

"I've been thinking about what you said about Ross killing Stacey."

Dupuy pointed to herself, surprised. "What I said?"

"A while back you were quoted saying he killed her out of simple jealousy. That's what you thought the motive was."

"That's what I thought enraged him enough to kill her."

At the time Stacey disappeared, she was still living with Ross, though they were in fact separated. She'd gotten a job at Blooming-dale's in Stanford Shopping Center and was going out at night with friends and, as it turned out, Bronsky. Ross may have strayed from their marriage first, but now Stacey was out and about, meeting new people, embracing a single lifestyle. As they worked toward a divorce settle-ment, Ross claimed they had an understanding. Maybe so, but they had sworn statements from three people—a fellow Bloomingdale's em-ployee, a manicurist, and Bronsky—who all said they heard him shout-ing at Stacey over the phone. More than once, he'd threatened to kill her—or used words that implied he could make her "disappear."

One night she came home late, leaving her car parked on the street in front of their house, not in the driveway, which she'd been doing ever since they were separated. She appeared to have slept in her bed in the guest cottage, but she wasn't anywhere to be found in the morning. It took Ross two full days to report her missing. His reason: He thought she'd gone to visit a friend in L.A.

"Pastorini thought he killed her because of money, not jealousy," Madden said, speaking of his old boss. "He didn't want to give up anything in a divorce. That, and he thought he might lose custody of their kid."

"Maybe," Dupuy remarked coolly, sounding and looking like her old self. "But once he got himself a girlfriend he started working on getting a bunch of assets out of his name. He was preparing for a di-vorce for months. Which is why I'm not sure her killing was premed-itated. A lot of people don't remember this, but when he took off, we were on the verge of charging him with fraud, not murder. We had him on the financial shenanigans."

She was right. A lot of people forgot that. They assumed that with all the circumstantial evidence and solid bits of physical evidence—Stacey's blood and hair in the trunk of Ross's car—they had a strong enough case to bring him up on murder charges. But it just didn't work without a body. It rarely did.

J.J. didn't seem to care about all that. "Do you know what John Lennon's least favorite Beatles song was?" he asked them.

"I don't know what *my* least favorite Beatles song is," Dupuy replied.

J.J. handed her his phone. "Do me a favor and get a video of this for me. I want to see how it plays."

Madden didn't like where this was going. That's the last thing he needed, some video popping up on YouTube or Facebook.

"That stays in the phone," he said. "No social media, understand? You will not screw up my investigation, I don't care who you are."

"Chill, Detective," J.J. said. "We're all responsible adults. Except the baby, of course."

"Have another mimosa, Hank," Dupuy suggested, fiddling around with the settings on the phone's screen. When everything was set, she pointed the phone at J.J. and nodded, indicating she was ready.

"And a three, two, one," J.J. cued himself, then started playing, plucking the strings on his guitar as he launched into a sweetly subdued acoustic intro. When the words finally came, his voice—quiet, soulful—wasn't what Madden had expected.

Well I'd rather see you dead, little girl
Than to be with another man
You better keep your head, little girl
Or I won't know where I am
Ah no, no, no

Madden vaguely recollected the original song, which was off one of the Beatles early albums. He fought to remember the title and then it came to him as the words came out of J.J.'s mouth: *You better run for our life if you can, little girl.* The original version had a much quicker, driving pace. But J.J.'s new rendition was just the opposite: slow and soulful. He'd turned an angry, misogynistic tune into a bluesy ballad. Madden wasn't easily creeped out, but he suddenly felt a little spooked.

Let this be a sermon
I mean everything I've said
Baby, I'm determined
And I'd rather see you dead
Ah no, no, no

When J.J. stopped playing, Dupuy tapped the phone's screen, then set the phone on the table. Madden noticed that tears had welled up in her eyes.

"What do you think?" J.J. asked.

"Haunting," she said. "I've never heard that song."

Madden clapped, giving him a short ovation. So, too, did the ground-radar technician, who'd removed his headphones and had them around his neck.

"The Beatles?" the guy called out. "'Run For Your Life.' Off *Rubber Soul*. 1966. You added the 'no, no, no', right? Really changes it. Awesome rendition, man. You play around here?"

"Thanks, dude," J.J. said. "Hey, what do you call that machine?"

"GPR," the technician said. "Ground Penetrating Radar."

"GPR," J.J. murmured to himself, then picked up his phone and pulled out the little stylus that was stored inside it and scribbled something on the screen.

"I write everything down now," he said when he was finished. "I let a lot of shit slip by when I was younger. They didn't have these phones back then. I got pages of notes in here. I'm going to write a book. Maybe have it come out at the same time as the new album. One supports the other. You married?"

Not surprisingly, the question was aimed at Dupuy, not Madden.

"Is that for your notes?" she asked.

J.J. laughed. "No."

"Let's just say negotiations are ongoing."

"Yeah, I've been there," he replied. "Was engaged twice. Didn't knock anybody up, though. Good thing, because I'll tell ya, the best business decision I made was not to get married. My lawyer said don't get hitched without a prenup. And I listened. That's the one rule of showbiz. Get a good lawyer and listen to him. Or her, as the case may be."

Madden didn't know exactly why Dupuy and her on-again-off-again boyfriend of the last several years, Ted Cogan, hadn't tied the knot, but he was pretty sure money or prenups weren't the hold up. However, she didn't say anything to refute J.J.'s comment; she let him reminisce about his two brushes with near-catastrophic financial ruin.

"One of my bandmates recently had to declare bankruptcy," he said.

"Drummer?" Madden asked.

"Yeah, major bummer. I felt for the guy. But it was his own fault."

Dupuy took a long drag on her wine glass. Madden could see she was growing a little weary of their houseguest. Some of the sheen was wearing off. What a shame.

After draining what was left of his drink, he looked over at the ground-radar technician, who was now staring at his screen intently.

"I sincerely doubt this guy is going to find anything," he said, thinking aloud.

Almost as soon as he said it, the technician pulled his headphones off his ear and stepped away from his machine. For a moment, Madden was concerned he'd heard him and was somehow offended. But it wasn't that.

"I've got a couple of hot spots," he called out to them. "Like I said earlier, I can't tell you what's there, but if you want to start digging while I do the other side, that's fine by me. I'm curious myself."

Madden sat up in his chair, a bit shocked.

"Are they big enough to be a body?" he asked.

"Could be," the technician replied. "I'm just reading the topography. It can sometimes show metal. Have a look if you want."

Madden followed him back over to the machine. To the untrained eye it was hard to interpret what the wavy lines meant.

"They both aren't too deep," the technician said. "Around four feet. You digging or you getting someone to do it?"

Madden wasn't exactly sure how he was going to handle the excavation. He had Shelby's landscaping crew scheduled to come in that afternoon.

"I'll start and let's see how it goes," he said.

"I'll help," J.J. called out gamely.

Madden ignored the comment. He thanked the technician and

headed to his car, parked out in front of the house. On the sidewalk, he paused for a moment and looked around. All the cars parked nearby appeared empty. There wasn't any sign of the tail he thought Shelby had put on him.

He opened his trunk and retrieved Shelby's gleaming gift shovel along with a tripod and digital SLR camera he planned to use to document the excavation.

When he returned to the backyard, J.J. was gone. Dupuy said she'd sent him into the garage to look for a shovel.

"I don't want him digging," Madden said.

"Come on, Hank. Maybe he'll take his shirt off."

"Stop."

After he used the camera to shoot some still images of the site, he set up the tripod in the middle of the lawn and put it into video mode. He told Dupuy to stand behind the camera while he rolled up his sleeves and began scripting out what he wanted to say in his mind. After thirty seconds or so he declared himself ready and took up a position in front of the camera. The shovel, head up, stood by his side. He asked her how he looked.

"A little American Gothic," J.J. said, returning to the deck with a less glamorous digging tool than Madden's. "I like it."

"I didn't ask you," Madden quipped.

"Just talk, Hank," Dupuy said.

And he did. He said who and where he was, why he was there, and noted the time and date.

Then he started to dig.

13/ Getting Woozy

CANDACE EPSTEIN DIDN'T DIE. FIVE DAYS AFTER SHE WAS HIT SHE WAS in the ICU at Mount Sinai St. Luke's Hospital on a ventilator with multiple medication drips and bandages around her head that extended across the right side of her face. Thanks to her daughter, Fremmer had made it onto the approved visitors list, but he also discovered he had an inside contact: A friend from spinning class, an anesthesiologist who worked at the hospital and helped run the ICU as a critical-care physician.

The extent of her injuries was staggering. The impact, or really three impacts, if you counted the windshield and the pavement, had left her with a broken femur, fractured pelvis, and a "closed-head injury"—a skull fracture and subdural hematoma. A neurosurgeon had performed a "bolt" operation, installing a device in her head to relieve pressure on her brain from intracranial bleeding. She'd also ruptured her spleen, which had been removed, broken six ribs and had a bilateral pneumothorax—torn lungs in non-medical speak.

His anesthesiologist friend Ethan Bernstein said she was lucky to be alive. He'd seen other "peds vs. cars" who arrived in her condition and most didn't make it. She still might not make it.

Ped vs. car—pedestrian vs. car—was how first responders and hospital trauma teams referred to patients like Candace. The term also showed up in YouTube video titles, although in Candace's case, the publicly released video of her being struck was labeled with a more literal descriptor: "Woman pushed in front of car in New York." It had more than five million views in less than forty-eight hours.

He didn't stay at the hospital long. Delivering a bouquet of flowers and some clichéd words of encouragement, he'd become profoundly unnerved. Years ago, he'd spent several days in the hospital with his ex-fiancée Denise, who'd suffered a broken neck in a body surfing accident. That was a clusterfuck. She was paralyzed from the chest down. But the damage was limited. Mostly internal, not external. He wasn't looking at a shattered human being, someone who was unrecognizable.

After he left the hospital Fremmer picked up the 1 train over by Columbia at 116th Street and rode it down to 79th Street, then scootered to the Starbucks on Broadway and 75th Street. Spotting his favorite table in the back corner vacant—a rarity at this hour—he went in and set up shop, opening his laptop to check on Candace's e-books, all of which had become Amazon bestsellers. He'd just opened her Kindle Direct Publishing dashboard when he felt the Bluetooth headset in his right ear vibrating, announcing an incoming call. He looked at the Caller ID on his phone and recognizing the number, clicked the answer button on the headset.

"This is Max."

"Mr. Fremmer, this is Charlie Mould. I got your message. You wanted to speak to me about Ron Darby."

"Yes, thanks for returning my call."

"I didn't quite understand what you were saying in the message," Mould said. "Are you his attorney? Or do you work for his attorney?"

"I work *with* his attorney Carlos Morton," Fremmer replied, speaking louder than he usually did into the headset's microphone. His top-of-the-line Plantronics model picked up his voice and cancelled out ambient noise so well that he could talk in a low voice and callers could hear him clearly, even if he was in a noisy room. "I don't know if you heard about what happened up here in New York—"

"Yeah, I heard," Mould said. "I've been reading about it. I've seen your name in the press, which is why I was a little confused. You know the victim. You're her book doctor?"

"More of her co-publisher, but that's not worth getting into. I went into the police station to answer some background questions about her and ended up meeting Ron. I got concerned he may be getting a raw deal so I put him in touch with Mr. Morton, who's a lawyer friend of mine."

"Raw deal in what way? You think they got the wrong guy?"

"Knowing what I know that was my gut reaction."

Mould seemed surprised by the assertion. He wasn't the first.

"Really?"

"Really," Fremmer said. "Anyway, the reason I called is that we got a hold of an old Great Valley High yearbook from down there in Malvern. Someone put it up online. And we looked up Ron and we were kind of surprised to discover that he played on the football team in high school. You were the captain and also a friend of his."

Fremmer didn't actually know whether Mould was Ronald's friend in high school. He was making an educated guess.

"*A* captain," Mould corrected him. "There were three of us."

"Sorry. A captain. And you and Ron were friends?"

"Yeah, sure. But that was a long time ago. I haven't seen him in probably thirty years."

"What position did he play?"

"Ron? He played defensive back and some wide receiver. A lot of us played both ways. I played safety and running back."

"And back then, what kind of guy was he?"

"What do you mean? Like was he a nutjob?"

"Well, more like did he show any signs of having mental health issues?"

"Not that I saw. He was as normal as anybody else, I guess. He dated a cheerleader, did pretty well in school, was popular. I mean, we drank and smoked pot and did some crazy stuff. But it was the seventies. There was a lot of crazy stuff going on, though when you see what's going on with kids today, it doesn't seem so crazy."

"And about when would you say he started having issues?"

"Well, he didn't make it through his first year of college, so I'd say then. Well, I shouldn't say he didn't make it. They didn't kick him out. But I think the story was he just didn't go back after the summer of his freshman year. He said he was going to take a year off and work. And then he just never went back. And it was very frustrating for his family. He was smoking a lot of dope and just sitting around, you know?"

"And you saw him then?"

"I saw him around a little," Mould said. "During the summers. When I was home. But we started moving in different circles. He started getting, you know, antisocial. And then he kind of disappeared. His parents passed away. His father first and his mom about three or four years later, I believe. And after that I didn't hear anything about him except that he was kind of drifting around doing odd jobs. Went out to California, I think. Or maybe Arizona."

"And he never came to you for anything?"

"You mean for money?"

"Or a job?"

"Back when I was still in college we talked about it once or twice. My family is in the supermarket business. I worked in that business for a while. But the kind of jobs we talked about didn't interest him. We're talking stock boy. My dad made everybody start at the bottom and prove themselves. Even I had to."

"And now you have your own craft beer company?"

With the Internet it was hard to keep secrets. Before he ever got on the phone with Charlie Mould he knew a lot about him. But the flipside was Mould also knew a lot about Max Fremmer. Or certainly more than he was saying. One Google search would have brought up a wealth of information.

"Yeah, we specialize in Belgian-style beers," Mould went on. "To tell you the truth, it's been hard to keep up with demand. Been a real boom in craft beer here in central PA the last few years."

"Well, let me ask you this, Mr. Mould—"

"Charlie. No one calls me Mr. Mould."

"OK, Charlie. No one calls me Mr. Fremmer either. Let me ask you this. And this is the real reason I called. While you played football with Ron did he take any bad hits? You know, get laid out or anything like that?"

The line went silent for a moment.

"You're asking whether he got concussed?"

"Yeah."

"Funny you should mention that because it's something I've been giving some thought to myself. Not about Ron. But just how it pertains to me because, you know, sometimes, I have those little moments were I can't remember something and it makes you wonder whether it's just getting old or something else. I played some in college, too."

"But how 'bout Ron?"

"I mean, back then we all got concussions and no one thought anything about it. They held some fingers up and if you got the correct amount you went back in the game. We called it getting woozy. But yeah, I distinctly remember him getting knocked out at least once. They had to hit him with the smelling salts and all that. And one time he didn't remember playing in the second half. He had a sack and scored a touchdown and the coach gave him the game ball. The next day, he asked me why he got the ball. And I said, 'You were awesome in the second half.' He didn't remember any of it."

"So you can definitely say that on two occasions he had what would typically be construed as a concussion by today's standards."

"Yeah, and there were probably other times. A lot of the time it's you going to make a tackle and the guy's knee catches you in the head. The knee to the head causes a lot more concussions than you realize."

"And you'd be willing go on record about those two incidents you were talking about?"

"On record? With who?"

"Well, for instance, if I had a reporter call you would you be willing to speak to her about what you just told me."

"What kind of reporter?"

"Someone from *The New York Times*."

"*The Times*?"

"Yeah. I don't know if you've noticed, but Ron's getting put through the ringer in the tabloids. He's become the poster child of the city's homeless problem. They're all over the mayor. It'd be good to humanize him a bit."

"Where is he now?"

"He's in the psychiatric ward at Bellevue. They're conducting what's called a 730 exam to see if he's fit to stand trial."

After Fremmer left the police station, Ronald had been taken downtown to Central Booking in the basement of the Tombs, a detention complex that got its nickname from the Egyptian Revivalist style of Manhattan's original house of detention built in 1838. That original building had been demolished long ago but the sobriquet stuck with all subsequent structures that replaced it.

He was arraigned the next day on attempted murder charges. At the arraignment, Morton had asked for and was granted a 730 exam to be conducted to determine whether Ronald was fit to proceed. According to article 730 of New York Criminal Procedure Law, an incapacitated person was defined as "a defendant who as the result of mental disease or defect lacked capacity to understand the proceedings against him or to assist in his own defense."

At Bellevue, a designated state hospital, two qualified psychiatric examiners had been assigned to evaluate Ronald and submit their findings to the court within thirty days. However, with all the media scrutiny, Ronald's case was on the fast track and Morton thought he might be back in court soon, perhaps within a couple of days. He also thought the DA was ready to go right to a grand jury if Ronald was declared fit.

"How do you think they're gonna rule?" Mould asked.

"Well, I think the problem is Ron goes from saying some pretty whacky stuff to having some pretty coherent moments. And the truth is you gotta be pretty batshit crazy these days not to stand trial. So we're preparing for him to be indicted."

"Maybe he didn't mean to push her in front of a car," Mould said. "I mean, from the video, it's clear he pushed her. But maybe he didn't see the car. Maybe he just pushed her and she ended up in the street, you know?"

"It doesn't really matter. Whoever pushed her caused her injuries. It doesn't matter whether he intended to or not. He's going to end up with an attempted murder or murder charge and he's looking at a doing a lot of time if they can prove he did it."

"And what good is my speaking to this reporter going to do?"

"I think people are sympathetic to the whole concussion angle these days."

"You can't blame football for what he did. You got thousands of guys who played football and they aren't pushing people in front of cars."

"We're not trying to blame football," Fremmer said. "We're just trying to give him a past. All people are seeing now is a disheveled, mountain man type guy. All they're seeing is his mug shot. But like you said, once upon a time that same guy dated a cheerleader. People need to know that guy and how he ended up living in the streets."

"I get it," Mould said. "And sure, I'll speak to that reporter if you want. Our Belgian White was actually in *The Times* a few months back. Got a nice little bump from that. Speaking of which, your victim friend got a couple of big plugs for that smut she writes. My wife says her e-books are on the Amazon bestseller list. She downloaded the first one. Says it isn't bad but it's no *50 Shades*."

"Well, that's a high bar to get over," Fremmer said, glancing at the dashboard on his laptop screen. It showed in real time the sales of all her titles. He'd been alternating between 99 cents, $1.99, and $2.99 to maximize revenue. Amazon took 70 percent of the sale price of any book priced below $2.99, but the numbers got reversed at $2.99 or greater. The trick was to get some sales at $2.99 while the book worked its way out of the bestseller list, then drop the price before it lost its Top-100 ranking.

"You come up with that title?" Mould asked, chuckling.

"Which one?"

"*Upload in Progress.*"

"I might have," Fremmer admitted.

"Well, I'm not the type of guy who gets all holier than thou about how people go about making their livings so long as they're not hurting anyone of course."

Just then Fremmer felt his headset buzzing. Morton's picture popped up on the screen of his phone.

"Hold on a sec, Mr. Mould, I have another call coming in."

"Charlie."

"Yeah, sorry. Charlie. I'll be right back. Don't go anywhere."

He then clicked over to Morton and said: "Hey, I'll call you right back. I've got one of his teammates on the other line."

"Anything there?"

"Yeah, I'll tell you in a minute."

"You ask him about raising some money?"

"No."

"Ask him."

"I'll call you back."

He clicked back to Mould and said: "Sorry about that."

He was still there. "That's OK," Mould said.

"That reporter I was talking about, her name is Christina. I don't know exactly when or even if she'll call, but I'm going to give her your number if you don't mind."

"Is there anything I shouldn't say?"

"No, say whatever you want. And if you have other people she can speak to, that'd be good. Which reminds me. Do you know if Ron's got any family or friends who'd be willing to support his defense? Mr. Morton is working pro bono on this, as am I, but I know he'd like to hire some quality investigators to hunt down any sort of exculpatory evidence that might be out there. He's got a couple of former detectives who usually work for him, but they don't like to work for free."

"He's got a sister," Mould said. "Maggie. But he put her through the emotional ringer from what I heard. She doesn't want to have anything to do with him."

"She married or does she still go by Darby?"

"I think she's married." He heard Mould put his hand over the phone and in a muffled voice say: "Honey, you remember the name of the guy who Maggie Darby married?"

Fremmer couldn't hear how Honey responded. But after a moment, Mould came back and said: "My wife says she thinks it's Gilligan. Like the show."

"OK, thanks. Like I said, it isn't for me."

"No, I get it. And I'll tell you what, depending on how things play out, I'll check with some of the guys who were on the team and maybe we can pass the hat. No promises, though."

"Totally understand. You have a good day."

He hung up and called Morton back.

"His teammate says he had at least two concussions," he told him. "And he's willing to go on record with that with that reporter I spoke to. I'm going to email her right now with his contact info. Hopefully she calls him."

"Well, it's something," Morton said. "Might help change the narrative. I'm going to venture that brain-damaged former football player plays slightly better with the public than mentally ill homeless person who stopped taking his meds."

"He dated a cheerleader in high school," Fremmer added.

"Booyah. Get me pictures. I'm seeing a young man in a light blue tux with ruffles. Did I mention that I got my second death-threat phone call this morning?"

"The price of fame."

"Just some crank. Was from out of state. But I want you to know that if I see a deal he should take, you need to help get him on board. Mr. Darby will not be a long-term client. Your ever hear of Kendra Webdale? There's a law named after her. She was a promising young writer when a psycho named Andrew Goldstein pushed her in front of a subway in 1999. Two trials and seven years later he finally pleaded guilty to manslaughter. He got twenty-three years."

"Have a little faith, Carlos. I saw Candace this morning, by the way."

"How she's doing?"

"She's a wreck but still alive."

Just then Fremmer looked up from his laptop and saw a young woman, rather stunning, wearing mirrored aviator sunglasses, her dirty-blond hair pulled back into a short ponytail. She was at the end of a short line of customers putting in their order. But instead of facing toward the counter she had her back to the line and appeared to be looking directly at him.

Morton said something about how it was miracle Candace was alive considering what he'd seen in the video, but Fremmer wasn't really listening. The woman had the high cheekbones and slim frame of a model, but lacked the height. She was wearing skinny jeans and an unzipped, tight-fitting short black leather jacket over a white T-shirt. A pair of fashionable platform shoes gave her two, maybe three inches.

"Do I know you?" Fremmer said.

"Hang up," she said.

"What?" Morton cut in, confused.

Fremmer stood up to face the woman. "There's a rather attractive woman here who wants to talk to me," he said to Carlos. "I don't know who she is but she seems to know who I am."

"Great, I'm getting death threats for representing this guy and you've got groupies."

"I'll call you back."

He took the headset off, clicked the call end button, and put the device in his pocket.

"Max Fremmer," he said, extending a hand. But she didn't take it.

"I need you to come with me," she said.

"Where are we going?"

"Uptown. To the Lucidity Center. Mr. Braden wants to talk to you. He's upset you haven't been returning his emails."

"Braden? I responded. I told him I don't have any manuscript. She never gave me anything."

"I know. He wants his money back. She's selling rather well these days."

"What's that got to do with me?"

"You're her publisher."

"I'm her book doctor."

The woman smiled. It was the first sign of emotion she'd shown. Fremmer liked it.

"You and I know that's just for SEO," she said.

Oh, man, he thought. *So clean, yet she plays dirty.* "Who are you?" he asked.

"I'm the muscle."

"I can see that."

"Come on, get your stuff, let's go. I've got an Uber waiting outside."

"I don't get into cars with strangers."

She looked at him for a moment, then put her hand up to the left side of her sunglasses and removed them rather deliberately, as if she'd watched *Top Gun* too many times.

"You don't want to piss me off," she said.

He noticed that between her eyebrows, she had a scar. It was circular, a little smaller than a dime. It didn't do anything to diminish her beauty but was slightly sinister.

"I'll make you a deal," he said. "Promise to have a drink with me later and I'll go with you."

"Are you sure that's a good idea?" she said.

"What do you mean?"

"I read your little memoir," she said. "You're an alcoholic, aren't you?"

He was stunned. "You read my book?"

"I picked up a used copy on Amazon. It was even signed. I enjoyed it. Self-loathing is a good theme. But here's the thing. I didn't really buy that you hated yourself as much as you said you did for wanting to leave your fiancée after the accident. Sure, you felt bad. You struggled with it. You drank. Your grades fell off at law school. You knocked up a one-night stand. Whoops. But I wasn't totally sold. There were times when I thought you were pretending to be someone who hated himself."

"That was the writing. You can't pretend to be a good writer."

"No, the writing's good. You know it is. Which is maybe why you hate yourself now."

He stared at her, transfixed. "Wow. If that's your fastball I'd love to see your curve."

She smiled one more time, then put her sunglasses back on.

"I'll have a drink with you," she said. "Tonight if you want. But get in the car. I've got things to do. And I know you do, too."

14/ Bang 'n Bolt

MADDEN WAS SWEATING. HE'D STRIPPED DOWN TO HIS WHITE V-NECK undershirt and was standing in a hole almost to his waist. He and J.J. had taken turns digging out a section about four feet wide and five feet long. They were down about three feet when the technician said they should be close and Madden told J.J. to get out of the hole so he could take over. A few minutes later he chopped into the hard ground with his shovel, took away a chunk of earth and spotted what looked like a lighter-colored rock.

He put on a pair of blue latex gloves he'd stowed in his pocket, asked Dupuy to hand him the smaller hand shovel, then got on his knees and began to dig carefully around the object of interest, alternating between the shovel and his fingers.

"Dude, that's a bone," J.J. declared, peering into the hole from his haunches.

It was. It was long and thin. Possibly a rib, Madden thought, clearing more dirt along its contours.

"You getting this, Carolyn?" he said, without looking at Dupuy, who was behind the camera.

"Camera's recording," she said. "Time is eleven seventeen."

An inch to the right of the bone he caught the edge of another fragment and gingerly began to clear around it. Soon they were looking at a short row of thin curved bones, what appeared to be a rib cage.

"This is freaking me out a little," J.J. said. "I didn't think it would. But I'm freakin' a little here. What if it is her?"

Madden wasn't going to say anything but he was freaking a little, too. *It can't be this easy*, he thought, momentarily seduced by a vision of yellow crime scene tape and television crews crowding the sidewalk opposite the house. He promised himself he'd be humble. *This isn't about me. I'm just finishing what the MPPD started. We said we'd find Stacey Walker and by God we have.*

"How far are you going?" Dupuy asked.

"'Til I'm sure we're looking at human remains," he said.

They both knew that meant finding the skull. But Dupuy was clearly becoming antsy. As a former prosecutor, she'd have preferred doing the handoff to law enforcement sooner rather than later. They'd have to get a forensic team in here and if they were looking at some sort of blunt-force trauma, Stacey's skull might be in fragments. You didn't want to be poking around with a shovel—even a mini one—with a situation like that.

"I think he strangled her," J.J. announced. "My money's on that."

"The only way you'd know that is if he crushed her windpipe," the ground-radar technician pointed out. He was standing behind J.J., sipping some sort of vitamin-water drink.

"Well, if everything else got ruled out, you'd have to go with that," J.J. said.

Madden looked up from the hole and glared at them. "I'd like to remind you both that we're filming here."

Just then he heard the faint ding-dong of what sounded like a doorbell. He couldn't tell if it was coming from their house or the neighbor's.

"Did you hear that?" he asked.

"What?" J.J. said.

They waited a few seconds, listening. When the bell sounded a second time J.J. still didn't hear it but everyone else did.

"Doorbell," Madden said, alarmed. They hadn't brought a tarp to cover the hole, which was stupid.

"Maybe it's Shelby," Dupuy said. "Who else knows we're here?"

"You want me to find out who it is?" the technician offered. "I'll go look around the side. Where I brought my machine in."

Like a lot of homes in the area this one had a side gate that led to the backyard through a short, narrow fenced-in alleyway.

"Yeah, go," Madden said, laboring to get out of the hole. "Quickly, please."

By the time he'd put his dress shirt on and tucked it into his pants the doorbell had rung another two times and the technician had returned from his reconnaissance mission.

"Cops," he said in a low voice.

And almost as soon as he said it they were pounding on the door, announcing themselves. "Palo Alto Police Department. Open the door, please."

"Let me handle this," J.J. whispered. "You guys keep the baby quiet. Carolyn—that's your name, right? Go inside and take your clothes off."

"Take my clothes off?"

"Yeah, get naked. I'll talk to them for a minute. And then you come to the door."

"Naked?"

From the way his eyes moved up and down her body, he seemed ready to roger that, but then restrained himself. "Grab a sheet or towel or something," he said. "You're cheating on your fiancée. I Airbnb'd the place. That's the backstory. Go."

"I take it you've done this before," Madden heard her say as she headed toward the house.

"Who do you think coined the term Air bang 'n bolt?"

"I didn't know it was a term."

"It's not something I'm proud of."

They disappeared into the house, leaving Madden and the technician in the backyard.

"Am I going to get in some sort of trouble for this?" the technician asked.

Madden held a finger up in front of his mouth, shushing him. Muffled voices. J.J. speaking, the police responding. A minute later Dupuy's voice joined the conversation. Some laughter, everything seemed to be going well, and then the sliding door opened and Dupuy came out dressed in nothing but a T-shirt that came down just below her panty line. Madden's eyes opened wide, the technician's jaw dropped a little.

"They want to see an Airbnb receipt," she whispered, going over to the stroller to check on the baby. "Any paperwork we can show them?"

Madden had the lease agreement in his sport jacket draped around the patio chair. He went to the coat and fished it out of the inside pocket.

"I've got a copy of the lease," he said quietly, unfolding the sheets of paper. "But Shelby's name is on it. What do you think?"

"I think they know we're looking for Stacey," she said. He looked up from the lease and saw that she was now bending down to check on the baby, causing the T-shirt to hike up precariously on her body. "They say a neighbor called to report some suspicious activity. But I'm getting the vibe someone tipped them off."

"Well, we're not letting them in," Madden said. "They'll have to get a warrant."

She took the lease agreement from him. "I'll keep them out," she said. "But call Shelby and tell him to get over here. We're going to need him."

"Did they know who J.J. was?"

"Not until he told them. They knew me, though. Apparently one of them was the arresting officer in that dog-napping case I worked on last year. Fancy that."

Madden winced a little. "Sorry."

"There is some good news, though," she said.

"What's that?"

"I get to regret having sex with J.J. Carradine without having had sex with him."

15/ The Agitator

FREMMER STUDIED THE ENTRANCE TO THE LUCIDITY CENTER ON WEST 100th Street but wasn't sure what to make of it. If not for a small brass plaque affixed to the right of the door underneath the intercom system, he would have thought he was looking at another residential brownstone on a block of residential brownstones. This particular building, however, in the well-gentrified neighborhood a little south of Columbia University didn't have a set of stairs or stoop leading up to the front door, the trademark of the classic Manhattan brownstone. Instead, the immense money-green front door was just off the sidewalk.

His beguiling escort pressed the buzzer on the intercom and addressed the ball-shaped camera integrated into the unit.

"It's me," she said.

A few seconds later a click and a short buzz indicated the lock had been released. They entered into a vestibule, a kind of mudroom with coat hooks and a bench on one wall. Fremmer relieved himself of his scooter but kept his backpack, preferring not to separate from his laptop and other gear.

She led him up a short wheelchair accessible ramp to a second door, which swung open as they approached it. Fremmer expected to see someone standing on the other side of the threshold to greet them, but there was no one, just a large, neutral-colored room with high ceilings. A staircase on the opposite side spiraled gradually up to a second floor. On the wall just in front of the staircase was an impressive, square-shaped aquarium with rounded edges that was lit to impressive effect, probably six by six. The door automatically swung shut behind, closing with a barely audible thud.

Aside from the aquarium, the room was sparsely decorated and lighted a little somberly. To his right was a long wood table and high back chairs waiting to seat a dozen people, maybe more, and to his left two couches in an L-shaped configuration around a wooden coffee table that matched the dining room table. A set of folding chairs, at least ten, were stacked up against the wall in the back corner. Fremmer guessed the room converted into a meeting space for larger gatherings.

It had no windows but an opening next to the staircase brought in some natural light from what appeared to be a kitchen and, judging from the sound of the door sliding closed, some sort of outdoor space.

Braden, looking fairly dapper in a blue sport jacket and jeans, came into the room.

"Ah, Mr. Fremmer, I see Rochelle was able to persuade you to make a little time in your busy schedule for us."

It was the first time he heard her name. On the car ride over she'd agreed to meet him later in the bar of 'Cesca, a restaurant on West 75th, but wouldn't tell him her name. Maybe she'd been trying to maintain some distance, or a veil of mystery, but she didn't seem too concerned that he now had something to call her.

"Do you live here?" Fremmer asked, doing his best to avoid staring at Braden's prosthesis.

"Sometimes," he said.

"So you run a business out of your home?"

Braden took the question in stride but didn't answer it directly. "We think of this as a center for enlightenment," he said. "We run workshops and seminars here, even do some research, but some of our clients stay with us for up to a week, sometimes longer. We offer intensive training sessions for those who are looking to get to the next level so to speak. Our clients come from around the world."

"Do you have the required permits to run a hotel out of your home? The proper insurance, etc."

Fremmer didn't care if the guy was missing part of his arm. He couldn't resist needling him. In his days as a high school basketball player he didn't start. While he had some skill, he earned his minutes for his hustle, and the coach would sub him in to raise his skilled players' intensity levels. Invariably, he went in and committed a hard foul almost immediately, riling the other team and energizing his own.

He became known as "The Agitator." That was his role. He fell into it as a sophomore hustling to get minutes. And while he scored more as a senior, even hitting twenty a couple of times, he never really grew out of the role of team agitator. In some ways, he still hadn't.

"Everything's in order," Braden assured him.

"Well, this all reeks of shadiness," Fremmer declared, holding both his index fingers up and twirling them in a circular motion. "I've got a lot of experience in the field of suspect entrepreneurial endeavors and this one's pretty damn suspect."

"Have you ever had a lucid dream?" Braden asked.

"I'm familiar with the concept."

"By familiar you mean you've experienced it?"

Fremmer nodded. "I have."

"How did it manifest itself?"

"I don't know. I was in a dream and I realized it and I said to myself I'm in a dream, I'll do whatever I want."

"And what did you do?"

Fremmer looked over at Rochelle, who had the faint glint of a smile in her eyes. She seemed to be enjoying herself, if only slightly.

"You want the R version or the unrated version?" he asked.

"However you're comfortable expressing yourself is fine," Braden replied. "We're not here to judge."

"Thanks. But if it's OK with you, how 'bout she goes first?" He nodded in Rochelle's direction. "To show me how it's done."

Braden motioned for her to go ahead.

"I had one a few night ago where I was in a spinning class," she began.

"Oh, you spin," Fremmer remarked. "You know I—"

"I'm next to the instructor," she went on in the present tense, ignoring him. "We're facing the class. And I see the class is looking at me. And I'm not sure why they're looking at me. And then I look down and I see that I'm in my underwear. I'm spinning in a thong and a regular bra."

Which isn't much less than what some people spin in, Fremmer thought.

"For a moment I'm really embarrassed. I can't believe that I came to class dressed like that. What was I thinking? And then I look down at my underwear and I notice it's a little translucent, I can see pubic hair."

Fremmer felt his Adam's apple rise and fall.

"When I see it," she continued, "That's my cue."

"Your cue?"

"That's my cue to know that I'm in a dream. You can train yourself to activate with certain visual cues that you've encountered in previous dreams. It doesn't always work but in this case it does. I realize I'm dreaming. So I look out at the class and spot a guy I like."

"You know him?"

"No, just a random, good-looking guy."

"Older, younger? What level of good-looking are we talking?"

"I don't know. Dark hair, pretty tall, smooth hard body, in his thirties."

"OK, generic good-looking guy. You aren't that picky, but you don't like chest hair. Go on. I'm fine with unrated by the way. Did I mention that?"

"So I unclip from my bike and go up to him and tell him to get off his bike, I need his help. He asks me what for and I say, 'You'll see.' And he gets off and follows me outside the spinning room. I lead him to the women's locker room. He stops at the door for a second and asks whether it's alright to go in. I say, sure, I got permission. And then I lead him into the steam room and we kiss a little and then I tell him to lie down on the bench and I pull off his biker shorts and get on top of him."

"Are there other women in the steam room?"

"No, I'm not into other people watching."

"Good to know," Fremmer said. "What happens after that?"

"I come."

"Well, that's a bit anticlimactic. How 'bout the guy?"

"I don't know. After I got off him, he was gone."

"Disappeared into the steam, eh? Vaporized?"

"Puff," she said, her fingers springing open like a flower in high-speed bloom.

"Rochelle has had documented orgasms in her sleep," Braden announced rather clinically.

Fremmer couldn't resist asking how one went about documenting that.

"There are sensors," Braden explained. "The most common is a vaginal photoplethysmograph."

"Of course," Fremmer said. "Pardon my ignorance. And I know Candace was fascinated by all this stuff. I saw some of it pop up in her fiction. But to be clear I'm not about to publish a nonfiction book on the subject. And I've never seen a manuscript of any sort. What was she writing for you anyway?"

Braden offered a faint smile, then pulled out a folded sheet of paper from his inside jacket pocket and handed it to Fremmer. It didn't take long for Fremmer to figure out that it was a simple one-page contract, not so different from the ones he'd drafted for his clients. It showed a short description of what she was supposed to write and when she was supposed to deliver the work.

"She was writing a history of The Center wrapped around a history of lucid dreaming," Braden said. "I was going to get someone else to write it, but she convinced me that she could do a better job for less."

Fremmer glanced over at Rochelle, standing poker-faced, the neutral bystander. He handed the paper back to Braden.

"So was it supposed to be a promotional vehicle?"

"Yes and no. We intended to sell it. As you can see, this wasn't a handshake agreement. It's fully documented. She's already three months late. I intend to be reimbursed as the contract states. And it's coming out of all the sales you've been making on her current titles."

Fremmer was stunned. He shouldn't have been, because Rochelle had already told him that's why Braden wanted to speak to him. But there was something about Braden's resolute, detached tone that took him by surprise.

"Are you crazy?" he said. "I'm trying to raise funds for her daughter. And it's not as much as you think. After taxes, after all is said and done, she's looking at fifty or sixty grand. Amazon's making more than she is."

"Well, maybe they'll forgo their cut for her sake."

"Believe me, I've been trying to get them to. I've made calls."

"The hospital expenses will eat everything up," he said. "She's better off being insolvent. You should disburse the funds and make me—and yourself—whole before the bill collectors come after her. If you want to make a contribution to her daughter, do it later."

"Will you do that?" Fremmer asked.

"We'll cross that bridge when we get to it. For now, I want my advance back. I'll give you 'til the end of the day to write me a check for $50,000. Or I can give you a PayPal account to transfer to right now if you want the miles on your credit card, though you'll have to pay the transaction fee."

"Are you kidding me? She won't see the royalties for over sixty days. And what are you doing paying her fifty grand? I could have got you someone for half that."

"If she were to die from her injuries, which I understand is still a strong possibility, it would complicate things. This needs to be done now."

"Or what? You gonna break my legs?"

"Not my style."

Fremmer laughed nervously. He didn't know what to think. If Braden was bluffing, he was pretty good at it. There was also some perverse logic to his demand.

"What if I find this manuscript?" he asked.

"So you do have it?"

"Did I say I have it? I asked what if I found it?"

"I'd take that into consideration, of course, depending on the condition it was in."

Fremmer chewed on that for a moment, then decided the whole thing was ridiculous. He told Braden as much.

"No, you're ridiculous," Braden shot back, showing some real temper for the first time. "First, you tell the police that I threatened Candace and then you told a reporter that Candace was advanced money to write a book about The Center but didn't deliver the book. You got me tangled up in this mess."

OK, so this is where all the hostility is coming from, Fremmer thought. "No, no," he said. "I just told the detectives that erotica wasn't the only thing she wrote. I gave that as an example. And as far as telling the police you threatened her, that never happened. I said she appeared to feel threatened but she didn't tell me by whom. They must have played you. That's what detectives and prosecutors do. They play people against each other. They take shots and watch for the reaction."

"I'm well aware of their methods," Braden replied more calmly. "Speaking of which, I see your attorney friend, the one I met, is now defending this homeless person who pushed Candace."

"Allegedly pushed."

"Whatever. Why would you encourage him to do that? You call me crazy."

"Look, the fact is someone was threatening her. She told me that someone had done something very bad that she knew about. Doesn't it seem strange that she would then get pushed in front of a car by a random homeless guy?"

"Chance," Braden said. "Bad luck. As you know, she could be very charming. But she also had her delusional moments. You know her fiction wasn't always fiction. You do know that, don't you?"

"That's what makes it good," Fremmer said. "If you felt she was so unstable, why'd you give her an advance to write this book for you? I thought she was just doing some accounting work for you."

"Did I say she was unstable? A little delusional, but then so are about fifty percent of Americans, particularly all the religious fanatics. Look, you say she told you someone was threatening her. Well, she told me you had her manuscript. If you're inclined to believe her, so am I."

The guy had a point, Fremmer thought. And it turned his stomach to think about it. If she was lying, then he'd made a grave error and sent Carlos on a fool's errand. *Christ,* he thought. *Maybe she was lying. Then again, maybe Braden is. But why?*

"You see it cuts both ways," Braden said.

Fremmer scanned his repertoire for a snappy comeback but before he could find one they were interrupted by a teakettle's low whistle emanating from the other end of the room—or rather beyond it.

"Come," Braden said, heading in the direction of the noise. "Let me at least offer you something to drink so I don't come off as completely rude."

Fremmer didn't really want anything to drink but he did want to ask Braden a few more questions, so he followed him but paused to look at the fish tank. It was a beautiful microcosm of a saltwater ecosystem, a miniature reef.

Braden was at the stove when Fremmer caught up with him. The kitchen was huge. Modern. White-tiled. High-end appliances. An island in the center, it looked like something you'd see in the suburbs or on The Food Network.

"If you don't mind my asking, how'd you lose your hand?" he ventured.

Braden didn't answer right away. He went to the cupboard and took out a mug.

"Antibiotic-resistant staph infection," he said, placing the cup on the island counter. "Long time ago. Going on twenty-five years. I got a fairly deep cut on one of my fingers. When I saw that it was getting infected I tried to treat it myself. A couple of days later I got a very high fever and had to go to the hospital. They treated it but nothing worked. I went from having this little cut to having to choose between amputation and death. They took most of my forearm to be safe. I'm lucky it was just that and not the whole arm. And that it wasn't my dominant hand."

Rochelle removed a tea packet from a box and tore it open. Handing Braden the sachet she said, "I think you're well acquainted with the illogical emotional ecosystem of tragedy, Mr. Fremmer."

Braden dropped the tea bag in the coffee mug and poured the steaming water over it.

"After you have something like this happen you can either think you're cursed or blessed," he said. "I went with the latter. What I want you to understand is that what we're doing here is potentially groundbreaking. Your mind is the greatest virtual-reality machine. Nothing can touch it. Not in our lifetimes anyway. And we've developed proprietary techniques and technology that allow us to safely and affordably live out our fantasies in a way that's virtually indistinguishable from reality."

"I personally prefer the real thing," Fremmer countered.

"We're not just talking about sex," Braden said, "though that's certainly one of the primary applications."

"Weightlessness," Rochelle offered. "Flight. The Superman experience. You want a cup?"

"No thanks," Fremmer said. He went over to the sliding glass door and looked outside at the walled-in backyard. Even a tiny outdoor space was a huge luxury in Manhattan. This one had a wooden deck off the kitchen overlooking a small Japanese garden with gravel paths, a water fountain, sculptures, well-manicured shrubbery and a couple of small trees. In the reflection of the glass, he could see Rochelle mouthing some words and gesturing with her hand, having a silent discussion behind his back.

"Very Zen," he said, then turned around and headed back to the island. "I bet you guys do a kick-ass barbecue. Veggie burgers on the grill. A little Enya on the outdoor speakers."

Braden laughed. "Despite appearances, we're less new-agey than you think. The garden is the way it is because it's easier to maintain. We don't get much light back there, which limits our landscape selection."

"How long have you known Candace?" Fremmer asked. "She told me she's been dabbling in this stuff for a while. She was also into psychics. Sorry, check that. She called them intuits. I told her they were the same thing, that they just changed the name for legal latitude. Which is kind of brilliant if you think about it."

Braden didn't answer right away. He fished out a half-used packet of artificial sweetener from a small bowl on the counter and sprinkled its remaining contents into his tea.

"A long time," he finally said. "Maybe twenty years. I'd just bought this place."

"OK. So now if I were your lawyer, or a detective for that matter, the next question would be what sort of relationship did you have with her?"

"But you're not my lawyer or a detective."

"Well, let's pretend I'm both. Did you ever Bill Clinton her?"

Rochelle laughed. Getting an actual laugh out of her was surprisingly gratifying. Braden wasn't so amused.

"Is that some sort of hip-hop term?" he asked.

"No, it's my own," Fremmer said. "Sorry, I've been trying to make that a verb for a while."

"Look," Braden said, "I have a reputation at stake. We have financial backers. We have a product coming out—"

"What kind of product?"

"A transcranial electrical stimulation sleep mask. Using electric currents, we can increase or decrease the intracerebral current flow in specific areas of the brain. The change in neuronal excitability is what helps facilitate lucid dreaming. We can significantly increase the odds of having a lucid dream."

"Really? And there's some sort of app that goes with it?"

"Yes. Android and iOS."

"Sweet," Fremmer said. "And you have clinical studies to back it?"

"We're working on that."

"Of course you are."

"We had to lay out a lot of upfront money to produce enough to bring our cost per unit down. So I'll just say this: You do harm to me I will do harm to you. I can't have malicious rumors spread about this center or me. Candace was a good woman—"

"*Is*," Fremmer corrected him.

"Yes, *is*. And I'm sorry about what happened. But she took money from me and she's going to give it back."

"I was kind of hoping you'd reconsidered," Fremmer said.

"There's nothing to reconsider."

"Well, at least give me a chance to see if I can find the manuscript."

"You have 'til the end of the day. You can make arrangements with Rochelle. She'll let you out."

With that Fremmer followed her back to the front door and picked up his scooter.

"I guess I don't get a ride back," he said to her.

"One-way ticket," she said. "I'll see you later at 'Cesca."

"Better make it eight. I may need the extra time."

"Don't forget your checkbook," she said.

"My older brother was afraid of snakes so I got one. I named it Scorpion."

"Sounds like a bit of overkill."

"We always named our animals with some other animal's name. Kind of an inside family joke. Our dog's name was Bear, for instance."

"At least they were both mammals," Madden commented.

"You have a dog?" she asked.

"For a little while. And then he got hit by a car. I remember being upset about it but I think my parents were more traumatized by having to tell me. It was my mother's fault. It happened during the day while I was at school. I had a weird childhood. With the polio, I was spoiled in a lot of ways. I was treated like this special person. Every once in a while horrible things happened to me. Like my dog getting killed. Even the sexual abuse. That was an isolated incident. It wasn't like I had a stepfather or uncle who was abusing me for years. The guy was my doctor. There was some lead-up. He tested the boundaries over a few visits, but when he really did it, when he raped me, it only happened once. I didn't go back to that office. I didn't tell my parents why I wouldn't go back. I just refused to go back."

Dupuy took a step forward and put a hand on his shoulder. "Did you write that in your book?"

"No, I didn't get to that part yet."

"Well, that's a good way to say it. A good way to get into it. I don't think you have to be that explicit. You just need to talk about how it impacted you."

She was right, he thought. Ultimately, what he needed was to talk to someone like her and just record the conversation, then transcribe it. He was kind of doing that already some evenings. But he wasn't talking to a person, just his phone.

"I've been kind of keeping a record of what we're doing here," he said after a moment. "I don't write anything down. But I come home and put my phone on the kitchen table and hit the record button and talk about what happened. Sometimes it's short, sometimes it's longer."

"That's good," she said, distracted. "It's good to get something down. What are they doing?"

The radar technician was now taking a picture of J.J. holding the dog's skull.

"I think I heard someone say something about an album cover," Madden said.

"When you saw the bones, did you think about the money?" she asked.

"I didn't, actually."

"Me neither," she said not altogether convincingly.

They sat in silence for a moment. Then he said: "At this point I think we have to shift our focus to finding Ross. He has close family members still alive. And a daughter."

"They all think he's dead, though. You spoke to them."

He had. But their conversations had been brief. As far as they were concerned, the case was closed. They had moved on with their lives— or at least they said they had.

"I'm going to have to go see them in person."

"And after that, what, you go to Vietnam?"

"Maybe. My wife and I have been talking about taking a trip. The only time I've been out of the country the last ten years is to Nicaragua, to visit her family."

Shelby saw them talking and walked over, Darren's story in hand.

"Nice little adrenaline rush there, eh?" he said, approaching the table. He made his left hand into a fist and banged it gently against his chest a few times. "Got the heart pounding, right? Digging up the pet cemetery while keeping the police at bay. Nice way to start the day. You look a little tuckered out there, Detective."

Shelby was being polite. He was exhausted. He'd be lucky if his back was only half shot tomorrow.

"I'm alright," he said. "Just sorry we didn't find her."

"Sounds like your boy Bronsky was misled."

"When you got no favorites, you bet the long shot," Madden said.

Shelby responded with what sounded like a cross between a snort and a laugh. "You don't have to tell me," he said. "I'm an angel investor. All we do is bet long shots."

Madden knew Shelby had a fund. Not a big one, but big enough. All these guys did.

"You want a bagel?" Madden asked.

"Nah, I'm out. Got a conference I need to pop into. They're interviewing me. On stage. My landscapers will be here soon to start cleaning up this mess. Or they can keep digging if you want."

"I wanted to ask you something," Madden said. "But I was waiting to do it in person. You have someone following me?"

"Why would I do that?"

"I don't know."

"You sure you aren't being paranoid, Detective?"

"You sure you aren't lying to me?"

Shelby smiled. "Not about that. You mind if I take this?" he said, holding up Darren's short story.

"You paid for it," Madden said. "How 'bout the snake? You want him, too?"

"No, thanks. Freddy's all yours."

"I was going to bury him again along with the dog, although your friend J.J. seems to be quite attached to him."

Shelby looked back at J.J., who still had Finnegan's skull in his hand.

"He's found his muse, Detective. If you're lucky he'll write a song about you. And you, too, Ms. Dupuy. Immortality beckons. But time's a tickin'. I'll give you another couple of weeks to make some progress."

"But your contract says I have six months to find them," Madden said.

"It does."

"So why'd you say I only have a couple of weeks?"

"I have a chronic case of impatience. I take these pills to control it, but they don't seem to work."

"A contract's a contract," Dupuy interjected.

Shelby nodded in agreement. "But you can always write multiple contracts with multiple people. Last I checked, your contract didn't include an exclusivity clause. And I believe that it would be your fault that it doesn't have one, wouldn't it, Ms. Dupuy?"

The comment left Dupuy looking a little dumbfounded, which wasn't a good look for her.

"You realize he can quit at any time," she said, recovering her composure. "And you still have to pay him."

Shelby smiled. "You a quitter, Detective?"

"There's been someone else on this from the start, hasn't there?

That's how it works with you, doesn't it? You guys put two competing teams on a project to double your chances of success."

"Didn't they tell you that in the Valley it's all about collaboration? Working across teams. The free flow of ideas. Open offices. Flat org charts. Bah."

"You didn't answer my question."

"My company had thirty-one employees when I sold it. There was only one team. But remember my background, Detective. I am an enabler. My mission is simple. I have faith in you. Your baby's crying, Ms. Dupuy. I believe it's feeding time."

17/ A Guiding Hand

Fremmer was late. He bolted through the two sets of doors leading into the restaurant and pulled up in front of the hostess stand to survey the bar area. His eyes darted around frantically, his heart beating hard after running the last few blocks. The restaurant was busy but not hopping, so it wasn't hard to pick out individual people.

"Do you have a reservation?" asked the hostess from behind her podium.

He managed to tell her no before covering his mouth and letting out a series of short coughs. Recovering, he said: "Did you see a single woman come in about fifteen minutes ago? Medium height, very attractive. Oh, there she is."

Out of the corner of his eye, he saw Rochelle in a booth by the window.

"Sorry," he said, sliding into the bench across from her. "I didn't have your phone number or I would have texted."

"I wasn't worried," she said. "I don't usually get stood up. And someone already bought me a drink, so you're off the hook."

Fremmer looked around for his competition. "Who?"

"Some guy up at the bar. He asked to be on the standby list. I told him it was closed but he sent it over anyway."

Fremmer thought he spotted the guy. But it was hard to tell. He noticed a few barstool straddlers looking in their direction, and based on the frequency of their glances, they seemed to have already written him off as boyfriend material. They were ready to pounce at the first opening.

It didn't help that he looked like he'd thrown on some clothes he'd found sitting in a hamper and then sprinted four blocks because he was late. He had showered, shaved, and exchanged the dual-layered long-sleeve T-shirt for a button-down Oxford, but he was still in jeans and his Fred Perrys, a get-up that would have fit in better at one of the more collegiate bars up on Amsterdam like the Gin Mill or Brother Jimmy's. Establishments that focused on serving alcohol not food.

"Well, thanks for waiting," he said, running a hand up his brow, pushing a light layer of moisture up into his hair. "Can I still buy you a drink?"

"Did you find it?" she asked.

"Wow, no foreplay."

"Overrated," she said.

"Let me get a drink first. Been a long day."

He flagged down a waitress and ordered an Old-fashioned with Bulleit, then asked Rochelle what she was drinking. It looked like a vodka or gin tonic. She'd almost finished it.

"I'll take what he's having," she told the waitress.

"You also want Bulleit?" she asked.

"Excuse me?"

Fremmer answered for her. "Yes, the same."

After the waitress left, Rochelle admitted she wasn't much of a drinker.

"It doesn't help you with lucid dreaming?" Fremmer asked, only half joking. "I heard it helps some people."

"It can," she said. "Alcohol gives you REM rebound once its effect wears off. It'll delay your first few cycles of REM sleep but then REM gets more amplified later in the morning, which can increase the chance of having a lucid dream. But not everybody's brain chemistry is the same."

They continued talking about things that might help or hurt the chances of having a lucid dream until their drinks showed up. He reached for the glass as soon as the waitress had set it on the table and took a long swig.

"How old did you say your kid was?" she asked.

"Thirteen."

"You have him stay at his friend's place whenever you think you're going to get lucky?"

"This one was already scheduled. But his best friend's mother has taken pity on me and thinks I should be more unencumbered to find a wife so she offers to take him whenever I want. They've got a very large apartment and only one kid. I sometimes think he'd prefer to live there."

"He have a girlfriend?"

"I don't know about a full-blown one but he's got stuff going on. I try not to poke around his Instagram too often, but I don't always succeed. The kids these days have different levels of attachment. You know, there's hanging out. There's going out. Then there's HU-ing, which I only learned recently is short for hooking up. And the girls are much more aggressive. One will just walk right up to him and say, so and so likes you, you're going to go out with her. They're very forward. But you're probably not so removed from that. What are you, twenty-five, twenty-six?"

Rochelle smiled. She picked up her new drink and looked down into it for a moment. "Thirty," she said. She picked up her glass and sipped it like it was a palate cleanser that would wash the bad taste from her mouth.

"Wow. Thirty. You're actually marginally appropriate." He left out the *for me*, but she knew he meant.

"What happened to his mother?" she asked. "The book ends with him two years old and her off in L.A. with a cocaine problem."

"Among other problems and other drugs," he said, wiping his brow again. "You talk about unstable, she was unstable. But very hot. As hot as you." He raised his glass in a pseudo toast and took a drink.

"But you were into her?"

"She was out of my league. Looks wise anyway. I had no illusions about being with her long-term. You take the trip and enjoy it while it lasts."

"What happened to her?" she asked again.

"She got her shit together," he said. "I don't know how, but she did. She got a couple of parts, then a real role on a sitcom. And then she married a high-powered entertainment lawyer. They've got a couple of young kids. She still does a little bit of acting, but she's basically a stay-at-home mom. Not something I ever pictured her doing."

"Does your son see her?"

"He has. Not often. But she comes through New York occasionally and they meet."

"Does she want him back?"

"She can't have him back. You read the book. I got full custody. That's ironclad. She had her chance. At first, she wasn't going to have him, then she was going have him and put him up for adoption. And then she was going to have him but said I wouldn't be in the picture. Finally, in the end, she ended up dropping the kid in my lap and saying, 'Sorry I really can't deal with this, I'm splitting, he's all yours.'"

"And you wanted her to have the baby all along?"

"Call me superficial but aside from being borderline insane, genetically speaking, she was grade A. Smart, an athlete. I wasn't going to do much better. I figured you put her with a B+ guy like myself and I might get an A-. I actually did better. He's a great kid."

"I think you read *Brave New World* too many times," she said.

"Probably."

"You ever come close to getting married again?"

"Not really. You?"

"I was never engaged," she said.

"You know what I mean."

She took another tiny sip of her drink. "I've been proposed to."

"Of course you have. I think three guys up at the bar are ready to get down on a knee right now. So what happened? Ring not big enough?"

"Rings are cheap," she said.

"What do you consider cheap?"

"Fifty grand is cheap, Max. You should really pay it."

"I should. But then I'd feel stupid. So I've got a proposition."

She gave him that hard look he'd seen before. Now it made him think he'd been naive to accept her earlier, friendlier tone at face value.

"Don't worry, it's not romantic."

"I'm not worried," she said. "But maybe you should get another drink to have on hand when I say no. You're empty."

He looked down at his glass. She was right. Only the rocks and cherry garnish remained. He hadn't realized he'd finished. By the time he looked up again she'd flagged down the waitress, who was at a nearby table. After he put his order in, she asked about his proposition.

"Shouldn't we wait for the drink?" he said.

"I don't need to."

"Well, I have a question for you first. You wouldn't answer it in the car. How'd you end up at this Lucidity Center and what's your role there?"

"That's actually two questions."

"Just answer me. I won't tell you what my proposition is until you do."

"Now you're getting childish."

He couldn't help it. He was good at it. He propped his elbows up on the table and folded his hands in front of his chin. He let his face rest against his hands and waited.

"I used to clean his fish tank," she finally said.

He laughed. "What do you mean?"

"Exactly what I said. I came in every month and cleaned his fish tank and then set up the new one when he got it. And then I did some cooking for his events. I was a chef. Not a *chef* chef. I did dinner parties for people."

"By yourself."

"I had another guy who worked with me. He still cleans Braden's tank and helps out around the Center. If I needed extra bodies for the parties, I'd bring in some of his actor friends. A lot of them worked in restaurants or as cater waiters."

"So you had a fish-tank cleaning business?"

"We worked out of a shop downtown. They'd send us out. It paid pretty well. We gave half of what we earned to the store, usually got a decent tip, and the store would give us a little percentage if we got the customers to order supplies or new equipment."

"Fascinating," he said. "And then Braden brought you into the business?"

She nodded. "He's a smart guy but he isn't so business smart."

"Where'd you go to college?"

"Maybe I didn't," she said.

"That would be good."

"Good for what?"

"For the memoir. Have you ever considered writing one?"

She laughed. "Oh, no. I'm barely literate."

"I bet I could get you a $50,000 advance for it."

"I hope that's not your proposition."

"No. But I bet I could."

Just then the waitress came back with his new drink and took his empty.

"Time's up," she said.

"OK, OK." He reached into his pocket and pulled out a high-capacity USB thumbdrive.

"What's that?"

"That's Candace's hard drive."

"Is the manuscript on there?"

"No. But she's got some notes, some recorded interviews with Braden, and a bunch of other stuff. All her emails are here. This is everything that was on her computer. I cloned it."

"What am I going to do with that?"

"I don't know. But I figured it's worth something to you guys. Because I know something shady is going on here. And it took me a lot to get this. I had to call up her daughter, who's a basket case right now. She's staying with a friend's family, and I had to speak to that family and convince them to let me into Candace's apartment and get me onto her computer. I'm a little shocked that the police hadn't taken it away. Do you know how hard that was?"

"What about the cloud?" she said.

"What about it?"

"Does that have the contents of her Google Drive?"

"She was old school. She didn't use Google Drive. Not with me anyway. She always sent Word docs."

"Thanks, but we'll pass. I'll take that check now."

"Look, can you at least call Braden and ask him?"

"Sure. But I know the answer already."

"Well, call him, please."

With that she picked up her drink and left the booth. He noticed then that she was wearing a skirt, not pants, showing a lot of skin, which hurt him a bit. She walked over to stand near the entrance. He watched her take her phone from her purse, tap the screen and start talking. She kept her back to him so he couldn't try to read her lips.

When she returned she slid back into the booth and said, "He says no deal."

"Take it or leave it," he replied. "I'm not writing you a check."

"Come on, Max. You're a good guy. I don't want to see anything bad happen to you. The truth is I kind of like you. Trust me, it's not worth $50,000. It's not even your money."

"Look, I don't get these vague threats. Let's wait to see if Candace wakes up. She's the one who needs to write you a check, not me. Like you said, it's not my money."

She smiled, then picked up her drink—or what he thought was her drink—and took a big sip.

"These aren't bad," she said.

"So, that's it?"

"For now."

"And then what?"

"That's up to Braden."

A little sigh of relief. She hadn't turned her cards over, but he suddenly felt better for calling the bet and throwing his chips into the pot.

She stood up to go.

"Where you going?" he asked. "You didn't finish your drink."

"I think we're done here," she said.

"You said you'd have a drink with me."

"I had two."

"You didn't finish either one."

"OK," she said, "I'll finish this one. But I want you to pretend this is a lucid dream."

"How so?"

"This is how you do it. Watch me. You shake your head." She shook her head like she was clearing cobwebs. "Then you take a drink. OK?"

OK, he said, and followed her example. At the time, it occurred to him that his drink was a little more watery than he thought it should be; it wasn't as fresh as he'd have liked. But he didn't give it much thought because it still tasted fine.

"Are you lucid?" she asked.

He shrugged. "No."

"Well do it again," she said, repeating the process and draining her glass in the process. He finished his, too, and after he was finished, he looked at her. When he did, she leaned forward and kissed him gently on the lips.

"You lucid now?"

"More so," he said.

She leaned forward and kissed him again, this time longer.

"Now do the next thing you want to do," she said. "Put your hand under the table. Put it on my leg."

He hesitated. *What game she was playing?*

"Come on," she said invitingly, "do it," and his resistance went out the door. He did as instructed. He put his hand timidly on her knee. He was suddenly back in high school. But instead of contemplating his next move, she made it for him. She slid down in the booth, slouching badly, his hand riding up the inside of her thigh.

"Keep going," she said. "Let it go. Let it go where it wants. Yes. Now you've got it. Now you're really lucid, aren't you?"

He was. He was completely lucid.

She put her hand over his, the skirt between them, and guided his hand into her crotch. That he remembered: her hand, guiding his. But everything after that was a blur. And then there was nothing. A void. Until he woke up on a bed somewhere with an oxygen mask over his face and someone slapping him lightly but sharply and asking him something he didn't understand.

"What'd you take, Mr. Fremmer? Can you tell us what you took?"

18/ Long Road of Dead Ends

CATHLEEN MILEKI, STACEY WALKER'S ONLY DAUGHTER, LIVED IN Petaluma, an exurb north of San Francisco in Sonoma County. Madden had only been to Petaluma once before. On the way to Calistoga for a wedding, he and his family had stopped there for lunch after running into a nasty patch of weekend wine country traffic just past Marin County, on a rural stretch of the 101 freeway where one didn't expect traffic.

Lesson learned, this time he set out before dawn on a weekday and made the drive there in ninety minutes. Thanks to Google Maps he knew exactly what Mileki's house looked like. He also knew that her section of town just to the west of the historically well-preserved downtown had survived the 1906 earthquake mostly intact. According to local real-estate brokers it was a desirable neighborhood.

Madden arrived there just as the sun was preparing to rise. In the predawn light he took in the view, which wasn't quite majestic, but the neighborhood had a nice, layered, terraced feel to it. The homes, a hodge-podge of architectural styles, sat on lots that were neither grand nor cramped. *American Graffiti* had been shot in Petaluma. So had other movies that called for a small-town, everyday America feel to them. Looking around the comfortable, middle-class neighborhood, Madden could see why Petaluma, California was such a popular location choice for Hollywood; it was emblematic of the middle-class American Dream.

The two-story house was set on an elevated lot on Rebecca Drive. Its short but wide driveway curved up the incline of the lot to a two-car garage. A fairly steep concrete staircase led up to the front door. Both the house and landscaping around it seemed well maintained and ecologically current, with drought-resistant plants, cacti and most of the front yard covered in small stones instead of grass to save water. The theme was more desert-influenced than Japanese rock garden, but it fell somewhere in between the two.

Two cars were parked in the driveway. Madden could see that the light was already on in the kitchen. Marcus, who'd given him Mileki's contact info and arranged the initial phone call, had told him Mileki was almost twenty-nine, married and had one child. He still talked to her occasionally.

Madden parked a little further up the street. It was just getting light out, the air was crisp—the outside temperature gauge in his car read 47. He watched the house and thought about what he'd do if the husband were home. *Was it better to talk to her alone or with him present?* He was still trying to decide when it was decided for him: At six-forty-five a young man came out, insulated coffee cup in hand, laptop bag in the other, bagel clenched between his teeth, got in his car and drove away.

Madden waited fifteen minutes, then decided he looked suspicious sitting in the car. He detected no activity in the house, so he got out, put on a pair of headphones and started walking, doing his best imitation of a senior citizen on his morning walk. The only problem was his version included a limp that made him stand out more than he'd have liked.

He power-walked up and down Rebecca Drive, and after a few passes he saw some movement in one of the front windows of the Mileki house. A child—he or she was young, maybe three or four—was scurrying about. He looked at his watch, almost seven fifteen. Just then his phone pinged with a new text message.

"U there?"

It was Dupuy.

"Y, and she is 2," he wrote back. "I'm still outside."

He always felt proud when he effectively shortened his texts. He wasn't good at it—and his kids made fun of him for trying to be "with it"—but he tried to condense whenever he could, even if he didn't always adhere to the proper shorthand terms.

"You sitting?" she texted back.

He wasn't. "Should I be?"

"Maybe."

She sent a link to a web page. He clicked on it. The text of an article loaded first, followed by an image of Shelby. Madden scrolled down on his iPhone and saw another photo, this one of Stacey Walker, and further down, one of himself. As soon as he finished reading the headline and the first few paragraphs he called Dupuy.

"Are you kidding me?" he said.

"Good morning to you, too," she replied.

"You think Shelby's behind it? You think he told him to write that?"

By "him" he meant Bender, who'd written an article on his website, onedumbidea.com, telling the story of Shelby hiring Madden to crack the famously unsolved Walker case. It was a scoop, of course.

"The way it's written made me think Shelby wrote it himself," Dupuy said. "Talk about blowjobs."

"He quoted me," Madden said. "I never said he could quote me."

"I think that's the least of your problems."

"What do you mean?"

"Just don't look at the comments. There are a lot of sick, mean-spirited people out there. You're getting trolled a bit."

That didn't sound good. He looked at his screen and a read a particularly bothersome paragraph to her: "Shelby says he's offering Madden a highly generous bonus commensurate with today's Silicon Valley standards if he solves the case. 'You look back at the bounties we were offering for Saddam's henchmen in Iraq,' Shelby says. 'I think it's time private financiers like myself—or our government—apply some of the same practices to unsolved murder cases in this country. We should have a deck of cold-case cards. I see this as a start to a larger program.'"

Madden's voice trailed off as he continued to read on his own. "Doesn't he realize this is going to make my job more difficult? People are going to think it's millions of dollars?"

"Isn't it?"

"Yeah, but I don't need all these crackpots trying to contact me. I really don't need that."

"That's probably what he wants," she speculated. "He gave you your shot, now he's decided to open things up, crowdsource the investigation. He's made you the conduit. It spices up the story, gives it a better hook. You're a minor celebrity after all."

"He could have just put up a million-dollar reward and called it a day."

"Boring. Remember, there've been other people who've put up rewards before. Ross's brother put up seventy-five thousand. Back then that was real money."

Madden looked up at the house. There was more activity. Mileki appeared briefly in the window, then stepped out of view.

"Well, thanks for that fantastic news," he said. "I'm going to go knock on this door now. Wish me luck. I hope she hasn't heard about any of this. What time did the story post?"

"Late last night," Dupuy said.

"Someone could have emailed her."

"It's not that big of a deal, Hank. It might help in the long run."

"Everybody's going to want a piece, Carolyn. The guys I used to work with back at the MPPD. Billings, for example, he's going to want in on this. Your old friends back at the DA's office. And who knows who else."

Silence on the phone.

"I'm not letting this one go," he said. "Bender's going to pay. I will make him pay."

"Well, I may have something for you there," Dupuy said. "But we can talk about it later. Call me after you speak to her."

"If I speak to her."

"Stop being so negative, Hank."

"How 'bout you stop being so chipper?"

He hung up, marched toward the front door. His anger had energized him. He rang the bell. A dog started barking.

"Who is it?" Mileki asked through the door.

"Detective Madden," he practically shouted. "Sorry to bother you at this early hour. I left a message last week saying I might be in the area and wanted to try to meet with you. Well, I'm in the area."

No response. Just more barking. He felt her looking at him

through the peephole, so he held up his driver's license. Then his private investigator license.

"Pete Pastorini says hello," he went on, saying the first thing that came into his head. "I told you he had a stroke. He's doing a little better now but he's still got some paralysis on—"

She opened the door.

"Stay, Dakota," she said, struggling to restrain the dog—a yellow Labrador Retriever. As soon as it saw the visitor it stopped barking and started wagging its tail, eager to greet the new guest.

She jerked back on Dakota's collar and told him to sit. He obeyed briefly, then popped right back up.

"I'm not sure now's a good time, Mr. Madden," she said. "I don't have any problem talking to you. I'm not sure what I can tell you other than what I have already said on the phone."

"It'll only take a few minutes. I'm headed up to Calistoga. You were on the way. I wanted to talk to you in person."

"Down, Dakota." The dog was now on its hind legs, trying to jump up on him. "OK. I'm taking my son over to his pre-school program in a little while, but I'll talk to you while I'm getting him ready. You came from Menlo Park?"

"Yeah. Left at five. Got here pretty quickly."

"Come in," she said. "Dakota, down. Chill out, animal."

It took a few minutes, but the dog finally did calm down. Cathleen led Madden into the kitchen, where she continued the task of spreading jam on a couple pieces of multigrain toast for her son. The kid, who had lighter hair than his mother, was cute—not a towhead, but close. He was sitting in one of those simple, ladder-style Scandinavian high chairs at a round table, waiting patiently for his breakfast. Maybe three or four years old, he was big enough to have outgrown a standard high chair, but the one he was in didn't seem babyish.

"Eli, this is Mr. Madden," she said, dipping a knife in the jar. "He's a detective."

"I know what a detective is," Eli said. "It's a special kind of policeman who doesn't have to wear a uniform."

"That's right," Madden said, impressed by how verbal he was.

"You look too old to be a policeman," the kid remarked.

"I am too old," Madden said. "I'm retired from the police force, but I work for myself now. I have to keep busy or I get bored."

"I got bored this morning," Eli said. "I had nothing to do."

She served him the pieces of toast on a blue plastic plate, along with a matching cup full of milk.

"He always says he has nothing to do when I take away the iPad from him," she explained. "I'm thinking of taking it away for good if he keeps saying that. You hear that, buddy?"

"No," Eli said.

She stepped over to the counter, picked up a remote and turned on a small flat-panel TV mounted below a cabinet near the refrigerator. The PBS Kids channel came on. Eli squealed with delight.

"I'm going to leave you alone for a few minutes, Eli. You OK with that?"

Eli didn't answer. He was already mesmerized by the TV.

Mileki motioned for Madden to follow her through the open doorway into the living room.

"I've got to get him dressed in ten minutes," she said. "So that's what you've got. I hope it's worth the detour."

It already was, he thought, looking at her. Part of him had been expecting someone more sullen, hardened, and emotionally drained. But she was just the opposite. She seemed bright and cheerful, not a line of worry on her face. She was fit and attractive, her light brown hair pulled up and clipped into a bun on top of her head. She had more than a little of her mother in her. The same perfect spacing of the eyes, a similar pointiness to their small noses. Madden knew right away that he liked her.

They sat, she on the couch and he on a club chair facing her, a little off to her left.

"Is it OK if I record you?" he asked. "I'm a little lazy on the note-taking these days."

That was fine, she said, so he set his iPhone down in the middle of the coffee table in front of her, purposely positioning it between a couple books instead of on top of one of them. He wanted it to blend into the table, making her forget it was there.

"Look, I've spoken to Pete a couple more times since I last spoke to you and gone through the file on the case, or most of it anyway." He didn't tell her how he got the file, but it turned out Pastorini had made a copy that he kept in a filing box in his garage. "And a few days ago I went down to Orange County to talk to your father's brother. He says he hasn't seen or heard from his brother since he took off. You may know this already but for many years after your mother disappeared Pete used to go down to your uncle's house around the holidays. Sometimes for Thanksgiving, sometimes Christmas Eve. And he staked the place out, figuring your father might show up." He was about to mention that Pastorini also received secret approval to monitor her uncle's mail through the post office, but he stopped himself, realizing that information was privileged.

"He told me about that," she said. "I know he spent a lot of time on the case. Please send him my regards. I'm sorry he had a stroke."

"He said that one time he just missed your father—or so a neighbor told him."

She rolled her eyes. "Do you know how many times someone claimed they saw my father? After *Dateline NBC* ran the story they got over five hundred calls."

"So I take it you're in the 'he's no longer alive' camp?"

She pointed to her head. "For me, he's alive in here. He'll always be alive."

"OK, but I have to ask. Has your father ever visited you—in all these years has he either visited you or tried to contact you in any way?"

"Some people claiming to be him have," she said. "But no, never him."

"You swear to that? You swear on your son's life?"

"Yes, I swear," she replied without hesitation. "I swear my father Ross Walker, who killed my mother Stacey Walker, never has visited me or contacted me in any way."

She sounded as if she were in court and had been coached by a lawyer. Perhaps he shouldn't have asked her to swear on anything.

"You're looking at me a little funny, Mr. Madden," she said.

"Just the way you responded. I didn't mean to put you on the stand."

"It's not that. Sorry. I've been through a lot of therapy. It's how my therapist taught me to accept what happened. I used to repeat that whenever I met with her. 'My father Ross Walker killed my mother

Stacey Walker and there's nothing I could have done to save her.' If you say it enough times, it loses its power over you. After what happened to you, did you ever go into therapy?"

"Excuse me?"

"After your sexual abuse."

He looked at her, blinking a few times.

"No," he said. "No, I didn't. I'm a private person. My therapy was my work. I never analyzed it much, but my wife says it was no accident I became a cop. If I'd been smarter maybe I would have become a doctor and tried to cure cancer or something."

"Well, you didn't let it eat away at you, that's the important thing. You hear about all those boys abused by their priests or team coaches and how they kept it inside them all those years. Some of them ended up on drugs or committing suicide. I think it's great what you accomplished. I saw they're making a movie about you with Kevin Spacey."

He felt his face redden with embarrassment. "There was some talk about that but it didn't happen."

"Well, you should make it happen. It's a good story." Her eyes lingered on him for a moment. "You do look a little like him. He'd be perfect."

"I was supposed to write a book," he said. "I can't even get that done."

"An editor at a publishing house once approached me about writing one. But I had no interest. I'd said all I had to say in Frank's book."

"He says he still talks to you occasionally."

"I've known him a long time. He was very sensitive to what I was going through. He was one of the few people who really knew my mother. They went to high school together."

"You grew up with your aunt then?"

"Yes, my uncle down in Laguna Beach was trying to get custody, but the court sided with my mother's sister. I grew up in Auburn, not far from Sacramento. And then I went to Chico State. My husband's from here though."

"We stop in the McDonald's in Auburn on the way to Tahoe when we go skiing," Madden said.

"Yeah, I think that's how people know it—from stopping for gas or at some fast food restaurant. But it's not a bad place to grow up."

"And you're a full-time mom now?"

"Mostly. I have a business organizing people's closets and homes. I basically help people throw stuff out. You said your job was no accident and mine probably isn't either."

"You don't seem to care whether we find your mother's body or not."

"After all the years of having people promising they'll find her, you tend to get a little jaded."

"I'm not promising anything."

"I know you aren't," she said.

"Would it make you feel better if she were found? Wouldn't it bring you some peace of mind?"

"I don't know. It would just confirm that she's dead. I assume she is, but the truth is as long as she isn't found, it leaves me with that tiny bit of hope that she's still alive."

He nodded. *Like the title of Marcus's book*, he thought. *Never found, never dead.*

"However, on a more practical level," she went on, "it would help get some money out of the insurance company."

"I meant to ask you about that," he said. "One of the things we as investigators talk about is how your father would benefit from your mother's death. One of the things cited was the insurance policy. When insurance is a motive the perpetrator usually makes the death look like an accident."

"I don't think it was insurance. I think he just didn't want to pay up in the divorce. And I think he wanted full custody."

"You were close to your father?"

"Yes. He coached all my sports teams. I played soccer and softball. And I can tell you he didn't think my mother was a good mother. He thought she was a whore, which is typical of abusive husbands. They're the righteous one and she's the whore who deserves to be punished."

"So you think he planned it?" he asked.

"Absolutely."

"But you ended up getting some money from his life-insurance policy?"

"Yes, when they finally declared him dead, I got some money. I was around fifteen. It took around seven years to sort it all out. You're looking at some of that money right now. It helped pay for this house."

"So, as you say, from a practical standpoint, wouldn't it be in your best interest for me to find your mother?"

"Sure. But I don't know how to help you. I've told you everything I know. And whatever I said back then is in the police report and Frank's book. Everything was fresher in my mind then."

"But you're twenty-eight now."

"I actually just turned twenty-nine last week."

"OK, twenty-nine. Do you look at things differently? Do you see your parents and what was going on between them, all the friction, the affairs, all that stuff, any differently? Has anything ever popped into your head where you say to yourself, 'Hey, I might have missed something important.' Or maybe think of a person the police should talk to?"

"I did that, Detective. I've been there. I was the one who remembered the name of the Mexican worker who was digging test holes on my father's property. I was the one who helped the police find him."

She was. He remembered that from the file. But it hadn't led to anything. Another dead end along a long road of dead ends.

"What happened to that property?"

"Everything got sold eventually."

"And it went to you?"

"Some of it. There were creditors who took a big chunk. My father had his debts."

"So you must be pretty well off?"

"I would have done better holding on to it. The land's worth a ton more today. But yes, for around here we're doing fine. We're comfortable. Someday I'd like to find an open lot somewhere and get one of those green prefab modern homes with all the renewable energy options built-in. But for now this is good. It's plenty big for the three of us."

The dog reappeared with a throw toy, dropped it at Madden's feet, and waited, his tail wagging, eager for the game to begin.

"Sorry, buddy, I can't play right now," Madden told him.

"That's right, Dakota," she told the dog. "His time's almost up. You have any other questions, Mr. Madden?"

He thought a moment. He'd come in with a lot of questions, but now he couldn't think of any of them. Part of him was just happy to see that she'd turned out as well as she had. After chasing bones for so many weeks, it felt good to connect with the closest thing to Stacey Walker in the flesh.

"I'm sorry," he said. "I'm just a little frustrated. I've only worked a few cold cases. What you hope happens is that after so many years you find little chinks in the armor. People die off. And a person who was afraid to talk starts talking. But I'm just not getting much. We had a new lead but it didn't turn into anything."

"I know," she said. "It is frustrating."

"Oh, before I forget, do you mind if I take a picture of you? You don't have anything online, no Facebook or anything, and my associate, Carolyn Dupuy—I don't know if you remember her, she was the assistant DA on the case—she's been working with me on this and wanted to see what you looked like."

"I'm sorry. I don't take pictures."

Madden wasn't totally surprised by her response. He figured there might be an explanation for the lack of photos but was still hoping to get a shot. And not just for Dupuy. It was always good to have a current photo of anyone closely involved in a case.

"Why?" he asked.

"I just don't want it to end up in a story somewhere showing me compared to my mother. It's not something I want people to see. As a child I saw myself in the newspapers. I don't want to see that girl again."

"But it won't end up in a newspaper or anywhere. I promise."

"I'm sorry," she repeated. "The only one who takes pictures of me is my husband. It's my policy. You'll just have to draw a picture for her. I do remember her by the way. Quite well. Please say hello."

With that, she got up from the couch.

"As I said, I'm really impressed with you, Mr. Madden, and what you've been able to accomplish. I'm glad we got a chance to meet. I'm rooting for you. I really am. If you get a good lead, something real, please call me."

It was time. Time to run the big play. It was why he was really here. To run the play, which was really two plays wrapped into one.

Some private dicks—or people who called themselves private dicks—didn't hesitate to use shadier techniques, like planting bugs or attaching GPS trackers to cars, both of which were illegal to do without a court order. He'd seen ads for tiny GSM bugs with SIM cards that would allow him to call into the bug and listen to what was going on in a room from anywhere. The good ones—the ones that worked— were expensive. But he wasn't Machiavellian enough to start bugging people's homes and cars. That wasn't to say he didn't have a few tricks up his sleeve.

"Just one other thing," he said, his eyes never leaving hers. He didn't want her looking down at the coffee table. "I promised to deliver a message from your uncle."

He reached into the inside pocket of his sport jacket and pulled out an iPod Touch, which he'd borrowed from his daughter. He hit the home button, input her code to unlock the device, then clicked on the Photos icon. He scrolled through the thumbnails until he got to the one he was looking for, which was actually a video, not a photo.

He hit play and handed her the iPod.

"Hey, kid, it's your uncle Robbie," the video started. "It's been a while."

He watched her watch her uncle. The video wasn't long, a little more than a minute, and was mainly a plea to see her again. Robbie and his wife missed her and thought about her often. They hoped she and her new family were doing well.

"Honey, we understand how you feel," Robbie said. "But like I've said a hundred times before, we're not the bad guy here, we just want to know you, you're family, you're all we have left of him."

The video stopped after that. Madden saw a tear stream down her face. Then another.

A pained look. "They look so old," she said.

He waited for her to say more, but she just handed him back the iPod and then wiped the tears from underneath her eyes with her ring fingers, careful to avoid messing with her makeup.

"I can't ask you to do something you don't want to do," he told her. "But why don't you speak with him? What do you have to lose? Maybe he'll tell you something you don't know."

She looked at him. "Tell me or tell *you?*"

"A lot of years have passed, Cathleen. He's your father's brother. If there's someone who knows where she's buried, it would be him. He may want to get it off his chest."

"Why didn't you ask him that when you saw him?"

"I did. Not exactly like that. But I did say I could get him immunity if he had any information, so he shouldn't worry about incriminating himself. Pete offered him the same thing."

"And how did he respond?"

"He said he didn't think his brother killed your mother."

"Of course he did. That's what he's been saying for twenty years. Oh, and by the way, he's also made some pretty negative comments about my mother. You pick up on that in your research?"

"Well, I think it's worth a shot," he said. "Think about it."

"I'm sorry, I can't," she said. "I spent a long time putting this behind me. As I said, I'm glad we met. But now I must politely ask you to leave. I've got things to do. Enjoy Calistoga. It's nice there during the week."

She led him to the front door, passing through the kitchen as she did. Madden's phone was still sitting on the coffee table, recording. But he didn't say anything, didn't even look in its direction. He just followed her out.

"Say goodbye to Detective Madden, Eli."

"Goodbye, Detective Madden," Eli said.

19/ 5150

FREMMER DREAMT HE WAS IN A HOSPITAL. HE WAS LYING IN A BED IN a hospital room and a doctor was talking to him, asking him if he could move his legs. First he tried to lift his right leg, then his left. Nothing. He concentrated, tried to wiggle a toe, but still nothing. But he was able to move his finger. In fact, he could lift his right hand. He could make a fist. "What's wrong with me?" he asked the doctor.

"You've been in an accident," the doctor said. "You fractured a vertebra in your neck."

He recognized the doctor. He'd seen him before in another hospital room. And that was when he realized he was dreaming. He'd put himself in the hospital bed. He hadn't been in an accident. *She'd* been in the accident. Not him. This was a dream.

"Tell her to come in," he told the doctor.

The doctor knew who he meant. He left the room and a moment later his ex-fiancée Denise walked in. She stood there, looking at him, tears in her eyes, overcome with emotion.

"I'm sorry," she said. "I'm so sorry, Max."

Fremmer smiled. She was in for a shock. His legs were limp, but using his good hand he swung them out over the side of the bed and sat himself up. He waited for the circulation to return to his legs. Then he stood and faced her, naked.

Her jaw dropped. She was wearing a long T-shirt, a kind of gown, and he lifted it up and touched her between her legs. He worked his fingers inside her. Then, when he thought she was ready, he swung her around and bent her over the gurney, hiking the gown up over her head, exposing her smooth, muscular back.

He looked over and saw a nurse sitting in a chair not far from the bed looking at them impassively. She was attractive. Hispanic. No, maybe Pacific Islander. Or African American. He couldn't tell. Her face was expressionless but she seemed interested because he wanted her to be. He nodded in her direction, acknowledging her presence. Silently, she took off her clothes and came over to him, pressing up against him. Moving in rhythm with him, she put her hand on his backside, adding force to his thrusts. How helpful! How exhilarating! But then she brushed against his arm and something hurt. The IV. It was still in his arm. He had a tube sticking out of him. Christ. The tube.

That killed it. He felt the dream drifting away. He'd had it. He'd been lucid. But now it was getting away from him. And then it was gone.

He woke unsure of where he was at first, only aware that he had a dull headache and felt tired. But once he looked around it didn't take him long to realize he was in a hospital room and that something bad had happened because both Carlos Morton and his son Jamie were there. Neither noticed he was awake at first. Morton was on his phone, tapping out a message, and his son had his headphones on and was working on his laptop.

"What's going on?" Fremmer asked and Morton looked up.

"Hey, buddy. How are you feeling?"

"Where am I?"

"You're in the hospital. St. Luke's. You were downstairs in the ER for a while last night and they got you into a room at like 4 AM."

He looked at the machines next to him and the curtain room divider, drawn open. Another bed to his left. Polished linoleum floors. Why the hell was he in the hospital?

"What happened?"

"You don't remember texting me last night?"

There was something foreboding in Morton's tone.

"I texted you?"

"Dad, you sent a text saying you wanted to die."

Jamie had pulled his headphones off and had stood up. He had a strange look on his face that was a mixture of fear, relief, and anger. Fremmer was always amazed at the kid's height, almost five-seven. But he looked taller standing there. He had a little bit of acne on his forehead, but objectively the kid was a stud, a poster child for the anti-abortion movement if ever there was one.

"What are you talking about?" Fremmer said. "Why would I do that?"

His visitors looked at each other. They didn't seem to believe him.

"Dad, you texted Carlos and another person last night and said you were sorry but you were tired of living. You said tell Jamie you love him and that you're sorry, but he could go live with his mother like he wanted to. I don't want to live with my mother. I don't know where you got that. I never said that. Why'd you say that?"

"We found you on the floor of your apartment," Morton said. "You'd vomited all over the place. The paramedics came. You were lucky you didn't drown in your own vomit."

Oh, Christ, Fremmer thought. "It was her," he murmured.

"Her, who?" Morton asked.

"Rochelle," he said. "The woman I told you about. The woman from the Lucidity Center who worked for Braden. The guy you met in the police station."

"So, you're saying you didn't text anyone?"

"No, she did."

"But it came from your phone," Morton said. "It definitely came from your phone."

He looked over at Jamie. Tears were streaming down his face. He'd become such a stoic, macho kid that it was weird to see him crying. Fremmer hadn't seen the floodgates open like this for five or six years. It was touching.

"Hey, buddy," Fremmer said. "Don't cry. Come over here and give me a hug."

Jamie came over to the bed and practically lay down on top of him. A sharp pain shot through his arm, which made Fremmer realize he had an IV in him. Aside from that momentary discomfort and the dull headache, he felt pretty good.

"I wouldn't kill myself. You know that."

His son got up and wiped his face, still perplexed.

"She must have drugged me," Fremmer thought aloud. "They say what was in my system?"

"GHB," Morton said.

Fremmer had heard of GHB, it was some sort of hipster drug, he thought.

"You weren't at a club last night, were you?" Morton asked. "They were saying it's known as kind of a liquid ecstasy in smaller doses. Liquid E. At higher doses it's a date-rape drug, though."

"There you go," Fremmer said.

"Why would she drug you?" his son asked.

"It's complicated. She and her boss wanted money from me and I didn't give it to them."

"You might want to tell the police that," Morton suggested.

Fremmer thought about it—thought about what he'd tell the police and what they'd believe. He had a flashback to the scene in the restaurant, wondering for a moment if it had been real. If it had, if he'd really groped her, someone probably saw it. Where did that put him?

"They were at your apartment last night," Morton went on. "The cops. Firemen. Paramedics. Quite a contingent."

"So is that detective, what's his name, Chu, aware that I'm here?"

"I assume so," Morton said.

"What about the press?"

"I think they may be working on a story. I got a call a little while ago. I said it was a private matter. FYI, outside of Jamie here, no one from your family has been contacted. I don't know what you want to do there, but your son said you wouldn't want them to know, especially your older brother in Connecticut."

"Thanks. Yeah, he already thinks I'm a fuck-up. He called to berate me about getting involved with our friend Ronald by the way. Can't wait to hear what he says when he finds out about this. In case you're wondering, I did ask him for a donation to the Carlos Morton legal fund. I have no shame."

Fremmer rubbed his face with both hands. He was strangely calm, not as upset as he should have been. Then it occurred to him how much his hospital stay and ambulance ride were going to cost. He had insurance, but it wouldn't cover everything. There were deductibles and partial payments. He'd probably have to lay out a couple thousand at best. He was starting to regret not paying off Braden. But he was more perturbed at Rochelle. The woman was diabolical. He'd underestimated her. What was so important for them to do something like this? It couldn't just be the money. It had to be something else.

"How'd she get into your phone?" Jamie asked, not yet convinced his father was telling the truth. "It has a password, doesn't it?"

Fremmer raised his finger.

"Yeah, but there's the fingerprint ID. She just put my fingers on the phone until the right one unlocked it."

"Oh, yeah," Jamie said.

"Where'd they find my phone?" Fremmer asked Morton. "Where was it in the apartment?"

"On the desk in the little alcove," Morton said. "In that home office area you have."

"And I was on the floor there?"

"Yeah."

"And how 'bout my computer? Was it out?"

"Yeah, it was on the desk, too."

Fremmer thought about that. If his memory served him correctly, which was questionable at this point, he thought he'd left his laptop in his bag. He hadn't taken it out when he got home.

"I bet she got into that, too," he said.

"I think we should tell all this to the police," Morton said. "They can figure out if someone was on your computer and exactly when."

"What will that prove?"

"Look, they're going to ask you what's going on, we heard you tried to kill yourself, and you're going to tell them the story you just told us, and little stuff like this will make it hold together. We get some video footage from the restaurant and some from your apartment building."

"There is no video from our apartment building so strike that off your list."

"I saw a camera."

"Doesn't work. The DVR it records to broke and the co-op board hasn't gotten around to replacing it."

"Great," Morton said.

Fremmer shook his head in disbelief. He needed to get out of here. As soon as possible.

"You leave my phone at home or do you have it?"

"I've got it," Jamie said.

Fremmer motioned for him to pass it over to him, but it wasn't in Jamie's pocket, it was in his backpack, so it took him a moment to fish it out.

It still had a twenty percent charge. Fremmer looked up his friend Bernstein and sent him a text, asking him if he was in the hospital.

"Who are you texting?" Morton asked.

"A doctor I know who works here. I need to get out of here and will probably need professional help to do that."

"They want you to speak to a psychiatrist as soon as you wake up. You're a fifty-one-fifty. You're in the psych unit."

"I'm a what?"

"Fifty-one-fifty," Morton explained. "That's the code for someone who's a danger to himself or a danger to others. If you're admitted as a fifty-one-fifty you have to be cleared by a psychiatrist to leave. They don't want to take the chance you'll do it again."

"Well, get him in here. Or her. I'll tell them I didn't try to harm myself."

He was now looking at the texts he sent Morton last night. Wow, she was good. They actually seemed convincing. Then he went back to the top of his messages and noticed something really disturbing. Indeed, he had texted somebody else besides Morton. Much to his horror that person was his former fiancée.

"Was Denise there?" he asked his son. "Was she at the apartment?"

"No," his son said. "But she called 911. And me. And she's here now."

"Where?"

"Out in the waiting room. She showed up a little while ago. She had some work calls to make so she didn't want to come in. They said you'd probably wake up soon."

"You're kidding me. So, she thinks I tried to kill myself, too?"

His son nodded. "She thinks she's the reason you tried to do it."

"Oh, man." Fremmer said. "That's not cool. That is so not cool."

20/ Harmless

AFTER MADDEN WAS USHERED OUT OF MILEKI'S HOUSE HE WALKED UP the street, got in his car and drove down the hill past the house. About a hundred yards down the street he made a U-turn and parked again, leaving the engine running. From that vantage point he'd be able to see her pull out of the driveway and intercept her before she drove away. Ideally, however, he wanted to time his return so he caught her before she left.

He looked at his watch. He decided to give her ten minutes. Any longer and she might think it weird that it had taken him that long to remember he'd left his phone behind. Or maybe she wouldn't. He didn't know. But ten minutes sounded about right.

In the end he let the clock run a little longer—an extra minute— then drove back up to the house and parked in front. Soon he was going through the same routine with the barking dog and her eyeing him through the peephole.

"I'm sorry," he said. "I didn't mean to disturb you again. But I left my phone. It's in the living room."

She opened the door but not all the way. She told him to wait there, she'd get it. "I'm not closing the door on you, I just don't want the dog to get out."

In fact, she did close the door, then returned a few moments later to crack it open again and hand him his phone through the narrow gap. She didn't seem to suspect anything. To her, the phone looked like it was off. The screen had gone to sleep but the app was still running.

Even if she'd turned the phone on the first thing she would have seen was the lock screen.

"Sorry," he said. "Thanks. Have a good day."

Back in his car he wasn't quite sure where to go, but at a stop sign he pulled over and searched Google for "Petaluma breakfast spots" and picked one that looked good. He clicked on its address, which in turn launched the Apple Maps app.

It took him only five minutes to get to the restaurant, a quaint little place with a country kitchen feel called the Tea Room Cafe on Western Avenue. It served huevos rancheros, which was all he was looking for.

After he'd settled in at a table, he texted his wife and let her know he'd made it to Petaluma and was OK. Then he texted Dupuy. "Spoke to her for a little bit," he tapped out. "Going to hang out in town until after rush hour. Call you in a few."

Waiting for his food to arrive, he opened the voice-recording app on his phone and plugged his headphones in. The restaurant was a little noisy but it was still early, so it wasn't packed, and his earbuds, a pair of Bose in-ear headphones his wife had given him as a birthday gift, sealed well and cut out a lot of ambient noise.

"OK," he said to himself, "Let's see if we've got anything here."

He jumped ahead along the recording's timeline until he got to the point right before Mileki asked him to leave. He let it run from there.

"Say goodbye to Detective Madden, Eli," she said.

The iPhone had an excellent microphone and her voice sounded clear and fairly loud even though she wasn't close to the phone. That was a good sign.

"Goodbye, Detective Madden," he heard Eli say.

Next, the more muffled sound of the front door to the house opening, then closing. She then returned to the kitchen and told Eli she was going to be turning off the TV soon.

"Can you make it louder, Mommy?" he said.

Shit, Madden thought.

"OK, but just for a few minutes. Finish your milk. I've going to make a call and then we're going to go."

The volume on the TV went up. For about ten seconds that's all Madden heard. Some silly PBS Kids show.

"Hey," he heard her voice again. "So I had a visitor this morning. The detective. Madden." A pause, then: "Yeah, at the house. He just left."

He had trouble hearing what she said next. Maybe she was moving around or maybe the mic was picking up too much of the TV show, he couldn't tell which it was, but her voice came and went. One-way conversations already sounded fragmented. This one even more so. He paused the recording and took a pen and small notebook out of his coat pocket so he could jot down what he heard. When he was sure the pen worked, he hit the play button and began taking notes, writing one line for each fragment of the conversation.

. . . *from Menlo Park. He was on his way to Calistoga.*

He's a little handicapped, you know. I felt bad. I had to . . .

No, the usual stuff.

. . . no, nothing. It's always the same thing.

He went to see Uncle Robbie. He made a video to show me.

It reminded me of one of those hostage videos. Except instead of pleading for his life he was pleading to see me. It was sad. He looks old now. I started crying.

He wanted me to go see him.

No. He thinks he's so desperate to have a relationship with me that he'll tell me where mom's buried. He offered to get him immunity.

Same story.

I know. For someone so decorated, he seems to be flailing. He said he was frustrated. But given his situation, it's great what he's accomplished. I told him that.

[A laugh]. I actually asked him whether he'd been in therapy. You should have seen his face.

It was strange to talk to someone that age who'd been sexually assaulted. I only know young people who'd been assaulted.

It was Pete's case. It wasn't ever his.

What I expected, I guess. Eli told him he was too old to be a police officer. I was kind of horrified when he said it but it was kind of funny.

No, no, it's OK. You don't have to. He's harmless. I just wanted to let you know. I don't think he'll be coming back.

No, I don't want you to say anything. I'll talk to you later.

Eli's good. You wanna say hello? Eli, say hello to papa.

Come on, Eli. Say hello. I'll turn off the TV if you don't.

The next thing Madden heard was a prolonged high-pitched scream. Apparently, Eli wasn't good with threats. He went nuclear. And that was it. The phone call ended. And there wasn't anything else after that. No other calls. Just the inane banter of a mother and her four year old. And then Madden showed up at the door and the phone was retrieved without comment.

"Sorry," he heard himself say. "Thanks. Have a good day."

He sounded pathetic, he thought. A lot of people had underestimated him over the years, but he found confidence in the knowledge that people underestimated him. This time was different, though. He'd allowed himself to be soft. He'd gone in feeling bad for her. That was a mistake. Christ, she thought he was harmless. What a goddamn insult! For a second he wanted to drive back up to the house and play the recording back for her.

Harmless, huh? Well, you got played. Played by a senile old detective.

The waitress brought him his coffee. She asked him something, but he didn't hear her because he still had his earphones on. He pulled them out.

"Excuse me?"

"You want a newspaper, sir?" she asked.

"No thanks."

After she left he put the headphones back on and called Dupuy.

"You get anything?" she asked.

"Yeah, a bruised ego."

"What happened?"

"I pulled the old leave-the-cell-phone-behind-while-it's-still recording trick. It worked a little better this time. She made some unflattering remarks to her husband about me."

Last week in Laguna Beach he'd done the same thing with her uncle Robbie and his wife, Jillian. They'd met at a restaurant and he'd gotten up to go to the bathroom, leaving his phone at the table. They'd talked while he was gone, but about superficial matters like whether Madden looked like Kevin Spacey. And then they had a discussion about the actors who'd played Ross, Stacey, and Cathleen in the re-enactment scenes in the *Dateline NBC* segment about the case. Both Pastorini and Marcus appeared on the show, playing themselves.

"The husband was there when you spoke to her?" Dupuy asked.

"No, she called him afterwards to tell him what a putz I was."

"Really, she called you a putz?"

"Not exactly. The funny thing is I went in feeling sorry for her and came out impressed by how together she was. Apparently, the reverse was true for her. She came in impressed with how together I was but came away feeling sorry for me."

"Is that objective Hank talking or oversensitive Hank?"

"I don't know. I'm tired. I actually want you to listen to the recording when I get back. It's kind of fragmented. There's a TV playing the background, so I couldn't hear everything. She didn't really say anything all that interesting but I thought her tone was slightly conspiratorial. I may be wrong, though. It's hard to know what to think when you're being insulted. She said I was harmless."

"Ouch."

"Yeah, it hurts. How 'bout Bender? You said you had something for me. What is it?"

"Some dirt. Ted heard something. You gotta talk to him about it."

"What kind of dirt?"

"Talk to Ted. He thinks Bender's trading prescription drugs for access to executives at some of these companies."

"Really?" That sounded juicy. He was suddenly in a better mood. "Who's his source?"

"Talk to him. He's still asleep. He's off so he's around. I'll have him call you when he wakes up."

"I'll be back by around noon."

"How's Petaluma?"

"I like it. It seems unpretentious. Got a bit of a southwestern flair. Or maybe it's just western. At least it's got some old bits and pieces. Some history. You know, they filmed *American Graffiti* here. I think I'll do the tour later. A couple of the locations still exist. I've gotta get a picture."

"I didn't realize you were such a fan."

"That movie launched a lot of careers."

"Speaking of pictures, you get one of her?"

Back to reality. "No," he said.

"Did you ask or just forget?"

"So she thinks I'm harmless and now you think I'm senile?" Madden said, only half kidding. "I asked. She says she doesn't do pictures. Doesn't want them to end up in the paper or on social media. Something about not wanting people comparing her to her mother."

"Does she look like her?"

"Yeah."

"A lot?"

"There's a definite resemblance. Similar eyes. Similar nose. She's a good-looking woman."

"Sounds like she turned out OK."

"Better than OK. And she got there by looking forward, not back. Which is why we're an intrusion."

"Well, wait 'til the Bender story gets out there. She's really not going to like you then. She's going to think you put him up to that."

Christ, she was right. All of a sudden he didn't want to go back. He wanted to keep driving. Maybe he'd really head up to Calistoga and hole up somewhere for a few days. Just check out. He didn't even have to drink, though that's what one did in wine country, wasn't it?

"Hank, you there?"

"Yeah, I'm here."

"I said, 'At least she won't think you're harmless.'"

"No, maybe not."

21/ Unconditional Release

FREMMER WAS NEVER ALONE IN THE ROOM. WHENEVER HE WAS, EVEN for just a few minutes, Paulette came in and sat in one of the two empty chairs. She was less sexy than the woman in his dream, but resembled her just enough to make it difficult for him to look her in the eyes without feeling a whiff of embarrassment. Her job as a psych ward nurse—or at least part of it—was to make sure he didn't try to harm himself again. And that meant he wasn't allowed to be in the room by himself. Someone had to watch him at all times.

When she popped into the room this time Jamie was there, so it wasn't to keep him company.

"Sir, that friend of yours in a wheelchair is still out in the waiting room," she said. "She asked if she can come in now. What should I tell her?"

Until now Paulette had been quietly bland. But Fremmer detected a bit of attitude in her voice, like he could hear her thinking, *What kind of asshole treats a person in a wheelchair like that?*

"Tell her I'm too dangerous."

"Dad, you've got to speak to her," Jamie cut in. "She's been sitting out there for almost two hours. It's rude."

Fremmer didn't want Denise to see him like this. He'd sent Morton away and told him to tell her on his way out that he was in no condition to see anybody. That apparently hadn't worked. Fremmer's attempts to extricate himself from the hospital had been equally unsuccessful.

"Spoke to 2 docs," he texted his friend Bernstein earlier. "One was a shrink. They still won't discharge me."

"Patience patient," Bernstein said. "U r a liability. Be out in a little while. They're getting ready to close here."

Bernstein was in surgery. Fremmer pictured him there, sitting at the head of the operating table by the patient's head, texting on his cell phone. As a patient you didn't realize what was happening while you were lying there, cut open. But that was what anesthesiologists did. Most of the time they weren't doing anything so they texted. Or checked their email, stock quotes and sports scores.

"OK, tell her to come in," he said to his son. "But give me a few minutes alone."

He told Jamie to go find them some food. Maybe he could dig up a turkey club. He was starving.

"What are you going to say?" his son asked.

"I'll think of something."

"You can't be a dick, Dad."

"Me? A dick? What are you implying?"

"You know what I mean. Don't be your blunt self. Some people don't appreciate it."

"Some people do. And those are the ones you want to hang out with. But point taken. Ixnay on the blunt self. Now amscray."

In the thirty seconds he was alone he tried to make himself more presentable. He finger-combed his hair and popped a Lifesaver from the roll Morton had left behind. He still had the IV needle in his arm, but he'd been disconnected from the banana bag of fluids so he wasn't tethered to anything. He could have greeted her standing up but he thought that wouldn't look good considering he'd had Morton tell her he was in no shape to see anyone. So he stayed in the bed, propping himself up a few more degrees with a press of the button on the bed's remote control.

Paulette knocked first, and then held the door open so Denise could wheel herself in. *This isn't going to end well*, Fremmer thought as the door closed behind her.

"Hey," he said.

"Hey," she said back.

"You hear the one about the guy who hit the prescription pills a little too hard and texted his lawyer and ex-fiancée about wanting to kill himself?"

"You scared me, Max. You scared Jamie."

"I know. I'm sorry. I am a little surprised though."

"About what?"

"No flowers."

That got a smile. A tiny one. "I debated it," she said. "But then I decided it wasn't appropriate to bring flowers to someone who tried to kill himself."

"Probably not. But I'm glad you came. I'm sorry I kept you waiting. It's just that I'm feeling a little stupid and not so attractive. You look good, though, kid."

She did. From the waist up she looked exactly as she had all those years ago, maybe better. And with the bed in the way, that's all he saw, her upper half without the chair. Her tight shirt showed off her arms; she was in better shape than he was. A real-estate broker now, he'd heard she'd been doing some wheelchair racing, which made sense—she was a serious runner when they'd been dating. He hadn't seen her in four years. She'd been in a relationship with another wheelchair racer. They were going to get married. Then they weren't. She didn't post much on Facebook, but sometimes she liked the images he posted. Occasionally she made comments on them. He commented back. That was the extent of their relationship.

Instead of answering, she wheeled herself forward and pulled up alongside the bed. The chair barely fit between the bed and the wall. Before he knew it she'd taken his hand and was looking at him intently. He wasn't sure what she was looking for but it felt good to hold her hand. So good he wanted to cry. And then he did. He felt a tear go down his cheek. He couldn't believe it.

"If you still love me, why didn't you just tell me," she said.

"I don't know."

And then he heard Rochelle in his head saying, "Are you lucid? Are you lucid now?" And he really wasn't. He was completely unsure what was happening. He wondered if some residual GHB had suddenly kicked in.

"I've got to tell you something," she said.

"What?"

"The last few years . . ."

Her voice trailed off.

"What?" he said.

"I wanted to say something but I didn't. But the last couple of years Jamie's been coming to see me."

He blinked, startled. "Excuse me?"

"We have dinner sometimes. When you're teaching that six forty-five spinning class I take him to dinner and you don't know. I'm sorry, I should have said something. He reached out. He wanted to talk. So I agreed to meet with him."

"What did he want to talk about?"

"Your book."

"I didn't say he could read that. He's too young to read that."

"I know. I told him that. But he already did. I think he was curious. He'd met me a few times when he was younger but said he didn't really remember it. So I agreed to meet him. And he asked a lot of questions. About you. About us. But then he just started asking questions in general. I think he just wanted to hear a female voice. That's what I really came here to tell you. I knew you didn't try to kill yourself, Max."

"You did?"

"Look, I was concerned enough to call 911. I had to do that. But it wasn't like you. It was sloppy. You're not a sloppy guy, Max."

He wasn't so sure about that. "I'm not?"

"Sure, you seem like you're winging it a lot of the time. But when it comes to the important things you're meticulous. You want everything to be perfect. If you wanted to kill yourself, you would have done it right. All your affairs would have been in order. Remember what you used to say, 'If you're going to do it, do it with conviction. Always do it with conviction.'"

"I still say that."

"Well, this lacked conviction."

She was right, of course.

"So what was I really up to?" he asked.

"I don't know. Some guy feeling sorry for himself. Or being a pussy about his emotions."

He nodded. That made sense. He squeezed her hand a little tighter.

"I'm going to go now," she said. "But when you get through all this, I promised Jamie that the next time we go out you'd come with us."

"That'd be good," he said, "I lost my spinning classes, you know. I don't know if you've been reading the papers about this woman who was pushed in front of that car, but she—"

"I know. She's your client. I saw you on TV."

"I may have gotten out over my skis a little too far. This guy that pushed her, I thought he was innocent. Now I'm not so sure. And I roped my lawyer friend into this whole thing. I've got to raise some money for him. We've got to get him a proper defense."

"You also landed yourself in the hospital. What'd you take?"

"I'd rather not talk about it. The whole thing is embarrassing."

Just then there was a knock at the door and his friend Bernstein came in. He looked startled. He wasn't expecting to see Fremmer holding hands with a woman in a wheelchair, having a moment.

"Hey, you made it," Fremmer said.

"You want me to come back in a little bit?"

"No, it's OK," Denise said. "I was just leaving."

She introduced herself to Bernstein as she backed out of the room. Bernstein wasn't much taller than Denise sitting in the chair. He was still in his scrubs, a trim forty-six-year-old who still had a full head of mainly dark hair that looked like it hadn't been cut in a while. Fremmer knew him from his spinning class. He was a regular. They occasionally rode outside together, around the loop in Central Park or over the George Washington Bridge to New Jersey.

"I'm the ex-fiancée," she said.

"Oh," Bernstein said. "I have one of those. You're a lot better looking than mine, though. Who broke it off?"

Bernstein may have been the bluntest guy Fremmer knew.

"I did," she said.

"I thought so."

After she'd gone, Bernstein said, "Something tells me you were engaged while her legs were working. What happened?"

"Body-surfing accident. Mexico."

"C6?"

"Between C6 and C7," Fremmer said.

"Bummer."

"Yeah."

"Was she really the one who called it off?"

Fremmer nodded. "I handled things pretty well at first. And then I didn't. I couldn't accept it. She eventually got tired of the act and granted me my unconditional release. Put me on waivers."

"Mine was a banker," he said. "Still walking and making lots of money. Didn't like to give head. In retrospect, probably not my best life decision. Now I'm an underpaid middle-aged doctor working for sucky people at a sucky hospital trying to send three kids to private school with a wife who quit her job and stopped giving head after the kids started private school."

"Bummer."

"On a happier note, I do have some good news for you."

"What's that?"

"Your peds vs. car woke up a couple of hours ago. The attending just told me."

"She's awake?"

"Yeah, you wanna go see her? The daughter's with her now. If she's OK with it I can get you into the ICU."

"Let's go," Fremmer said.

"Let me get you discharged first. You good with me telling them this was a revenge-jealousy-gay thing? That's a language they understand. GHB and ass-fucking tend to go hand-in-hand. You throw a little homo erotica at them and everything suddenly becomes clear."

"Whatever it takes, man. Just don't talk that way in front of my son when he comes back."

"I'm just kidding," Bernstein said. "But I like your spirit. You're hardcore, Fremmer. That's what I like about you."

22/ Crime Drop

THE FIRST CALL MADDEN GOT ON THE BENDER ARTICLE WAS FROM his old colleague at the MPPD. Jeff Billings had been the junior detective on their team of three detectives. Now that Madden and Burns had retired, he'd become the veteran of the team at the tender age of thirty-four.

Madden was on the 101 near Belmont, heading back from Petaluma, when Billings called. He put him on speakerphone.

"How long were you going to wait to tell me?" Billings said straight off the bat. No hellos or how-are-yous.

"I figured you knew already," Madden replied.

"We did."

"The Palo Alto boys tell you?"

"Why would they tell me?"

"They saw me digging up a yard."

"You were digging up a yard?"

"Yeah," Madden said. "Bronsky's old place."

"You find anything?"

"Yeah, I found something. Just not Stacey Walker."

"I didn't know anything about you digging up a yard," Billings said. "But I did know you were working on the case. You know how I knew?"

"No, how? Shelby?"

Billings made the sound of game-show buzzer. "Wrong. Pastorini told us."

"He did? He wasn't supposed to."

"Real smart, Hank. Tell a guy who had a serious stroke to keep a secret. Did you ever think that might not be the smartest move?"

"Maybe not, but I hope you're OK with me telling him you said that."

The line went silent for a moment.

"Don't do that," Billings said.

Madden smiled. He and Billings had always had a slightly adversarial relationship. Sometimes things got a little tense, but Madden appreciated that Billings treated him democratically, that he was an equal-opportunity taunter. Most of the ribbing was good-natured, only rarely mean-spirited. Madden and the other guys took shots at Billings' vanity—he was something of a pretty boy, short, with sandy blond hair, the lean, chiseled body of a surfer, and a too-cool-for-school attitude. Billings would let it roll off him, or he'd accuse them of jealousy, which was partially true. Now that a lot of the old guard had left he'd become insufferable, or so Madden had heard from his old friend Brian Carlyle, recently promoted to commander, one step below chief.

"So if you knew, why didn't you say anything?" Madden asked.

"I don't need to go down that rabbit hole. Look what it did to Pastorini. For what? Seven, eight years he didn't spend Christmas with his family? I've got smaller fish to fry."

"What are you working on?"

"Getting awards."

"Seriously."

"Seriously. You know we've got crime down forty-two percent in Belle Haven. We haven't had a gang-related shooting in nearly four months."

"I heard," Madden said.

The Belle Haven neighborhood in East Menlo Park bordered East Palo Alto. Back in 1992 East Palo Alto had the highest per capita murder rate in the country. Belle Haven had long been Menlo Park's little pocket of suburban blight and its main supplier of violent crime. That was changing, though. Fast. Insane real-estate prices pushed people to consider sketchier properties. When Facebook moved in across the freeway nearby, Belle Haven and East Palo Alto had seen their fortunes rise. Facebook funded one full-time patrol officer on the MPPD and had paid for the construction of a new service center at the cross section of Hamilton Avenue and Willow Road.

More controversially, the department also had three cars equipped with automated license plate readers that went around capturing license plate data and uploading it to a server managed by the Northern California Regional Intelligence Center, part of the Department of Homeland Security.

But Billings was taking full responsibility for the drop in the crime rate.

"We Moneyballed that shit," he said. "Came down to three houses creating eighty percent of the problems. I've been embedded, man. Vested and embedded, working with the neighbors to curtail anything that looks suspicious before it metastasizes into something nefarious."

"I miss you, Bills. So, now that you've eliminated crime, what's next?"

"Well, I wanted to talk to you about that."

Madden didn't like the tone. It sounded like he was about to deliver some bad news.

"What'd you want to talk about?"

"I don't know if I told you but I'm writing a book."

"About what?"

"About the murder cases we worked on together."

"You know I'm working on a book," Madden said, a bit shocked by Billing's revelation.

"Yeah, I know. But I heard it wasn't going so well. And I was approached by someone to write it."

"Someone who?"

"Your agent, I guess."

"To write my book?"

"No, to write a book about the cases," Billings said. "I was there, too. I was as much a part of it."

"Are you kidding me?"

"Look, I've made a lot of progress. But it's missing your point of view. I think it's important for you to be a part of it, particularly since you're the main character. I'd like to sit down with you—"

"Sit down with me?"

"Yeah, get you on tape. Interview you. I'll make you a deal. We'll help you out on the Walker case, get you whatever you need. You know, support your efforts. That's going to be our official stance with the media. We're taking the high road. The chief wanted me to tell you that. We're all about collaboration these days. Working together with businesses, the community—"

"I don't need your help," Madden said.

"Yes, you do. There might be something you missed. We can be helpful, Hank. You know that."

He was right. Angry as he was, he didn't take the offer for granted. He thought about it a moment, took a break, then said:

"Look, I actually do need some help with something. It's related. The guy, Bender, who wrote that article last night. I need you to investigate him."

"For what?"

"I'll tell you later. I've got another call coming in. It's my wife. I gotta get it."

He ended the call and waited for his wife to click in.

"Hey, hon," he said, "How do you feel about selling the house and moving to Petaluma?"

She wasn't in the mood for jokes, even if he was half serious. "Hank, someone from the *Chronicle* newspaper is calling. She's on the home line. What am I saying to her?"

Though her English was good, she sometimes didn't get her verbs —or their tenses—quite right.

"Tell her I'll call her back."

"What's going on?"

"Nothing. Just some unwanted publicity. Nothing bad."

Just then a text came in from Carolyn. "Chronicle calling me," it said. "What should I say?"

He didn't usually text while he drove but this time he made an exception. "Wait," he wrote, "on my way."

"Hank?" his wife said.

"Yeah, I'm here."

"The money Shelby will pay you . . ."

"Yes?"

"How much is it? It says a lot."

Oh, no. She'd read the article. That's the last thing he needed, his wife on his case.

"Yeah, but I actually have to find her, which I don't think is going to happen at this point."

"Why not?"

"I've got nothing. I'm no closer to finding her than the day I started looking for her two months ago. Don't believe what you read. It's all a farce."

"What's farce?"

"A lie. It's not real. People like Shelby don't live in a real world."

23/ ICU

T HE INTENSIVE CARE UNIT ON THE SEVENTH FLOOR OF ST. LUKE'S HAD
a horseshoe design, with a series of conjoined, glass-fronted
rooms built around a central nursing station. A level-one trauma center, Bernstein had worked at the hospital for over ten years. Now that
Mt. Sinai had taken over both St. Luke's and its sister hospital, St.
Luke's–Roosevelt, where he also worked, Bernstein told Fremmer he
was considering a move. They'd made too many big changes, including renaming the hospitals and reducing his salary.

"It's good they brought you here," he said in a low voice as they
rode the elevator to the ICU. "But you'd have been fine at Roosevelt.
Your peds vs. car, not so much."

This hospital was about twenty-five blocks farther from both his
apartment and the location where Candace had been hit. Even so,
they almost always brought major traumas to St. Luke's. Roosevelt
just wasn't equipped for it.

"They brought John Lennon to Roosevelt," Bernstein went on,
not caring that there were other people in the elevator, including another doctor, who was looking straight ahead, pretending not to listen. "He wouldn't have survived regardless, but he had no chance
there. Zero. I know the guy who held his heart in his hand. He's a
good doctor. Good at what he's good at anyway. But not the guy you
want treating a gunshot victim who has minutes to live. Zero chance
he was going to save him. Norman McSwain. Now that guy maybe.
Ever hear of him? I worked with him in New Orleans during my res-

idency. The man pioneered trauma. Saved people who couldn't be saved. He was amazing. He might have been able to save Lennon."

The elevator doors opened on seven and Fremmer said goodbye to Jamie. Then he and Bernstein stepped out and into the ICU. Fremmer was on the approved visitors list, but Jamie wasn't. Bernstein didn't want to complicate an already complicated situation by trying to bring him. He would wait for them in the lobby.

Fremmer noticed Candace's daughter, Mia, standing against the wall with her face in her hands, crying. She was a sporty girl who went around in indoor soccer shoes with every outfit and was going to be very attractive one day, but was in a little bit of an awkward stage, gangly, with braces and some acne. Her friend's mother Anna, the same woman who had helped him get access to Candace's computer, was consoling her.

Mia's tears quickly gave way to full-throttle sobs. Fremmer thought something terrible had happened, that Candace had died. He kept his distance until Anna noticed him standing there and made eye contact.

He didn't know quite what to say, so he said nothing as she walked towards him. In her Athleta leggings and tight-fitting light blue sweat top, she looked like she was on her way to a yoga class. This was a woman who knew how to take care of herself, Fremmer thought. She was probably around fifty, but looked remarkably fit. Not a gray root was showing in her short strawberry blond hair, her skin was smooth and her makeup flawless.

"Hey," he said.

"Hey," she said back. She took his arm and led him further away from Mia. "She's having a tough time. They tried to lower her expectations, but she just wasn't prepared. I probably shouldn't have brought her."

"What happened? I heard she woke up."

"She did. But she didn't know who Mia was. They don't even know if she even knows who she is. It's like one of those *Twilight Zone* episodes."

Now she was dating herself a bit.

"But she's able to talk?"

"Sort of. She didn't say much. But apparently her speech center wasn't damaged. It's here somewhere," she said, tapping the left side of her head. "In the frontal lobe. I'm learning a lot about how the brain works. She can see and hear. They say those are all good signs."

Bernstein came toward them and Fremmer introduced him.

"You mind if I speak to the girl for a minute?" Bernstein asked.

Anna was happy to offer her consent. She'd been eager to step in and help after the accident, but Fremmer sensed that she was starting to get overwhelmed. She'd thought someone from Mia's father's family would take over, but no one had come forward. Mia had been relying on her friends' parents for support, definitely not a sustainable situation.

"Hey, Mia," Bernstein said. "Remember me? I'm Dr. Bernstein. I'm a friend of Max's. I take his spinning class. I met you briefly the other day when you were visiting your mom."

She nodded.

"Look, I know it's tough but you've got to look at the bright side. Your mom woke up. She woke up now and that's a good sign. I've seen patients who've been in comas for two, three months. Sometimes they never wake up."

Mia nodded.

"This is going to be a long process," he went on. "It's going to take a while for her to get better. They may have to do more surgeries but eventually she'll be moved to a special rehabilitation facility."

"What if she never knows who I am?" Mia asked.

"I know it's troubling, but it's not something to be worrying about right now. The important thing is that she was able to see you and say something to you. What school do you go to?"

"P.S. 87."

"You're what, in fifth grade?"

"Yeah."

"I went to public school. I bet they don't have a lot of Escalades in front of P.S. 87 in the morning, do they?"

She shook her head. "No, not really."

"Don't laugh, but that's how my wife rates a school," Bernstein said. "She counts the number of Escalades out in front in the morning. That's pretty silly, isn't it?"

She smiled, exposing her braces. "One of my friends on the soccer team has a driver. Sometimes I get a ride to practice with her."

"You know Max's son Jamie? He's a little older than you."

Her eyes brightened hearing the name. She said she'd met him before. He was a year older. Or maybe it was two years, she forgot.

"Well, he's downstairs waiting for us," Bernstein said. "I've got to get something to eat. You guys want to come down with me and say hello?" he asked Anna. "I think it'd be good for both of you to get out of here for a bit. It can get oppressive. I know Jamie would like to see you."

Fremmer wasn't sure about that, but he didn't say anything, especially since Mia seemed to think it was a good idea. She and Anna went back into the ICU to collect their bags, and when they did, Bernstein turned to him and said:

"I'm going to leave you with a nurse I know. You go in there and see if she's responsive to you at all. Just talk softly. I'll check on her later. They may put her back in a coma, but you didn't hear that from me. It's a good sign she woke up, though. I wasn't lying to the kid."

Fremmer nodded. Bernstein handed him off to one of the ICU nurses, a young Asian woman, who took him into the ICU. Only about half the beds appeared to be filled, and other than the beeps of the machines, the room was quiet.

Candace was sleeping. Fremmer studied her face for a moment. Aside from the fresh bandages covering part of her head and face, she didn't look any different from when he'd seen her the other day.

"Hey, kid," he said quietly. "I heard you woke up."

With that her eyes fluttered open. She looked at him.

"Remember me? I'm the guy who helps publish your e-books. Max Fremmer."

She stared at him. He didn't seem to register.

"They're all bestsellers now," he said. "All four of them. You're my first author to have a bestseller."

As soon as the words left his mouth he regretted saying them. He was glad no else had witnessed his idiocy.

"Max," he said a little louder. "Frem-mer." He carefully enunciated his last name, as if that would help. "Do you know who I am?"

She shook her head ever so slightly. She seemed to have no idea who he was.

"Well, I'm a friend. I'm a friend who's here to help."

God, that sounded stupid, he thought. But what was he supposed to say?

"You were hit by a car," he went on. "I'm sure they've told you that. It was bad. Very bad. You're in a hospital. Do you know what hospital you're in?"

"Stanford?" she whispered.

Stanford? Is that what she said? She'd spoken so quietly that he barely heard her over the beeps. But that was what he thought he heard. There was a town upstate in Duchess County called Stanford. Maybe she'd spent some time there. He knew people who rented summer houses there—or near there. But a hospital?

"Did you say Stanford?" he asked.

A slight nod. He decided to go with it.

"Is that where you live? In Stanford?"

"Menlo Park," she said.

"Menlo Park? Menlo Park, California or Menlo Park, New Jersey?"

Edison had invented the light bulb in Menlo Park, New Jersey. A lot of people thought the one in California was named for Edison's Menlo Park but the opposite was true. Now probably wasn't the time for him to point that out to her, but it did cross his mind.

"California," she said.

"You live in Menlo Park, California?"

She exhaled hard. It took some effort for her to speak.

"My husband tried to kill me," she said.

"Your husband? Who's your husband?"

"Ross," she said.

"He pushed you in front of a car? You remember that?"

"No. No. He tried to choke me."

She grimaced. None of this made sense. For a few fleeting seconds, he thought they may have made a mistake and had somehow got the identity of the victim wrong, that this wasn't Candace after all.

"Your husband Ross tried to choke you? What's your name?"

Her eyes locked on him. He could see fear.

"Who are you? Are you a cop? Where am I?"

"You're in St. Luke's Hospital," he said. "You've been hit by a car."

"Go away," she whispered.

"I'm a friend. I'm here to help. I publish your books. I'm a book doctor."

"I don't write books. Please . . ."

She then let out a noise that was a mixture of a groan and a scream, the noise a wounded animal makes. Not ear-piercingly loud, but loud enough for everybody on the ward to hear her.

"Go away," she said again.

Soon there were two nurses and a doctor in the room with him, pushing him out of the way.

"What did you say?" the Asian nurse who'd brought him in asked.

"I didn't say anything," he said. "I told her who I was and that she'd been hit by a car."

"You better go out now," she said.

He went to smooth his hair back with his hand—it was a nervous tic.

"Is she going to be alright?" he asked.

When he reached up to fix his hair, his sleeve came down a bit and she noticed he still had his patient wristband on.

"Sir, are you a patient here?"

He looked at the band. He'd forgotten to cut it off.

"No. I was. Not anymore, though. They thought I tried to kill myself but I didn't."

Now she was looking at him with fear.

"I'm going," he said. "Don't worry. I'm going."

PART 3

23/ Kevin Spacey Calling

A MONTH AFTER BENDER POSTED THE ARTICLE MADDEN WAS BACK IN the hardware store, doing his usual Tuesday shift. He was in the middle of helping a customer find a drill bit that penetrated stainless steel when he felt his phone vibrate in his pocket. Text message alert. It could wait.

"I'd go with titanium," Madden told the customer. "The cobalt is good, but you might as well go with the titanium."

After the man walked away with the titanium bit, Madden took his phone out and looked at the text. It was from Pastorini. Madden couldn't quite believe what he saw.

"Kevin Spacey called," the message read. "Call him back. He's been trying to reach you."

A phone number followed the message. *Kevin Spacey was trying to reach him?* The area code wasn't from the Bay Area but it seemed familiar. And then he realized why. It was the same 347 number he'd seen a few days earlier. Someone had left two messages with Billings at the Menlo Park police department. In both cases, whoever had called had left a number but no name. Madden hadn't called back.

"The actor Kevin Spacey?" he texted Pastorini.

He had to wait a little while for a response. "Yes," the reply came back.

Something felt off. He decided to call him. He owed him a call anyway.

"Hey, buddy," he said. "Kevin Spacey? Are you sure about that? You spoke to Kevin Spacey?"

"I spoke to his assistant. A guy named Drew Masters." Pastorini's speech was getting better but wasn't perfect. He still sounded a touch drunk, with some slurring of his words—he had a hard time with the letter "s"—and he spoke more slowly than he used to.

Was is it possible? Kevin Spacey?

"Why did the assistant call you?"

"The MPPD wouldn't give out your number," Pastorini said. "I'm listed."

"Did he say why he was calling?"

"No. I'm watching a movie. I'm not your secretary. Call me later."

Madden took the phone away from his ear and looked at the time. It was 11:12 AM, 2:12 PM in New York. Spacey might be at lunch, but Madden could always leave a message with the assistant.

Fremmer had just stepped out of the Pacific Aquarium and Pet shop on Delancey Street, where he'd been inquiring about Rochelle, when he saw the 650 area come up on his phone. He'd used an app called Burner to create a temporary number that couldn't be traced to him. He could delete the number at any time and create a new one. *It's gotta be Madden,* he thought, *this is it.*

"This is Hank Madden," the caller said. "Who's this?"

"This is Drew Masters," Fremmer said. "I called you about setting up a meeting with Mr. Spacey."

"Yes, I got the message."

"Well, hear me out for a minute. My name isn't really Drew Masters and I'm not Kevin Spacey's assistant."

"You're not?"

"No, I apologize for deceiving you. I only said that because I knew you wouldn't return my calls. You're not so easy to reach. But here's the deal, Mr. Madden. I found Stacey Walker."

Silence.

"To be clear, this is not a crank call," Fremmer went on. "No one's trying to punk you. I assure you I'm totally on the level here."

"If you're not Drew Masters then who are you?" Madden asked.

"I can't tell you that right now. But call me Drew for now. I need to know if you have some sort of contract with Hal Shelby? I read one story that said you had a six-month window to find Stacey Walker. Was there some sort of legal document involved?"

"Yes. But I haven't been actively working for him for the last month."

Fremmer pumped his fist victoriously. *Houston, we have a contract.*

"Yes, from some of your later quotes you didn't seem so happy with how things had played out," he replied calmly. "But the contract stipulates six months, right? There's a date on the contract that says if you find her within such and such a time frame you get the bonus?"

"There is," Madden said. "I have a signed legal document. Why are you asking me this?"

"Because I want half that bonus, Mr. Madden. And I want half the bonus if we find her husband Ross. Basically, I want half of everything. And I need you to get on a plane and come to New York tomorrow so we can get to work on this."

"Tomorrow?"

"Yeah, by my count we only have a few weeks to get this done."

"Are you for real?"

"One hundred percent," Fremmer said. "I'll give you specific instructions on where to go later today. You pay the airfare and I'll reimburse you for your hotel after we sit down and sign our own contract. Don't bother trying to trace this number because I've taken steps to remain anonymous. After we get something down on paper I will tell you exactly who am I. But for now I need to remain anonymous to protect my interests. I haven't said a word about this to anyone. Do we have an understanding?"

"We do. But I still don't believe you. You know where she's buried?"

"Yes. I can tell you exactly where when you get here. Have you ever been to New York?"

"Only the airport."

"Well, May's a good time to come," Fremmer said. "Not too hot, not too cold, not too many tourists. I look forward to meeting you. I've read a lot about you."

"I can reach you at this number?"

"For now."

"Well, let me think about it and I'll call you back later."

"There is no thinking about it, Mr. Madden. You're getting on a plane. Otherwise, I'm going to have to try to make my own deal with Hal Shelby and I don't want to do that. I'm going for the whole kit and caboodle. And that means you are, too."

24/ A Gramme is Better Than a Damn

FREMMER WASN'T LYING TO MADDEN WHEN HE SAID THAT HE HADN'T told anybody about his discovery. After his conversation with Candace in the ICU, he did the first thing a lot of people would do under the circumstances: he Googled. He input the words "Menlo Park" "Ross" "husband" "choked" and "killed" into the search bar on his phone. The search results confounded and amazed him.

The first item was Bender's story on onedumbidea.com, posted almost a month earlier. It was about a wealthy Silicon Valley entrepreneur that hired a well-known, retired local detective in Menlo Park to help solve a twenty-year-old cold case involving a man named Ross Walker and his missing wife, Stacey. The entrepreneur said he'd offered to pay the detective a huge bonus if he found Stacey or Ross Walker. Sounded like seven figures.

Could the Ross that Candace was talking about be the Ross in the article? And if so, didn't that make her Stacey?

As soon as Fremmer got home, he dug up a picture of her on his computer that he'd taken of her at an Apple store a couple of years ago. He'd wanted to use the shot as her author photo on Amazon, but in the end she hadn't let him. He realized there were almost no photos of her online, just the small one posted on her LinkedIn page that the media had been using.

He compared his photo to the pictures of Stacey Walker from twenty years ago. Her initial thought was that it wasn't the same woman. The young Stacey had blond, straight hair. Candace Epstein had dark curly hair.

He kept looking, studying the features. Pretty soon he started to see the resemblance. It was in the eyes. A little in the nose, too, though it looked like Candace had some work done. The cheekbones seemed a little higher, the nose a little smaller. It was her. Had to be.

Making that connection didn't send a shiver up his spine, that came a few minutes later. He clicked through more articles about the case, and read one about the discovery in Vietnam of Ross's partial remains along with some personal effects including his passport. Fremmer soon realized that by "partial remains" they were talking about multiple bones, and those multiple bones added up to one hand, a wrist, and a forearm. One arm up to the elbow.

Fremmer read every article he could find on the subject of Ross. Over the years people had become divided over whether he was really dead. Some thought he'd chopped his arm off to fake his own death. Others thought that was crazy. Fremmer was in the middle of a piece when one line stopped him cold. It was a quote from Pete Pastorini, the lead detective in the case.

"Do I think there's a guy walking around somewhere with one arm who got away with murder? Sure, it's possible, but the more likely scenario is Ross Walker is dead."

And then it hit him: Braden. *He had one arm. The guy had one fucking arm. Staph infection? Yeah, right. The bastard chopped his own arm off. It's him. Has to be.*

Suddenly, it all began to make sense. Or at least he thought it did. When Candace told him she knew someone who'd done something very bad, the kind of thing that put a person in prison for a long time, she'd been referring to her previous life. Who was the someone? Braden? Maybe. But if she were Stacey and Braden were Ross, then no one was murdered. Could they both still be alive? Had it all been an elaborate scheme? And if so, to what end?

And what about Ronald? Was he connected to her past? And the alleged manuscript Candace was supposed to deliver, was there something in there implicating Braden in, well, something? And Madden's investigation, what was the timeline there? Could she have been pushed because of some fact or event he'd uncovered?

Fremmer's brief *ah-ha* moment suddenly morphed into a dizzying array of unanswerable questions and conjectures. He wanted to speak to someone about his recent discoveries, but that little piece about the bonus kept gnawing at him. There might be real money there, he thought. It could go straight into Jamie's college fund. And he'd be able to give something to Morton. Make it worth his while for taking on Ronald, who was scheduled to be back in court that week.

He needed Madden. First, he'd have to get him to agree to split the reward, then convince him to come to New York to see if he could identify Braden as Ross and take a DNA sample from Candace.

And what about Rochelle? He wondered if she knew who her boss really was. Or if Rochelle were her real name. A day after he got out of the hospital he'd received a get-well card from her with the odd inscription, "Remember, a gramme is better than a damn. 'Til we meet again, Rochelle."

The phrase sounded familiar. She spelled *gramme* the British way, so it had to be a literary quote. Google, the great curator of quotes, solved that part of the puzzle in less than half a second. Huxley. Rochelle had sent him a get-well card with a quote from *Brave New World*, a reference to one of the novel's many hypnopædic slogans promoting the utopian use of soma. Narcotics for the greater good.

God that was hot, he thought. But he didn't get the tone. What did she mean, "'Til we meet again?" Was she threatening or flirting? After all she'd already put him through were they just going to let him off the hook? That made no sense. Then again, maybe she'd gotten into his computer and lifted whatever file she was looking for. But what was it? What was she looking for?

What was her real name? Where did she live? He had to find her. The simplest way to do that would be to stake out the Lucidity Center, wait for her to show up, and then try to follow her back to her apartment. Except that he didn't have time for stakeouts.

Then he remembered that she'd said she once worked at an aquarium shop. That could have been a lie. But it was worth a shot. There were only a couple of dedicated aquarium stores in the city and only one downtown. It was on Delancey Street, not too far from the courthouse, where he had to go anyway for Ronald's mental competency hearing.

The hearing went pretty much exactly as Fremmer had expected. Ronald was escorted in the courtroom. Morton made an impassioned sixty-second statement about the hidden dangers of multiple concussions worthy of a Will Smith movie, and the judge announced his ruling. And just like that, Ronald was deemed officially fit to stand trial and sent off to Rikers Island, not the best place for a guy like him.

After the judge's ruling, *The New York Times* reporter asked Fremmer and Morton if she could meet with Ronald once he got settled at Rikers. She was still working on a story about his past and his history of concussions, but she couldn't tell Fremmer when it would be published. Candace was back in a medically induced coma so media interest was starting to wane. Her books had fallen off the bestseller lists. The case was entering a new phase. Morton called it the Hurry Up And Wait phase.

The shop was easy enough to find. A shiny plastic shark hung in a state of suspended animation in the front window, draped in something that resembled seaweed and surrounded by various colored coral and driftwood. The sign above the storefront began with some Chinese letters bracketing a reef fish. Below that were the words "Pacific Aquarium and Pet" and a phone number. Fremmer thought it looked like any other shop in Chinatown that sold knick knacks or maybe even edible fish.

The shop owner immediately remembered the young woman Fremmer described.

"Are you police?" he asked Fremmer.

"No, just an ex-boyfriend. I don't have her full name. She said her name was Rochelle."

"Her name not Rochelle. Her name Isabelle. Isabelle Hruska. I write it down for you. She worked for me long time ago. She take money from you?"

"She wanted money from me."

"You better check. Where she now?"

Fremmer was suddenly concerned. *What'd that mean? Check what?* "I know her from the Upper West Side."

"She live near here when she work for me. But she moved. I thought she good person but she not good."

No shit, Fremmer thought.

"What happened?"

"She thief. That's all I say. I give you name. She have guy she work with. He do psychic business. I give you his name, too. You no tell anybody. OK?"

Once Fremmer finally got a hold of Madden, five days after his conversation with Candace in the ICU, the ball began to roll. For all his hemming and hawing Madden got on a flight the next morning.

Fremmer told him to make a reservation at The Lucerne, a boutique hotel on the corner of 79th and Amsterdam. They'd meet for dinner at Nice Matin, the upscale bistro just off the lobby of the hotel. He'd be the guy at the bar wearing the Mohegan Sun T-Shirt. Double Down, the graphic said. He couldn't miss him.

And he didn't. Promptly at 8 PM, Madden walked into the restaurant and looked directly at Fremmer, who was sitting on a stool with his back to the bar.

Fremmer smiled. "Welcome to New York, Detective," he said.

25/ Escape Clauses

MADDEN DIDN'T KNOW QUITE WHAT TO MAKE OF THE GUY. SITTING on the stool with his elbows resting proprietarily behind him on the mahogany bar, he projected an air of confidence. Or arrogance. At first glance he looked younger than Madden expected, anywhere from late thirties to mid-forties. As he got closer though, Madden noticed the scattering of gray in his beard stubble. He knew plenty of guys like this in California. The outfit—ironic T-Shirt, expensively distressed jeans, retro tennis shoes—and the attitude—simultaneously laid-back and intense. Guys like Shelby were driven by that underlying intensity. Madden could see the same zealous quality in the eyes of this Drew Masters, or whatever his name was. The guy was focused. He knew what he wanted. He was a businessman.

"Thank you for coming, Mr. Madden," he said, greeting him with a warm, easy-going grin.

"Hopefully I won't regret it. I'm not in the habit of taking a call from a complete stranger one day and then getting on a plane and flying across the country to meet him the next."

"Well, I'm glad I was able to persuade you. I wouldn't have made you come if I didn't think it'd be worth your while."

"We'll see about that."

Another warm smile from Mr. Double Down, a.k.a. Drew Masters. There was something a little smug about it.

"Inside or outside, Detective?"

"Excuse me?"

"You want to eat inside or outside?"

"Inside, I think."

The place felt crowded though it was only about three-quarters full. Double Down got up from his stool, picked up his backpack from the floor, and signaled the hostess, who gathered up two menus and led the two men past the bar to one of the larger four-tops in the back.

Nice service, Madden thought. "I'm guessing you're a regular here?" It was more of a statement than question.

"Here and every Starbucks on the West Side," Fremmer responded. "Just water for me, no ice, please," he told the hostess.

Madden said he wanted the same.

"We should order now. You must be starving, and we don't have much time. Tell our server I'll take the steak frites medium rare," he told the hostess. "You want the same? You seem like a meat-and-potatoes guy. Best thing on the menu. You're not a vegetarian, are you?"

"No," said Madden. "But why the rush?"

"I have to get home to my son," Fremmer explained. "His homework helper said he'd stay until I got back. But we have some work to do after we finish here."

"What kind of work?"

"I need you to pretend you're a private investigator, which shouldn't be hard."

"What for?"

"You'll see. Did you bring Shelby's contract?"

He did. Madden took it from his inside coat pocket and handed it across the table. Fremmer read through it once, his eyes darting around the page. Then he went through it again, more slowly the second time.

"What are you looking for?" Madden asked.

"Escape clauses."

"Are you a lawyer?"

"Yes."

That surprised Madden.

"What kind?"

"The kind that slips escape clauses into contracts."

"How's it look?"

"Not bad. You didn't get an exclusive, which means he could have made the same deal with someone else. Or with me right now. But other than that, I think we're good. You're seeing my poker face right now, but trust me, inside I'm doing cartwheels. It's more than I thought. I wasn't expecting the extra million for finding both of them. You OK if I keep this?"

Madden didn't care what he did with it. He'd received his last monthly fee. As far as he was concerned, he was finished with the contract. Until yesterday anyway.

"Tell, me something, Mr. Masters—"

"Drew," Fremmer cut him off. "No one calls me Mr. Masters."

"Because it's not your real name."

"Not just that. No calls me by my real last name, so why should anybody call me by my fake one?"

Madden rolled his eyes. "OK. So, *Drew*, tell me this. If you think you can make a deal with Shelby, why don't you?"

"You and I know both know he's a prick. But putting that aside, which I'd do under the right circumstances, I need your help, Mr. Madden. This is an intricate and delicate situation. Do I look like a detective? Do I look like I've got law-enforcement connections in Northern California? That's why I need you. You're the pro, not me."

"You've seen how far that's gotten me with this case."

"I've done my homework, Mr. Madden. For someone so unfortunate you've been quite fortunate. You're a sympathetic character. Polio, drop foot, a victim of sexual abuse, you're the embodiment of the American spirit: grit and perseverance."

"No, I'm not. And I don't want people to think of me in those terms."

"Humble, too, eh? You just can't help yourself. All I'm saying is that Shelby knows he has to pay you because of who you are. And if you get paid, Mr. Madden, you know what that means?"

"What?"

"I get paid. Which brings us to the sub-contract I've drawn up for the two of us. It simply stipulates that should you fulfill the terms of Mr. Shelby's contract I get half of the payout within seven days of your receiving payment, whatever that amount may be."

Fremmer reached down into the backpack at his feet and brought out his own one-page document.

"You'll see that my name has been redacted from the copy you're looking at. But as soon as you're ready to sign, I have four unredacted copies prepared and a notary on standby in the restaurant to make it official."

Madden looked up from the document. *Did he say in the restaurant?*

"You have a notary here? I didn't know they provided such services."

"She works at the First Republic on 76th Street. Does all my notarizing. Very service-oriented, the folks at First Republic. I'm picking up the check for her and her sister. They're sitting two tables to our right."

Madden looked over and saw two attractive if somewhat heavy-set Hispanic women. Both wore glasses. One waved at him, presumably the notary. At that moment, Madden allowed himself to believe for the first time that this might actually be real.

"You don't mess around do you, Drew," he said.

"No, I don't."

Madden perused the document one more time. To be safe, he should have had Dupuy take a look at it. But things were complicated enough with him verbally offering her a bonus if they found Stacey or Ross that he didn't want her to know about this. The terms also seemed pretty straightforward. And his curiosity was killing him. Why was this guy being so careful about protecting his identity before he signed something? It didn't make sense. What was the big deal?

"Well, let's do this," Madden said. "I came here to see what you've got, so let's see it."

With that, Fremmer removed the redacted document and replaced it with the four copies of the unredacted version. As Madden read over the new document, Fremmer waved to the notary, a signal to come over.

"Hank Madden, meet Marjorie, the best damn notary in the city." Marjorie came equipped with her stamp, pocket embosser, and a glass of wine. She acted like she did this all the time.

The whole operation took less than five minutes.

"So long, Drew Masters," Madden said once Marjorie had gone.

"Nice to meet you Max Fremmer. Now tell me, why all the secrecy?"

Fremmer didn't answer right away. Instead he said, "I'm gonna to need your permission to record our conversation. What I'm about to tell you is well, sensitive, and a detailed record of evidence will benefit us both."

He was taking no chances. Only when Madden had consented— and announced his stated consent along with the exact time, all recorded on Fremmer's iPhone—did Fremmer begin to explain.

"If you knew who I was, if you Googled me, the stories that would come up . . . you might be able to put two and two together. I couldn't risk that."

"What kind of stories?"

"I wear many hats but one of them is book editor slash publisher. I have a client, Candace Epstein. She writes erotic fiction for me. Under a pseudonym. About two weeks ago she was pushed in front of a car. She's been in the ICU ever since. I'm pretty sure she's Stacey Ross."

Madden was stunned. *Stacey Walker in the hospital? Is that what he said?*

"I thought you said you knew where she was buried."

"In a manner of speaking," Fremmer replied. "She buried herself here. In New York. But she never died."

"How do you know it's her?"

"Look," Fremmer began, "her injuries were severe. She wasn't expected to survive at first. I'm one of the few people, maybe the only one, who's spoken to her. She briefly woke up after being in a coma for five days. But only for a moment. She didn't know who she was. She thought she was in Stanford Hospital in California. Then she said something about living in Menlo Park and that her husband Ross had tried to choke her. That's when she became all worked up and they made me leave the ICU. I didn't have time to ask any more questions."

"As I was leaving the ICU, I hit Google to see what came up. When I put Ross and Menlo Park in there, a lot did," Fremmer explained, "including the article that Tom Bender did about you and Shelby. And then I did some comparisons."

Fremmer reached into his backpack for his iPad, turned it on, handed it to Madden. He studied the image on the screen—two women side by side.

"My client Candace is on the left. Stacey Ross is on the right."

Two different women—the older Candace with dark, curly hair, and the younger Stacey with straight dirty-blond hair—yet there was a resemblance. They were not a perfect match, but as far as leads went, it was pretty promising. Still, Madden didn't completely buy it.

"Did she tell you she was Stacey Ross? Did you record the conversation like you're doing now?"

"No," Fremmer said. "I didn't think to do it. I was just hoping she might tell me something about who pushed her and why."

"I don't know," Madden said. "It might just be some weird coincidence. She might have read the same article you read and woke up thinking she was part of the story. As you said, her brain is pretty scrambled."

"I thought about that," Fremmer said. "But look, it's pretty simple to confirm. Just take this back with you to California . . ."

He pulled something else from his backpack, an envelope that he placed in front of Madden on the table.

"What's that?" Madden asked.

"That's a DNA swab I took from her at the hospital a couple of days ago. They've got her back in a medically induced coma. She has a daughter in California somewhere, right? See if you get a match. And I assume that the police may have some of her DNA samples still stored in some evidence room somewhere."

Fremmer was right. It was that simple. Why hadn't he thought of that? Then it hit him: If she were still alive, what did that mean? It meant Ross hadn't killed her. So why had she disappeared in the first place?

"I'm sorry," Madden said after a moment, feeling a little dizzy. "I don't know what to say. I wasn't expecting this."

"Gets your head spinning a little bit, right?" Fremmer said. "Well I've got something else guaranteed to blow your mind."

"Yeah?"

"I know a guy who's missing part of his arm. He and my client are friends. Maybe even more than friends."

"Which arm?"

"The right arm. And by that I mean his left arm."

"Is he Ross?"

"I can't tell. His name is Braden. Candace has known him for years. He runs an organization called the Lucid Dreaming Center out of his apartment about twenty-five blocks north of here. Hand me the iPad, I'll pull up some photos."

Madden passed the tablet to Fremmer, who scrolled through his photo library until he found the image he had in mind, a shot of an older gentleman Photoshopped next to a twenty-year-old newspaper image of Ross. Madden could see no resemblance between the two men. Well, maybe there was a slight resemblance, but he felt none of the feeling he got when he looked at Fremmer's client next to Stacey.

"You ever meet Ross?" Fremmer asked.

"I saw him at the station house once," Madden said. "But I never interviewed him. And it was a long time ago."

"If you saw him again, do you think you'd know it was him?"

"Maybe. I watched enough interviews to know his voice. Why?"

"Well, one of his associates stole some money from me. After we pay her a visit, I thought we'd go see him. And by 'we' I mean I'm bringing you along as my newly hired private investigator."

"How much she steal?"

"Fifty thousand."

Madden let out a low whistle. *What was this guy trying to rope him into?*

"How'd she do that?"

"Drugged me and had me write a check."

"You couldn't stop payment on it?"

"I didn't know it existed. The last thing I remembered before waking up in a hospital room on suicide watch was having a drink with her at a neighborhood bar. That was six days ago. I only noticed my bank account was short fifty grand yesterday, after the check had cleared."

"Ouch," Madden said.

"Yeah. I'm trying to be cool because I just met you and don't want to make a bad first impression. I'm actually pretty upset. Doing my best not to punch a wall."

"You want to do this tonight?"

"Yeah, right after we eat. It's been a rough few days. I'll tell you all about it over steak frites."

"I might need a drink a first," Madden said.

"I'd join you," Fremmer said. "But the way I feel right now, if I start I might not stop."

26/ Money Not in the Bank

BELLIES FULL AND STORIES TOLD, MADDEN AND FREMMER SET OFF TO find Isabelle Hruska. Fremmer had tracked down her address— 23 West 73rd Street, an elegant pre-war co-op between Columbus Avenue and Central Park West. The building was so swanky, it even had a name: The Park Royal. Fremmer had walked past it countless times before on the way to the park. Somehow Isabelle had managed to wrangle herself an apartment in one of the only doorman buildings on a block of brownstones. He was a little surprised that she'd pulled off such an admirable New York real estate coup. And then again he wasn't.

"What's your plan?" Madden asked as they walked east on 73rd.

"Make her give the money back."

"How will you do that?"

"I'm not sure."

"That doesn't seem like much of a plan."

"I'll improvise. I took some classes when I first came to the city."

"What kind of classes?"

"Improv. Acting. I wanted to be a litigator. Someone told me it would help. A lot of litigating is acting. You're playing for an audience."

"But you didn't become a litigator."

"No, but it actually helped. Taught me the secret of confidence."

"Confidence to do what?"

"To try to get fifty grand back without a plan. Just play off me. I don't think things will get ugly, but if they do, you've got skills, right?

I know you're a little handicapped but you got some training as a cop? Takedown moves and holds and shit like that?"

"I carried a gun," Madden said. "People tend to do what you say when you have a gun."

"That's not really the answer I was looking for."

"Don't worry. I can handle myself."

"Just make sure I don't do anything stupid," Fremmer said.

"That I can do."

A uniformed doorman greeted them at the front door of the Park Royal. Beyond him Madden took in the spacious lobby with its arches, porticos and intricate plaster decorative accents.

"May I help you gentleman?" the doorman asked. A sign on a pedestal facing them read, *All visitors must be announced.*

"Yeah," Fremmer said casually, as if he was a close friend. "We're here to see Isabelle." A beat, then: "Hruska."

"She went out earlier but I think she came back. Is she expecting you?"

"Why don't you call up and ask her. Tell her it's Max. Max Fremmer. Tell her I have that check she was looking for."

The doorman, a light-skinned black guy who could have been any number of ethnicities, dutifully rang her.

"There's a Max Fremmer here to see you," he said. "He says he has that check you were looking for."

A pause. After a moment, he spoke again. "Yes, here. Now. In the lobby. He's standing right here."

Another pause. He held the receiver to his chest.

"She says to leave it with me."

"Tell her to come down and get it."

Another conversation. This one a little longer.

"She says she can't come down right now."

"Tell her I'll wait." Fremmer nodded towards the seating arrangement in the middle of the lobby, four tufted leather burgundy club chairs atop a huge Persian carpet. "That looks comfy. Tell her I have all night. And all day. I can wait all month, the rest of my life. If she doesn't like that, she can ring the police. I'm happy to have a chat with them."

The doorman put the receiver back to his ear and mumbled a brief translation to Isabelle. Fremmer distinctly heard the word *police*.

"OK. You can go up," he said. "Ninth floor. 9G. To your left off the elevator."

In the elevator, Madden said to Fremmer, "So you did have a plan."

"To get her to talk to me. Not to get the money back. But I figured that would throw her off. That I was coming with a check. Now she knows I know who she is but she's wondering why I said I had a check. Maybe she's thinking I'm an idiot and don't know she already took the money. Which is pretty much what happened. I'm guessing the whole suicide thing was just a diversion to give the check time to clear."

"Whose suicide thing?"

"Mine."

"You tried to kill yourself?"

"No, I told you I didn't."

"Sorry," Madden said. "You were talking fast. It was a lot of information."

"Come on, man. Keep up. You're not in Mayberry anymore."

The elevator doors opened on the ninth floor. Fremmer led Madden down the long hallway to their left, per the doorman's instructions, and there she was, a few doors down on the right, standing in her doorway, wearing a tank top and leggings, no makeup and a pair of tortoiseshell glasses. The new look threw him off for a second—was Isabelle his Rochelle? She was just as sexy, but in a different, maybe better way. *Fuck me*, he thought, it's her.

"Hello, Max. You didn't tell me you brought company. This your father?"

"This is Henry. Former ace detective, now ace private investigator."

"Oh," she said. "I thought for a second you were gonna introduce me to your family. I don't know if we're quite ready for that, do you?"

"Come on, Isabelle. Cut the crap. The game's up. I'm onto you and your schtick."

"Really, I thought you were the one with the schtick, Max. Last I checked you wanted to get your schtick inside me. You want to see the pictures? That was quite a party we had the other night."

"Shame I don't remember it, especially since it cost me fifty grand."

"You get my note?"

"I did."

"You like it?"

"I like you, Isabelle. Maybe better than I liked Rochelle. But I'm still going to have to send you and your friend Braden to jail."

She laughed. "That's not going to happen, Max, and you know it. If anybody's going to jail, it's you."

"For what?"

"For stalking me. I saw you hanging out in front of the Center the other day."

"That wasn't me, Isabelle. Maybe you weren't wearing your glasses. And I didn't follow you back here. He did."

Madden gave her a little salute but didn't say anything. She bit her lip a little.

"Henry's good," Fremmer went on. "A real pro. He's costing me a lot of money."

"Even worse," she said. "You have a private eye stalking me. Move on, Max. Before you hurt yourself—or anybody else—more than you already have. Think of your son. He's a good kid. I saw the pictures. And you showed me those nice videos on your phone."

He took a couple of steps toward her before Madden held him back.

"You took fifty thousand from his future," he said. "Think of that."

"You'll get it back," she said. "Your client owed money. You're her manager. You control her finances. She has lots of money coming in." She nodded in Madden's direction. "He talk at all?"

"When he needs to," Fremmer said.

Just then he heard the sound of a door opening across the hall.

"Everything OK, Isabelle?" Fremmer and Madden turned to check out the source of the voice.

"Yeah, Gary. Thanks for checking. These guys were just leaving."

"I'm just trying to put the kids to bed here," Gary explained, only slightly irritated.

Fremmer looked over at Madden. If the detective had any opinions on the progress of their situation, he wasn't ready to share. Fremmer knew from the many articles he'd read that Madden was one of those guys who'd overcome his weaknesses by working harder and being better prepared than everyone else. Preparation called for a plan, some kind of script, which they didn't have. Fremmer's gut told him to keep going with the improv. It was time to bring Madden into the game and run a play for him.

"You're kicking us out? I haven't gotten to the good part yet," Fremmer told Isabelle.

She looked at him skeptically. "Really?" she said. "There's a good part? I can't wait to hear it."

"You want to keep doing this out here in the hall or you want to invite us in? I'd hate to disturb Gary and the kids again."

"I don't want to invite you in, Max. I want you to leave."

Before she could slam her door and retreat into the apartment he took a step forward and placed his hand on the doorjamb right next to her head.

"OK, have it your way," he said. "My associate Carlos Morton hired Henry here to assist us with the discovery phase of the case against Ronald Darby. You know Ronald, the homeless guy who allegedly pushed Candace into the car?"

"I think all of New York knows Ronald."

He leaned a little closer to her so his lips were just a few inches from her face. "Well, Henry here has been going through surveillance footage the police collected," Fremmer began in his quietest inside voice. "He's been sitting in a little room looking at a computer monitor sifting through hours of video taken from various cameras in and around Central Park West and 75th Street on the day Candace was hit. It's tedious work. But Henry here is a nationally recognized expert in . . . what's the technical term for that, Henry?"

"Video forensics," Madden said. "Or forensic video analysis."

"Yeah. Video forensics. Henry actually invented it when he was on the police force. Anyway, he's been going through hours of footage. And he found something. Something I think you'll be very interested in."

"What's that?" she asked.

Fremmer placed one foot in Isabelle's doorway as he pulled his phone from his pocket. "Let's take a look. Photo library open. Scrolling, scrolling. Ah, here it is," he announced, holding up the screen for her to view.

"You know this guy?"

She stared at the picture. Fremmer detected a split second of recognition in her eyes. She knew exactly who she was looking at.

"This is your friend Zander. He used to be your partner in the fish tank cleaning business and from what we've learned, you two had a little side business of ripping people off from time to time. Now Zander doesn't clean fish tanks anymore. He's gone into another line of work altogether. He's what you call an intuit. He runs a business out of his apartment. I had an appointment with him this morning. Very impressive. He doesn't use standard Tarot cards. He uses art postcards he's collected from around the world. It's brilliant, quite frankly. You go in there and ask him questions about your life and he flips these postcards and tells you what he sees in them and how they apply to your current predicaments. You know what was one of the cards that came up for me?"

She shook her head.

"Two guys in some sort of bondage situation. I think the card was from Amsterdam or Berlin. According to Zander, I'm a masochist who has to learn to be less submissive. I need to start asserting myself and quit being pushed around—to fulfill my potential. So here's the deal, Isabelle, or whatever your name is. Henry here found your friend Zander in that video footage. And as far as Candace goes, we think we have the smoking gun."

"What are you talking about?"

"Look, we know Braden is involved," Fremmer said. "But not for the reasons we thought before. Look at the video. The guy who pushed her appears to have full use of both his arms. Braden would never push her himself. He'd have someone do it for him. And that someone was your friend Zander dressed up as Ronald, who he knew from the neighborhood. He knew where Ronald hung out, and he knew every item of clothing Ronald owned. So Zander dressed up as one of the neighborhood homeless guys and pushed Candace into on-coming traffic."

For a moment, just a flash, Fremmer saw real fear in Isabelle's eyes. And then it was gone.

"You're out of your mind," she said.

Again, the door across the hall opened and an exasperated Gary popped his head out.

"Sorry," Isabelle said before he could complain. "I guess we got a little too carried away. Come on in, guys," she said, and reluctantly waved them into her apartment.

They followed her into the entrance foyer into the living room. The apartment was spacious by New York standards. Not a huge apartment, but well appointed, with all new furnishings and finishes, including a freshly remodeled kitchen. A small stack of magazines—*Vogue, Elle, New York Magazine*—was fanned out on the coffee table and a vase full of fresh peonies and hydrangeas stood on the small dining room table. The place was camera-ready, Fremmer thought. She was a total neatnik.

There was no offer to sit, no small talk. She started right in on them.

"You're crazy," she said. "Why would Braden want to kill her?"

"We can't discuss that right now," Fremmer said.

"It involves another case," Madden explained. "Another crime that took place a long time ago."

"What other crime?"

"A murder," Madden said.

"That Braden is involved in?"

"That's what the authorities in California are telling us."

"California? Braden never lived in California."

"How well do you know him?"

"As well as you can know a man without sleeping with him."

"And he told you he never lived in California?"

"I know for a fact he didn't. He lived in London for a few years and Boston before that. I know people who knew him in both places."

She might be telling the truth. She had no reason to lie about that. He didn't know what to do. Fremmer looked at Madden. He'd lost his momentum. She'd been frazzled, he was sure of that. But how to get back the advantage?

"Look," Madden said suddenly. "I'm going to tell you the truth. Can we sit down for a minute. My leg hurts. Childhood polio. I was one of the last cases in the U.S. and I've had this messed up foot that's now turned into a messed up leg. And my back isn't great either."

He sat in an armchair and motioned for her to sit down opposite him on the couch. "Just sit down, both of you. For a minute."

They sat—Fremmer on one side of the couch, she on the other, well apart.

"I'm going to be honest with you, Isabelle," Madden continued. "That's your name, right? Not Rochelle, not something else? That's your real, legal name?"

"Yes, that's my real name," she said.

"OK. Now that we've got that straight, here's the situation. I only recently met Max. He brought me in a few days ago to look at this video. It's new evidence, part of discovery. Now we've also dug up some video of our own and we're going to turn it all over to the police. Soon. I'm looking for anomalies, right? Anything that proves their client might not be the same guy in the video. And Max here gives me a picture of this Braden fellow. But I don't see him. He's not in any of the videos. I've got a couple of interns from John Jay working with me but we can only cover so much and go back so far. A few days, right? Maybe a week. Anyway, yesterday Max comes to me with a picture of this fellow Zander. He asks me to look for him. And lo and behold, one of my interns spots him. He's there. A couple of days before the victim gets pushed, I see him crossing the street in the same spot. And I see this Ronald fellow nearby."

"So what," she said. "Zander lives in the neighborhood. Uptown a little more but why wouldn't he be around there."

"Look," Madden said. "We're just giving you a heads-up. A chance to say something. If any of these people are involved in a crime and you know about it, that makes you an accessory to that crime. And this is attempted murder, and maybe even murder from what I hear about the condition of the victim."

"I had nothing to do with Candace getting pushed in front of that car. You understand me? Nothing. If you're recording this conversation, that is my answer on the record. Now, I'd like you to leave. Or I will call the police."

"Just one more question," Madden said.

"What's that?"

"Why'd you take fifty thousand dollars from this guy?"

"I didn't take. He gave it to me. He repaid his client's loan."

"OK, let me rephrase that. Why did you go to all this trouble to get this money?"

"First of all, it wasn't all that much trouble. Second, we have a new product we need to start shipping next week. But we got behind. We were this close to defaulting, which would have left us with nothing. You get it?"

Madden nodded. Then he stood up, signaling Fremmer to do the same.

"We're going to go now," Madden said. "But we're walking out of here empty-handed. You didn't give him his money back. And that means you're on my shit list. And you don't want to be on my shit list. You also don't want me thinking it ever occurred to you that your buddy Zander had anything to do with the crime Ronald is accused of. Save yourself while you still have the chance. Goodnight, Miss Hruska. Sleep well."

27/ Evidence Bag

"Loved the quiet intensity," Fremmer said when they got back out on the street.

"The what?"

"You got that whole Clint Eastwood thing going. I gotta say I didn't see it coming. I should've, but I didn't."

Madden took the compliment in stride. "That stuff you said about Zander, was it real?" he asked.

"Did it sound real?"

"You had me going."

"Well, the truth is . . ." Fremmer started to say, but something had distracted him.

Madden looked ahead and saw a woman, maybe early thirties, maybe a bit older, in a short black sleeveless dress coming toward them.

The woman said hello to Fremmer, and they stopped.

"Hey you," she said, then kissed him on the side of the cheek. "Were you on vacation? They had a sub teaching your class this week."

"I'm off the schedule for now," he replied.

"What? Why?"

"Talk to the manager. Put in a good word, would you?"

"Are you kidding me? I can't believe they did that. To you of all people. What happened?"

"Long story."

"I'll totally talk to the manager. And my friend Amy will, too. She loves your class."

"Thank you. And thank Amy," Fremmer said, and with a slight nod of his head he and Madden started walking together again.

"The key is fully believing what you say as you say it," he went on as if their conversation had never been interrupted. "The truth is my friend Carlos did hire an investigator who's trying to determine exactly where Ronald was that morning. Too bad he didn't carry a cell phone. That would have made it easy to track him. But we're basically left with any video we can get a hold of. And the cops are out in front on that. They've already collected footage from the same locations the investigator's going to. It's easy for them to get it. People want to cooperate with the police."

"They haven't turned it over yet?"

"The DA's office is taking its sweet time because it can. But now that the judge has ruled Ronald's fit to stand trial, they'll have to turn over what they've got pretty quickly."

"And the meeting with Zander?"

"Didn't happen yet," Fremmer said. "Drew Masters tried to make an appointment earlier today but couldn't get one 'til tomorrow afternoon."

"So where'd you come up with the stuff about the postcards?"

"From his website. And Yelp. He's got about fifty reviews, most of them quite positive. Of course, you never know who wrote them."

This Fremmer guy was strange, but he had a quick mind. Madden was impressed. He still didn't fully grasp the whole story, had yet to learn all the players and the roles they played. He knew all about Fremmer's connection to the victim, of course, and Fremmer had explained his conversation with Ronald in the holding cell well enough. What Madden didn't quite understand was why Fremmer got involved in Ronald's defense in the first place.

"You saw her reaction to your Zander theory," Madden said. "There was something there. Did you just come up with that?"

"About Zander trading places with Ronald?"

"Yeah."

"Look," Fremmer said, "I can see four possible scenarios. One, Ronald had one of his Looney Tunes moments and pushed her. Two, someone paid Ronald to push her. Three, he actually knew her and pushed her for some unknown reason. And four, someone who looked like Ronald pushed her. If the latter's the case we're looking at a premeditated situation and the question becomes, what's the motive? I can think of a lot of possibilities. The ex-husband is out the picture, he died over five years ago. But I suppose it's possible she could have rubbed one of these guys she gave handjobs to the wrong way. Pardon the pun."

"Handjobs?"

"Oh, did I neglect to mention that? She had this thing where she'd surreptitiously jack off guys in Apple stores. Research for her books. She'd cover up the action with a backpack or a coat. She put an ad on Craigslist and found plenty of willing participants. The books were fiction, but they were based on a lot of truth. Remember the book *Looking for Mr. Goodbar*? Her stories reminded me of that, minus the rough sex."

A little bell went off in Madden's head. He remembered hearing something about an accident and an author that wrote books about a woman who gave handjobs to strangers in Apple stores. Did he read about it or did someone tell him? Maybe it was his wife. That would explain why he'd half tuned it out. She was always sending links to articles she'd found about strange crimes. The online version of the *Chronicle* seemed to feature some bizarro story every day. Clickbait, they called it.

"I do remember that book," he said. "Roseann Quinn. That was the name of the real murder victim, the one the book was based on. She had polio as a kid, walked with a slight limp. I'll never forget someone telling me that."

"She lived a couple of blocks from here on 72nd Street on the other side of Broadway. The bar was across the street from her apartment. I forget what it was called then. I knew it as the All State Cafe. Used to go there all the time. It's something else now."

The memory of Quinn took Madden back. When was it that he'd heard about her? Was it college? No, it was after that.

"Anyway, you did great back there," Fremmer said. "I think we got under her skin. I bet she called Braden the second we left."

Madden would have liked to do the leave-the-cell-phone-recording routine with Isabelle, but she seemed pretty tuned into the possibility that one of them might be trying to record her—probably because she also used her phone as a weapon.

"Why didn't we go see him first?" he asked.

"Mainly because I didn't want to show up too late at her apartment. But I think it works better this way. If she called him after we left, he may not be so surprised we've come to see him, too. If he isn't so surprised, he may be more likely to let us in."

Madden didn't necessarily agree with Fremmer's logic, but he knew that on this case, for now anyway, he was along for the ride.

They walked two long blocks along 73rd Street to Amsterdam Avenue, then turned right and headed north. In the middle of the block, Fremmer stepped off the sidewalk into the street.

"It's a perfect evening for a stroll," he said, raising his right arm. "But Braden's place is twenty-five blocks uptown. We'll take a cab."

Madden studied the Maps app on his phone so he had some idea of the city's layout. And he'd read enough books and articles about the city to have a semblance of familiarity with some of its streets and neighborhoods. He knew he was on the Upper West Side near Central Park, but his overall ignorance about the place put him way out of his comfort zone. Too many impressions he had of the city were formed from movies he'd watched as a young man, when it was far grittier. Of course, he'd seen plenty of more recent shots of the city. It seemed like every other movie and TV show was made in New York, with the city playing a major role, so he knew it had changed drastically. Yet some of those early impressions were indelibly etched into his memory, clashing with the tamer version of the city he now experienced. It was a little like expecting to go on a safari in Africa and ending up at the San Diego Zoo instead.

More than anything he was struck by the number of people out on the streets. And how everyone seemed so collegial. It was almost ten on a Tuesday night and there were people everywhere, sitting outside at restaurants, strolling along the sidewalks, even grocery shopping. Palo Alto and San Francisco were bustling on Friday and Saturday nights, but they tended to empty out fairly quickly on weeknights, particularly earlier in the week. Back in his younger days he sometimes felt a little uneasy walking around the city late at night without his gun.

He felt much safer here.

And the other thing that stood out was the number of people out walking their dogs. That surprised him. All the dogs. This had to be prime dog walking time.

"They film *Taxi Driver* around here?" Madden asked as they got into a cab.

"Not here so much. The campaign office was down on Columbus Circle. But they shot *Three Days of the Condor* a couple blocks over on Broadway. The alleyway where Redford gets shot? That's now a really expensive garage behind the Ansonia on 73rd and Broadway. And then he runs up Broadway past the Beacon. You remember that?"

"Vaguely," Madden said. "I remember the movie but not the scene."

"Well, you can watch it on your phone when you get back to your hotel. You tired?"

"I'm OK. It's only seven for me."

"Good. So, this is the plan."

"There's a plan this time? I didn't know you did plans."

"I do a plan when the plan calls for a plan."

"Well, let's hear it then."

"We get Braden to drink something and then we take whatever he drank from."

Fremmer pulled a couple of large Ziploc bags from his backpack. They were folded down into a smaller rectangle.

"One for you," Fremmer said as he handed one to Madden, "and one for me."

"That's the plan?"

"Yeah, you check him out, then we get a DNA sample. A fingerprint or two wouldn't be bad either."

"What about the fifty thousand?"

"We'll deal with that as we go along. But I somehow doubt we're going to leave there with that, not without someone putting a gun to his head. But a cup we can do. He likes herbal tea."

"What if he isn't there? Or doesn't want to let us in."

"I don't know. That's not part of the plan."

"Well, do you have a contingency plan?"

"I do," Fremmer said. "But you don't want to hear it."

28/ Contingency Plan

FREMMER PRESSED THE BUZZER AND WAITED A FEW SECONDS. NO ANSWER. So he waited another few seconds and pressed the buzzer again.

Still nothing. He buzzed again, this time longer. Then one more time for good measure.

"Maybe it's broken," Madden said.

"I was just here a few days ago. It was working fine. He's not answering."

Fremmer looked up. There was a light on upstairs. Someone was home.

He hit the buzzer again, but this time he held the button down and didn't let go.

"What are you doing?" Madden said.

"I'm trying to piss off whoever's inside."

He heard the inner door open, then footsteps. Mission accomplished. The main door opened and Braden appeared before them, his face flush. He was not happy.

"Stop it," he said.

Fremmer finally let go of the buzzer. "Thanks for coming out, Victor. Now, why don't you invite us in so we can have a friendly chat? Don't worry, I'm not here to talk about the fifty thousand you took from me."

"Who's this?" Braden said.

"My private investigator, Henry."

Braden offered his hand to Madden. "Victor Braden," he said, shaking Madden's hand. "I don't know what he's paying you, but it's not worth it. He's a complete lunatic."

Fremmer watched Madden's face as he took Braden in. They were standing a few feet apart. Madden looked him directly in the eyes. He didn't say anything, he just stared, which made Braden uncomfortable.

"How'd you lose your arm?" Madden asked.

"Excuse me?"

"The arm, how'd you lose it?" repeated Madden.

Madden may have set a speed record for the missing hand question.

"That's a bit personal, considering you've just met, don't you think?"

"No," Madden said.

"I've got visitors in town from Germany. I have to get back to them. If you touch that buzzer again, I will call the police."

"Just answer the question," Madden said.

Braden nodded in Fremmer's direction. "He knows the answer, ask him."

"I want to hear it from you."

Braden looked at him disbelief. "A staph infection, OK? Many years ago. There, you satisfied?"

"You sure about that, Ross?"

Braden looked at him, befuddled.

"What?"

"Come on. Don't tell me you forgot your own name?"

Braden seem genuinely bewildered.

"What are you talking about? You're as crazy as he is, aren't you? Both of you need to get out of here now. You understand me?"

Well, this isn't going according to plan, Fremmer thought. *Time to go to the contingency.*

"We are sorry to disturb your little soirée," Fremmer said, stalling.

"It's not a soirée."

Fremmer looked to his right and saw what he needed: a woman coming up the street, walking a small dog. He took a step closer to Braden. Then he got right up in his face.

"You know what, for all your highfalutin lucid dreaming crap you're a two-bit criminal," he said, purposely letting his saliva fly in Braden's face.

Braden made a move to push him away, and Fremmer suddenly turned into a basketball player looking for an offensive foul, letting Braden throw him against the pavement, violently. His backpack blocked the fall a little, but he hit his hip and shoulder harder than he intended. His head touched down, too, which also hurt. He lay there for a moment. Braden looked at him, then at the would-be witness. He had a panicked look in his eyes.

"I didn't do that," he said to the woman with the dog, pleading his case. "I didn't push him that hard."

Before she had time to answer—and before Braden had time to get out of the way—Fremmer got up and slammed him in the face, square in the nose. The force of the punch didn't immediately drop him, but his back banged up against the closed front door of his townhouse. His legs then buckled and he kind of rode the door down to a seated position, his butt on his doorstep and his knees pressed up against his chest. He held his hand up to his nose. In a matter of seconds he was bleeding profusely.

Fremmer had a handkerchief ready.

"Here," he said, kneeling down to hand it to him. "Press it against your nose. Lift your head up."

Braden looked up at the dog walker, who looked both startled and alarmed.

"He tried to hurt me," Fremmer said. "You saw it."

"You broke my nose, you son-of-a-bitch," Braden mumbled through the handkerchief.

Fremmer let him hold it to his face a little longer. Until it was good and soaked. Then he took it away, ripping it from his grasp.

"Let's go," he said to Madden, who also seemed pretty astonished by what he'd just witnessed.

They walked over to Broadway, where Fremmer pulled out his Ziploc bag and put the handkerchief inside, sealed it, and handed it to Madden. Then he hailed a cab.

"So, that was your contingency plan?" Madden asked Fremmer after he'd closed the cab door.

"Yeah, you like it?"

Madden started laughing. "You know, he's right. You are a lunatic. There's only one problem."

"What's that?"

"I don't think that's Ross."

"No?"

"No."

Fremmer took a couple of seconds to consider the ramifications of Madden's statement. "Well, it felt good anyway. And at least we now know for sure it isn't him, don't we?"

29/ Ask the Void

MADDEN WOKE THE NEXT MORNING LATER THAN HE WANTED TO. HE was supposed to meet Fremmer at nine-thirty at a coffee shop on Amsterdam between 78th and 79th. He had to rush to get over there on time.

Nine-thirty came and went. No Fremmer. As Madden sat waiting he thought about their encounter with Braden. People changed a lot in twenty years, they'd seen that with Bronsky, but they didn't change that much. He remembered Ross Walker as a bigger man than Braden. Not necessarily that much taller, but he thought they had different bone structures. Plastic surgery could change someone's look, sometimes radically, but Madden thought he'd have been able to tell if Braden had had major work done. He just looked like he'd had a facelift/neck lift combo, and some hair plugs. Whoever had done the work had done a good job, but Madden could still tell right away there was something off about his face—something didn't quite look natural.

Their voices were different, too. Braden's voice was more affected and not as deep as Ross's. That was something he could have altered with practice. But Walker never struck him as the type of guy who would practice to be someone else or completely change his persona. The fact was if Fremmer had hit Ross Walker like he had, Walker would have made him pay for it afterwards. Missing hand or not, he would have tried to put Fremmer on the ground.

Madden once heard a story about Walker assaulting a guy on a golf course in Santa Clara. The guy had complained that Walker's group was being loud and disruptive; they were intoxicated. When the guy got in Walker's face, Walker head-butted him. They ended up wrestling to the ground and trying to pummel each other. The guy filed charges against Walker, but those were dismissed because the golfer and his playing partner refused to cooperate with the investigation. Everyone involved assumed that Walker had threatened further physical violence.

Last night, back at The Lucerne, Madden had told Fremmer what he knew about Ross and what he thought about Braden.

"I never had any close interactions with him so I can't tell you one hundred percent. But my gut says it isn't him."

He could see this upset Fremmer, and he understood why. If Braden wasn't Ross Walker then maybe Candace Epstein wasn't Stacey Walker. That possibility had also crossed Madden's mind. "But," he told Fremmer, "my gut also tells me the Stacey connection is real."

He warned him that DNA tests didn't happen as quickly as they did on TV crime shows. Madden could pull some strings to try to expedite matters, but he couldn't just walk in and say, *Here's a DNA sample we plucked off some woman in a hospital in New York, would you mind comparing it to those Stacey Walker samples you filed away? And while you're pulling evidence, could you go ahead and pull some of Ross's samples?*

Just the thought of all the miles of red tape gave him a headache. Moving through official channels meant questions about whether the DNA samples were obtained legally. Braden certainly hadn't willingly offered his sample. Neither had Candace. There were proper procedures for acquiring DNA evidence, and the police and forensic labs took those procedures seriously. Had Fremmer thought about all that?

He said he had. "But I figured we'd worry about it later," he told Madden. "The most important thing is to get some hard evidence for Shelby. I was worried the contract had some onerous verification requirements but it's pretty vague."

"Do I even want to know how you obtained a sample from Candace?" he asked Fremmer.

"That part was easy. I bought a DNA test kit at Walgreens, went to visit Candace in the ICU, and when I was sure nobody was looking, I swabbed the inside of her cheek."

"So how do you prove where the swab came from?"

"I recorded the entire procedure on my phone. I propped it up on the counter and hit record. The video file can be our witness if Shelby asks for more proof. Now you just have to get your own cheek swab from her daughter and then we send both into swabtest.com. It's like $100 per test. They can have results in three-to-five working days, so we'll have what we need to meet Shelby's requirements for verification before the contract expires. The police can sort out the rest later. We can't be late on this. From what I've read about Shelby, he won't pay if you miss the deadline."

Madden didn't have the heart to tell Fremmer that he didn't know how the daughter would respond to a request for a DNA sample. She might not love the idea. Also, Madden didn't like the fact that Fremmer was so focused on the money. He understood it but didn't like it.

Where was Fremmer anyway? He was sure they said nine-thirty. After ten minutes of waiting at the shop, Madden began to worry. They'd talked about Madden returning to California as soon as possible, but the earliest flight he could get a seat on was a red-eye that night. They'd meet for breakfast, then Madden could do a bit of sightseeing. He at least wanted to visit the 9/11 Memorial and Museum of Natural History.

At nine-forty-two his phone rang. It was Fremmer calling from the same 347 number. He hadn't changed it yet.

"Sorry," he said in a low voice. "I was about to leave to meet you when this detective showed up. It's taking longer than I thought, I might not be there for a while. I know you want to get down to the Memorial. Maybe you should just go ahead and we'll meet later before you go to the airport. We still have to discuss your book."

"Where are you? They pick you up?"

"No, I'm still at home," Fremmer said. "He's in the kitchen. I'm in the bathroom."

"This about Braden? He's pressing charges?"

"No. Not yet. But that dog walker or someone else called 911 last night."

"What'd you say?"

"Not much."

"Don't say anything," Madden advised.

"Now you sound like a lawyer."

"You probably need one," Madden said. "You should call your friend."

"I did. He said the same thing."

Madden didn't reply right away. He was thinking about Fremmer's cockiness; it worked both for and against him. In this particular case he thought it could get him into trouble.

"You're not going to bring up anything about your thinking Candace is Stacey, are you?"

"Under normal circumstances I probably would. But I can't. You're the one who has to take credit for finding her. I don't want to muddle that."

Madden thought it was a good sign that Fremmer sounded so rational. "If things get tight," he said, "or if the clock looks like it's going to run out on us, I'll just leak it to the press. I have a connection at the *Chronicle*." Madden was referring to the reporter who wrote the article based on Bender's piece on Shelby. "But before I tell anyone I want a few days back in California to see if I can make some progress in the search for Ross."

Fremmer was OK with that. "Just do me a favor."

"What?"

"When you go to the Memorial, look down into the reflecting pools and think about him."

"Who?"

"Ross. Look down into the void in the middle of the pool and ask where he is. It will tell you."

"Are you being serious?"

"No. But I know you're going to do it. The void does that to you. Makes you ask questions you can't answer. And who knows, maybe it will tell you. Maybe you'll think of something you didn't think of before."

An hour later Madden was staring into the north reflecting pool of the 9/11 Memorial and thinking about Fremmer's theory of the void. He was right. The void does do that to you. It was bigger than it looked in the photos. The pool was massive. But it didn't tell him anything about Ross.

Then something strange happened. He was sitting down on one of the plain square slabs of concrete that served as benches at the memorial site, when his phone rang. It was Dupuy. He'd noticed a missed call from her when he got out of the subway, but he hadn't called her back. He hadn't spoken to her in almost a week.

"You'll never guess who called this morning, back to back, literally within ten minutes of each other," she said.

"Who?"

"Your buddies Bender and J.J."

"Really, what'd they want?"

"Bender's looking for a new lawyer. He wanted me to represent him. I passed, of course. Referred him to a colleague."

She seemed to have already forgotten that Madden was the reason Bender needed a lawyer in the first place, that he was one who'd tipped Billings and the MPPD off to Bender's Adderall cache.

"I don't suppose he's become aware that your boyfriend and I are the reason he needs a lawyer?" Madden asked.

"I don't think so. He mentioned something about still trying to figure out who tipped off the police. He sounded really stressed. I felt bad for a minute. It's quite the scandal. I assume you've been reading some of the articles."

He had. The problem with a guy like Bender, a guy who'd built himself into a Valley powerbroker the way he had, with so much bluster and arrogance, was that everything was hunky dory until you tripped and fell. Now that he was down, all the people he'd alienated, insulted, or just plain ignored, relished seeing him lying there, prone and injured. They put their boots on and were now getting their kicks in, ribs first, then face.

Reading the articles, Madden at first enjoyed the furious indignation he'd helped ignite ("Blogger Accused of Trading Adderall for Access Fighting Charges and Fellow Bloggers' Wrath," was the latest headline he'd seen). But the more he read, the more he began to realize that a lot of these people now going after Bender were just as pompous and irritating as Bender himself. He wasn't sorry he'd given

Billings the tip, but he was sorry he hadn't gotten as much pleasure as he thought he would from seeing Bender in a bind. He also realized the condition wouldn't last. Notoriety had a power unto itself. Bender would rise again. He probably wouldn't be quite the same, but he'd return, slightly reinvented.

"How 'bout J.J.?" Madden asked, wanting to move on to a new topic.

"He called my office. He wants to have coffee and talk about the case. You know, he's still living in that house. He rented it for the rest of the month. He's written four songs already. He's looking for new material to work with. He asked if you wanted to come along."

"Thanks but no thanks. You go ahead and be his muse."

She was silent a moment.

"Hank?"

"Yeah."

"You know after J.J. called I listened to that file you gave me again. That recording you got of Cathleen, Stacey's daughter."

"Why did you listen to it again after he called? You weren't going to discuss that with him?"

"It crossed my mind for a second but you know I wouldn't do that without asking."

"The answer's no."

"No, I know. But I listened to it again and that's really why I've been trying to reach you. There's that part right at the end, the part where she asks her kid to talk with 'papa.' I listened to it with better headphones on this time and it struck me as kind of funny. Is the father Italian or European or something?"

"I don't think so. She said they met at Chico State."

"Well, listen to it again. You still have it, right? It sounds like *paw-paw*. Like the paw of a dog. When I heard it this time it just made me think that maybe she wasn't talking to her husband."

Madden was suddenly lost to thought. He thought he'd heard papa. But maybe she was right. Maybe it was *paw-paw*? But what did that mean?

"Hank, you there?"

"Yeah."

"Where are you? What's that sound in the background?"

"I'm out of town," he said. That wasn't a lie, but what he said next was. He hated to do it. "I'm out at the beach. Half Moon Bay."

"Playing hooky, huh?"

"Don't tell my wife. I'll call you when I get back."

"Listen to that again."

"I will," he said.

30/ Repercussions

Dᴇᴛᴇᴄᴛɪᴠᴇ Tʜᴏᴍᴀs Cʜᴜ ᴅɪᴅ Fʀᴇᴍᴍᴇʀ ᴛʜᴇ ᴄᴏᴜʀᴛᴇsʏ ᴏꜰ ᴄᴀʟʟɪɴɢ him before visiting him this time, but it turned out to be not much of a warning.

"Instead of trying to track you down at one of the seven Starbucks in the area, I thought I'd call first and arrange a meeting," Chu explained. "We need to talk, Max. I think you know why."

"I agree, Detective," Fremmer said. "I was actually going to call you today. Where do you want to meet? Don't say the station house. That didn't end so well for me last time."

"How 'bout your apartment?" Chu said. "Right now. I'm out in front."

Fremmer was on the third floor of a six-story brownstone, standing in his large eat-in kitchen, the nicest part of the apartment. He opened the window, stuck his head out, and looked down to the sidewalk below. Chu wasn't kidding.

"So you are," Fremmer said, talking into the phone as he looked down. "You bring me a coffee?"

"I thought you'd make me some," Chu said.

"Just give me a few minutes to get properly dressed."

"And call your lawyer buddy Morton?"

"That, too," Fremmer said.

He debated going down to meet Chu, but after having a quick conversation with Morton, who he told to stay close to his phone, Fremmer decided to let him come up. He looked at his watch. Nine-fifteen. He'd been all set to meet Madden. Now he was sorry he delayed his departure to prepare his gym bag. While he wasn't currently teaching any classes, he still had a free membership at the gym and was allowed to work out after the morning rush was over. He thought it'd be a good idea to show his face, try to make amends with the head fitness manager, who was based at the 76th Street Equinox.

But now here was Chu, once again showing up at an inopportune moment.

"Hey, bro," the detective said when Fremmer let him into the apartment. "Good to see you again."

He shook Fremmer's hand, then looked around, tilted his head up, and keenly and audibly sniffed the air.

"You cleaned up nice," he said. "Place smells a lot better than it did the other night. I heard they found you lying in your own vomit. I read the police report."

"Yeah. Not one of my finer moments," Fremmer replied. "I'm sorry you weren't here to witness it."

"I was worried about you."

"I'm sure you were. Coffee?"

"No, thanks, I already had some."

Fremmer decided to make a cup for himself. If Chu had wanted one, he would have made a full pot, but since it was just him, he fired up the Keurig one-cup machine instead.

Chu asked him if he could record their conversation.

"No," Fremmer said. "Let's keep this off the record. I'm doing that for your benefit, because you're going to end up telling me some things you don't want to."

Chu laughed. "Why would I do that?"

"Because I'm not going to tell you anything unless you do. It's called quid pro quo."

"I'm not sure you're in any position to make deals, bro."

"You don't know my position, so I don't think you're in any position to judge what deals I can make."

"Last I checked you'd OD'd on something and were texting your ex-fiancée and lawyer about killing yourself. And last night you got into a fight in the street with a one-armed man in his sixties. You ended up breaking his nose."

"You ever been hit with a prosthetic hand? I got news for you. It hurts."

"What were you doing there in the first place?" Chu asked. "He says you were upset you had to pay back your client's advance. He says you wrote them a check a few days ago but you now regretted it and said you felt conned. There was a woman involved."

"Yeah, the same one who slipped me some GHB and then texted my lawyer and my ex-fiancée telling them I wanted to pack it in. Did he mention that?"

"Any reason you didn't tell me that sooner? I told you to call me anytime."

"I was busy trying to recover from a hefty dose of GHB and everybody thinking I tried to kill myself.

Fremmer checked the Keurig to see if the water had heated up. He retrieved a Green Mountain K-cup from his coffee drawer, stuck it in the machine, and hit the button for a medium-sized brew.

"Sorry, Max, but I'm having a hard time buying that."

"If I were you, I would, too," Fremmer said. "But hear me out for a minute."

He then began telling Chu about his dealings with Braden and Rochelle—aka Isabelle. He told him about how she'd virtually kidnapped him in an Uber at the Starbucks on Broadway and 75th Street and brought him to the Lucidity Center, which Braden, in case he wasn't aware, ran out of his home.

He then described his experience of having a drink with her at 'Cesca and what transpired afterwards, almost nothing of which he remembered. When he woke up in the hospital, he'd theorized she wanted to get into his apartment so she could lift something from his computer. But it turned out she just wanted him to write a check. And he hadn't realized he'd written one until several days later, when the check had already cleared. He showed Chu a digital copy of the cashed check he'd obtained two days ago.

"It's my handwriting, it's my signature, but I can tell you I would never have made out a check to those scumbags had I not been drugged. That'll teach me never to keep much money in my checking account. Before this, low interest rates gave me no incentive to put money in a savings account."

"Tell me about it," Chu said.

Fremmer thought he detected a slight smirk. "You're not believing any of this, are you?"

"I'm listening," Chu said. "What I have learned over the years is that when someone tells you a story that's so outlandish that you don't think it could be made up, it may not be."

"Look," Fremmer said, "I'm trying to get 'Cesca, the restaurant I was at when she drugged me, to give me security footage from that night. They're not exactly eager to do that. I was going to pay someone off but I'm a little short on cash right now. But I bet you could get it without a problem."

"Oh, we got it already," Chu said.

"You did?"

"Yeah. It shows you guys having drinks and then sucking face pretty hard. She's a hot little number. I met her last night. She said you guys boned."

That threw Fremmer.

"She told you that?"

"Yeah, she said it was part of the deal. Said you agreed to pay back the advance on the condition she have sex with you. She had some video. On her phone."

"Was I awake in the video?"

"Frankly, I wasn't looking at you too much, bro."

"What'd she say her name was?"

"Isabelle, Rochelle, I'm not sure," Chu said. "I gotta check my notes."

"That'd be a good idea. She tell you what she did for Braden?"

"Helps manage the business," he said. "Been working for him for about four years."

Fremmer looked at his watch. Christ, he'd forgotten about Madden. It was nine-forty.

"Pause it there for a minute," Fremmer said. "I'll be right back. Just have to go to the john."

He quickly ducked into the bathroom down the hall, turned on the water, and called Madden.

"Where were we?" he asked Chu after he returned to the kitchen.

"We were talking about what your girlfriend did for Braden."

"She's not my girlfriend. If she were my girlfriend I wouldn't have to pay her $50,000 to have sex with her, would I?"

"So you admit to that?"

"I can't admit to something I don't remember, can I? She give you any theories as to why I might have wanted to kill myself?"

"You got depressed, bro."

"Over what?"

"Paying a woman $50,000 to have sex with you."

"I agree. That would depress me. If I knew I'd done it."

"No joke," Chu said, "I had a guy who paid a woman that kind of money to have sex with him. If I told you who he was, you'd know the name. He wasn't depressed about it, though. He's a billionaire."

"Thanks, Detective. That makes me feel better. If I wasn't missing a few zeroes off my self worth I'd be a happy clam and we wouldn't be having this conversation."

"Look, bro. I hear you. I'm listening. But you're not doing yourself any good going around punching people in the face. You're lucky the witness said Braden pushed you down first. And you're lucky it didn't happen in his apartment."

"You seem to be aware he's running a business out of his home. It's practically a hotel. He tell you about that?"

"The downstairs is permitted for a business. When he bought the building a long time ago it had a business down on the ground floor. It's grandfathered in. And frankly, we got bigger fish to fry than worrying about what he's running through there. It's not like he's selling drugs—"

"Well, in a way he is," Fremmer countered. "He peddles those supplements. And the whole promise of learning how to lucid dream is kind of drug, right? And then he's got this electrostatic doohickey headband coming out. That's apparently why he needed the quick cash infusion. He's gotta be mortgaged to the hilt."

"What I'm saying is he's not doing anything illegal. The lucid dreaming stuff is real, bro. I've had them. They're awesome. If I could take a pill and have one every night, I'd sign up for that program right now. Wouldn't you?"

Great, Fremmer thought. Braden had another a disciple. "Hey, maybe after his German visitors leave you can cash in your discount coupon for the Center's four-day workshop."

Chu didn't appear too happy with that comment.

"Look, I'm not going to arrest you," he said. "But this is a warning. You can't go on behaving like this and expect no repercussions. You have a kid. You end up messing up your life, they'll take him away from you. I had a buddy it happened to. He lost custody of his kid. It was sad."

Chu made a good point, which Fremmer couldn't fully appreciate at that moment. "You understand these people conned me," he said.

"I don't know what to believe, bro. Maybe you conned them. I don't know. I gotta keep an open mind. We're looking at everything. You may not think we are. But we've got a lot of people working on this case."

"How much video have you looked at?" Fremmer asked.

"A lot. We went back. Days. It takes hours. We got footage from at least six cameras. It's a lot of work."

"What are you looking for?"

"These guys—a lot of these homeless guys, they've got their little territories. They move around in a limited area. They sleep in the same spots. In his case, he slept over there on CPW, sometimes on the bench, sometimes just inside the park on the other side of the wall. And then he spends time on Columbus. And a little on Amsterdam. So we're looking at the area, the radius he moves around in. We're looking for him, seeing who he interacted with. Making sure there's no red flags. You'll see soon enough. It's tedious work."

"You look for Braden?"

"Sure. We looked for you, too."

Fremmer took his phone out his pocket and started swiping through the images in his photo library. "How 'bout this guy?" he asked, turning the phone over to Chu.

"Who's he?"

"He's an associate or former associate of Isabelle's. They used to clean fish tanks together and occasionally rob people. Isabelle Hruska is her full name. His name is Zander Bell. Nowadays he specializes in a different kind of rip-off—psychic readings from his apartment. I have an appointment to get a reading from him tomorrow afternoon. He look familiar to you at all?"

Chu looked at the phone and shook his head.

"Never heard of him."

"Well, you need to look for him in the video. And you need to ask Isabelle about him. My investigator put the screws into her a little bit last night and she got uncomfortable, which is saying a lot for a woman who's as put together as she is. Trust me. You need to run some checks on both of them."

He stopped talking and wrote their names on a piece of paper for Chu, just as the owner of the aquarium shop had done for him. Then he told Chu to hold on, he had something else for him.

Fremmer left the kitchen and went to the little alcove he used as his home office. He retrieved one of the USB thumb drives with Candace's hard drive stored on it. He'd made multiple copies and given a thumb drive to Morton to pass on to his investigator.

"You guys never took her computer," Fremmer said, handing him the thumb drive. "You got her phone but you never took her laptop. This is a copy of what was on her hard drive."

"Her whole computer fit on that?" Chu said, taking it from him.

"Yeah, it's a 128GB drive. Normally I'd bill you the forty dollars it cost me. But this one's on me."

Chu sighed. It was another thing to do. More paperwork.

"I'll have my guy take a look," he said.

"Look, I know the situation," Fremmer responded. "You think you've got an open and shut case. But it's more complicated than you think. I have some information I can't disclose right now that would change the way you think about everything if I told you what it was. You gave me a warning. Well, now I'm giving you a warning."

Chu looked him in the eyes. Fremmer looked right back. They held each other's gaze for a good five seconds.

"You're bluffing, bro," Chu declared after the stare down.

"Not about this."

"Then give me the information. Make me believe you."

"I can't," Fremmer said. "Not yet."

"Well, when you're ready, we'll talk. You know how to reach me."

"And you know where to find me."

31/ Dumb Luck

IN THE DREAM MADDEN WAS WALKING UP THE HILL TO THE DISH. HIS gait was remarkably smooth, he was hardly limping, and he reached the top more quickly than he thought. He felt good. A nice breeze was blowing. He wasn't perspiring. He wasn't even breathing hard.

He gazed out at the view. There were a few clouds in the sky, but the air was crisp and clean, the way it was after a big storm passed through, scrubbing everything.

Someone was standing next to him. He looked over and there was Frank Marcus, holding a drone.

"This is the latest thing," he said to Madden. "We put you on the drone and fly you over the property."

"So, you wear a headset?" Madden asked.

"No headset. It's in your own brain. The ultimate VR."

"I know," Madden said.

He was an expert now. He knew all about it. He told Marcus he'd been to the Center, met the founder.

"Well, I don't have to show you how then," Marcus said. He flipped a switch and the quadcopter turned on, its propellers humming to life. He handed the drone to Madden.

It didn't look big enough to carry his weight. *But this isn't real*, he thought. *This is a dream. It'll work.*

He extended his hand up, like he was hailing a cab, and held the quadcopter above him, careful not to let the propellers catch on his sleeve. He felt it pull him up gently until his feet lifted off the ground.

He hovered there a moment, a foot from the Earth. Then two feet. Then three. More comfortable, he went higher and let himself be carried forward.

Soon he was over the Valley. It was incredible. The most incredible thing he'd ever felt. Why hadn't he done this before? And then he looked down and noticed that all the houses and cars had disappeared. He couldn't remember if things had been in color before, but they weren't anymore. Everything was in black and white: He was looking at the nineteenth-century Valley. Haciendas. Horses. The dusty, dirt road that was the El Camino.

He guided the drone lower to get a closer look. The towns were barely towns. There was a house here and there. And there it was in all its magnificence: The Sharon Estate.

My God, he thought, *if this is the future it's a future I want to experience.* He descended a little more, wondering whether he should attempt to talk to one of the locals. Or was he better off staying aloft?

As he was trying to decide, something hit him. Not hard. But he felt a little jolt on his shoulder. A bird?

"Sir, can you raise your seat back, please?"

He opened his eyes and looked up to see a flight attendant. She had one hand on his shoulder, the other on the top of his seat.

"We're landing in a minute," she said.

"Oh, sorry."

He pushed the button on his armrest and the seat jerked forward, its new position satisfying the flight attendant. After she'd moved down the aisle in search of other offenders, he looked to his left, past the two people seated next to him, and glanced out the window. He was almost at the same altitude as he'd been on his drone ride. They were over the Bay—somewhere near Redwood City or Belmont, he thought. He could see cars moving along the 101 Freeway. The traffic on the southbound side—the reverse commuters from the city— was thick but had some viscosity, which meant it was still early.

He turned and stared at the tray table in front of him in its full upright position. How had he made it happen? How could he do it again? All he could think about was how it felt being outside the plane.

• • •

Madden decided not to go straight home when his flight landed in San Francisco. Instead he headed right to Petaluma to get a DNA sample from Cathleen Mileki, preferably with her permission. Once he had the sample he could contact his old friend Greg Lyons, the San Mateo County chief deputy coroner. Lyons was in charge of day-to-day operations at the San Mateo Sheriff's Forensic Laboratory and Coroner's Office. He could advise Madden on how to best process the samples—and how to do it as quickly as possible. The facility, in the foothills of southern San Mateo, wasn't far from the airport. He'd actually pass it on his way back home from Petaluma.

He and his one carry-on bag were off the plane at 7:35 AM, and in his car at long term parking by 8:00. Traffic on 101 was bad, but once he got over to the 280 freeway it moved well until he hit a bottleneck in San Francisco leading up to the entrance of the Golden Gate Bridge. It took him an hour and forty minutes to get to Petaluma— pretty good time considering he'd started at the height of rush hour.

When he arrived at Mileki's house nobody was there. Cathleen had probably taken her son to school and stayed out to run some errands or maybe go to the gym. At least that was what he hoped. He went back to the cafe he'd previously eaten at and ordered a croissant egg sandwich and coffee to go, then returned to the house, parking just up the street.

Sitting in the car he dozed off, he wasn't quite sure for how long, but when he woke up her car was in the driveway. Catching a fleeting look of her as she passed by the kitchen window, he felt his stomach tighten. He was suddenly nervous. He didn't know for certain if Fremmer's client was her mother, and he didn't want to raise her hopes if she didn't know about Candace. On the drive up he thought about the extremely delicate nature of the situation, but now that he was here, ready to go, that fragility seemed magnified. He worried that he wouldn't be at his best, maybe it hadn't been a good idea to come right off a redeye. Fremmer's go-go attitude had rubbed off on him, but that was now starting to wear away like a temporary tattoo.

He finished his coffee, then opened the paternity kit he'd left sitting on the passenger seat, removed the items he needed, and put them in his jacket pocket with the Ziploc evidence bag Fremmer had given him before their encounter with Braden. He got out of the car and made his way to the front door, climbing the concrete steps deliberately, his leg and back aching more than usual.

The door opened before his hand reached the doorbell. Cathleen, staring at him from the other side of her front door, appeared a little dazed. The dog started barking, but the barking wasn't coming from inside the house; he must have been out in the backyard.

"Really?" she said. "Today?"

He didn't know how to respond.

"Really?" she said again.

Cathleen looked like she was the one who'd just gotten off a red-eye. Her hair looked off, like she'd slept on it the wrong way, and her eyes were puffy and watery, like she'd just cut onions.

"Yes, sorry, me again," he said.

"Do you have a problem using the phone? You can't just keep showing up like this," she said, like he was a regular visitor. In fact, he'd only turned up once before. He counted his quick return to retrieve his phone as part of one visit. Maybe she saw it differently.

"Hopefully, this will be the last time," he said. "But I need something from you."

"Well, it's really not a good time. I just found out that my best friend died in a car accident last night."

"Oh, wow," he said reflexively. "Wow, I'm sorry."

A pained look crossed her face. She looked like she was about to cry.

"What do you want?" she asked.

"Can I come in for a moment?" he said gently.

"Just ask what you have to ask. I have a friend taking me out in a little while. I need to get myself together. I'm a mess."

"I really think you should be sitting down for what I'm about to tell you."

"I can't deal with any more bad news right now."

Was it bad? Maybe. Maybe not. "It's good," he said. "It just might shock you."

"Well, I'm going to have another drink then. You want one?"

That actually didn't sound like a bad idea.

"What are you drinking?" he asked, following her into the house.

"Screwdriver. I don't have any other mixers. If I drink, I usually drink wine. Too early for that, though."

A screwdriver sounded fine. She fixed him a drink, then refilled her glass with ice, vodka, and just a splash of orange juice. He watched her take a sip to check its potency, staring at her lips as they touched the rim of the glass. Maybe he wouldn't have to ask her for a cheek swab after all, he thought.

Just then he felt his phone vibrating in his pocket. He took it out to check the number. Fremmer. He clicked the volume button, sending the call to voicemail, and put the phone back in his pocket.

He caught her looking at her watch. "I'm surprised you're here," she said, "I heard you weren't working on the case anymore. You were frustrated by the sudden rush of publicity or something."

"I felt used," Madden said. "Maybe even slightly betrayed."

"Or was it fear of failure?"

"A little of that, too," he conceded. Under normal circumstances he'd never admit that, but he didn't mind admitting it to her. If there were ever a moment to curry some sympathy by showing his vulnerabilities, this was it.

His cell phone buzzed again in his pocket. This time he only felt a single, longer buzz. He took his phone out and saw that he had a text message. Fremmer.

"Call me," it said. "C died this AM. In shock. Not sure what 2 do. Need 2 speak 2 U."

Madden looked at the message, stunned. "C" had to be Candace.

His eyes went from his phone screen to Mileki. As soon as their eyes met he knew that she knew her mother was dead.

"Everything OK?" she asked innocently.

"You know," he said.

"Know what?"

"It's not your friend that died, is it?"

She looked at him, trying to meet his stare and hold herself together. But then her lip started quivering and she turned away.

"I'm sorry," he said. "I truly am. I just found out. That was someone calling me from New York. I came here to tell you I thought I'd found her. I wanted to get a DNA sample from you to confirm it. I didn't know whether you knew she was alive."

"Well, now she's dead again," she said angrily, practically spitting the words at him. "It's your fault. And that asshole Shelby."

What was she talking about? All his fault? How was he to blame?

Suddenly he felt a little woozy. He put his phone back in his pocket and leaned up against the kitchen counter. For a second he thought she'd put something in his drink. But then he realized he hadn't touched his glass yet. He felt faint. He could hear his heart pounding.

He tried to control his breathing. Inhaling and exhaling slowly through his nose, he ran through a mental checklist of heart-attack symptoms. His arms felt OK. No chest pain. He just couldn't breathe.

"Do you have an aspirin?" he managed to say.

She looked at him with some concern.

"Are you OK?" she asked. "You're white. Are you having a heart attack?"

"I don't think so. I just feel a little nauseous. I just got off a redeye."

He took a few more deep breaths and felt the nausea subside a little. It took another minute or so, but the wave that knocked him over retreated back out to sea, leaving him sprawled out on the beach. At least he didn't feel like he was drowning anymore.

Taking his arm, she led him into the living room and sat him in one of the club chairs. "I'll get you a glass of water," she said as she walked back into the kitchen. While she was in there he heard her phone chime, twice. She was texting someone.

She returned to the living room with the glass of water and a new demeanor. She seemed calmer. "Your blood pressure probably dropped," she said. "I used to have a problem with that. I fainted a couple of times."

Her voice was flat and unemotional, but her tone felt a little too friendly. *She's overcompensating. Who had she been communicating with?*

"Did you mean that?" he asked.

"Mean what?"

"That it was my fault? Did my investigation trigger something?"

She didn't answer. Instead she turned away and sat herself down on the couch across from him.

"I shouldn't have said that," she said. "I made a mistake. How did you find her?"

"Dumb luck. She said something to someone in the hospital. She thought she was at Stanford Hospital. And then she mentioned something about her husband Ross choking her. She didn't remember her new identity. And then someone contacted me, a guy who wants half the money Shelby's supposed to pay me if I find her. You know this only happened because that tech blogger wrote that article I was upset about. How's that for irony?"

"She woke up?"

"For a little bit," he said. "Then they put her back in a coma so her brain could heal. But I guess something happened this morning."

"She was having another surgery and she went into cardiac arrest, the news report said." Mileki stared straight ahead as she spoke. She seemed lost in her thoughts.

"Cathleen?" Madden said.

"What?"

"What happened to your father? What happened to Ross?"

"I don't know."

"I think you do," he said. "You knew about your mother. You knew the whole time, didn't you?"

She didn't answer, so he continued talking.

"This probably isn't the best time to bring this up, but I think you should be aware that you're an accessory to a crime. I'm not quite sure what that crime is yet. But you're going to have to come clean now, you understand? You're going to have to tell the world what happened. You can make a deal. You can stay out of jail."

A tear streamed down her face, then another. He watched them drop onto the rug.

"You have no proof of anything," she said.

"It doesn't matter what I have," he said. "When the police find out this woman in New York was your mother, all hell is going to break loose. They're going to find out if you had any contact with her. If you did, they'll prosecute you. And either way the press will make your life a living hell."

She didn't react. She just sat there staring at the coffee table.

"Why?" he asked. "Just answer that. What made her go to New York in the first place? Is your father still alive? Is his name now Victor Braden?"

That got her attention. Only her reaction wasn't what he expected. She looked up and let out a little laugh.

"You know who that is?"

She smiled. "The one-armed dream guy."

"Yeah, the dream guy."

"What do you think?" she asked.

"I don't know," he said. "I'm asking you."

She glanced at her watch again. *Was it really her friend or was someone else coming? Her husband? Or maybe the person she called paw-paw on the recording he'd made.*

"Who'd you text earlier?" he asked.

"My friend. I know her from Eli's school."

"I don't think so."

"You want to know why?" she asked.

"I want to know who you were really talking to earlier," he said. They seemed to be having parallel conversations. "I want you to know that my associate in New York knows exactly where I am. If anything happens to me, he'll pass the information on to the police."

"After that doctor did what he did to you, how did you feel?" she asked.

"Excuse me?"

"After he put his dick back in his pants, how did you feel?"

He looked at her. *Why the blunt language?* If she was trying to get under his skin, she was doing a good job of it. He stopped himself from lashing back at her, decided to play along and not get defensive.

"Relief, I guess," he said after a moment. "Relief it was over."

"And then what?"

"Humiliation. I felt humiliated. Embarrassed."

She nodded. "Why didn't you tell your parents?"

"He warned me not to. Said if I did, he'd make sure no one believed me. I believed him. But I also didn't want them to know. I thought my father would have been mad at me because I let it happen."

"But now you regret it, not telling them?"

"I do. Because he did the same thing to other kids. I could have stopped him. I should have stopped him."

"What if you had told them?" she said. "What would your parents have done? What would your father have done?"

Madden's eyes dropped to floor as he pictured his father's reaction. "He would have—"

He stopped mid-sentence, suddenly realizing where she was going. He looked up at her. She was talking about *her* parent. Except it wasn't her father she was talking about, it was her mother.

"Your father was molesting you?" he said. "That's what was going on? And she killed him?"

"No."

The answer didn't come from her, though. It came from a voice behind him. A familiar voice. Madden wheeled around in the club chair and saw Marcus standing there, pointing a small gun at him.

"I did," he said.

32/ The Oracle

THAT MORNING FREMMER GOT A CALL FROM THE 92ND STREET EQUI-
nox. The same fitness manager who'd berated and fired him the
week before was now begging him to come in. The instructor scheduled to teach back-to-back classes at ten and eleven had called in sick
at the last minute and they needed a sub ASAP.

Fremmer liked to think they called him thanks to the barrage
of requests from his regulars wanting him back on the schedule.
But the more likely scenario was they couldn't get anybody to come
in on such short notice, and Fremmer lived fifteen blocks from
the gym.

His first impulse was to decline the invitation—or at least play
hard to get—but then he thought better of it. Double sessions were
hard to come by and not only could he use the money but he needed
the exercise.

In the middle of the second class he saw Detective Chu's number
come up on his iPhone. Fremmer had all his Spotify playlists set up on
an iPod Touch that he connected to the studio's audio system. He used
an app on his iPhone as a timer for the interval-based sections of his
programs or "courses," as he called them. He let Chu's call go to
voicemail and called him back when he finished class, a few minutes
after noon.

"You saw the news?" Chu asked.

"No, what?"

"Your client passed away early this morning."

"Candace?"

"Yes. I'm sorry."

"Are you kidding me? What happened?" He was asking and Googling at the same time.

And there it was: *Victim of Homeless Pusher Dies.*

"The report we got was from the hospital was that there were complications from surgery. We were preparing a statement, but the media beat us to it," Chu said.

Fremmer didn't even know she was having surgery. Why hadn't Bernstein called him? Oh, Christ, it was Thursday. Bernstein never worked Thursdays.

Apparently Morton had just heard too because now he was calling him. "Hold on a sec," Fremmer told Chu, "I have to take this call.

"I gotta call you back," he said to Morton. "Sorry."

"You heard?" Morton asked.

"Just now. I was teaching a spinning class. I'm on the phone with Chu. The detective."

"They're upgrading the charge to murder two," Morton said. "I just spoke to the DA's office."

"Fan-fucking-tastic. I'll call you right back."

Fremmer got back on the phone with Chu, who told him the same thing about the DA upgrading the charges. But that wasn't the real reason he was calling.

"It'd be good if you could stop by the station," Chu said. "I'm not asking you to come in, but it would be good if you happened to stop by because you felt like talking to me."

Chu was clearly speaking the way he was for a reason. Fremmer didn't know quite what that reason was yet, but he went along with it.

"Always love to chat with you, Detective," he said.

"You still have an appointment with Zander today?" Chu asked.

"Yeah. Assuming he doesn't cancel. Why?"

"Well, we checked him out like you said to and well, we found some interesting shit. Dude's pretty shady. He's got a record."

"Can't say I'm shocked to hear that. How 'bout the woman? Isabelle?"

"She came back clean."

"She's not," Fremmer said.

"We spoke to her. She told us some things about Zander. Did you know he works for the Lucidity Center?"

"Yeah, I think he still cleans Braden's fish tank."

"Apparently he also handles a lot of their bookings and manages the website. He also gets a commission for bringing people in, acquiring new customers so to speak. He's been involved with the Center almost as long as Isabelle has."

"Interesting," Fremmer said.

"We're going through the thumb drive now. We need to talk you before you go to that appointment. We also found something else."

"What?"

"We've got Zander near that intersection on CPW a week before your client got hit. It looks like he said something to Ronald and took some photos of him with his phone."

Photos? Fremmer thought. *What had Ronald said back in the holding cell? Something about a guy taking a picture of him. The Oracle.*

"You got him on video?" Fremmer said excitedly. "You got that?"

"Just come by, OK? I'd rather talk face-to-face," Chu said.

"I'm at the gym. Just have to take a shower and I'll be right over."

Fremmer needed to pull himself together. He felt awful about Candace worrying about her daughter, feared that her death would impact his attempts to reveal her true identity, and was exhilarated by the prospect of Zander as a suspect. He was also a bit paranoid. Maybe Chu was messing with him, giving him enough information to get him to the station. But why? He needed to call Madden. Madden would have answers.

But the first thing he had to do was call Anna, the woman taking care of Mia, Candace's daughter, and to ask how she was doing. What could he do to help?

"It's hard to tell how she's really taking it," Anna reported. "Part of her thinks it's maybe better she passed away because she'd never be the same again."

After that conversation, Fremmer decided to decompress in the steam room for ten minutes. It was all moving too quickly. So much so that he forgot about Madden. He was a few blocks from the police station when he finally tried to reach him. Getting no answer, he sent a text.

33/ View To A Kill

MARCUS WALKED OVER TO CATHLEEN, PULLED HER HEAD TO HIS chest with his free hand, and the two hugged warmly.

"I'm sorry," he said to her. "I tried to get here sooner. I got in the car as soon as I got the Google alert. I was hoping you wouldn't see it."

"I saw it after I got out of the gym," she said. "I thought it was a mistake. I thought she was improving."

That solved the mystery of how Marcus had gotten there so fast. Madden realized that he was already en route when she texted him about Madden's unexpected visit. But Marcus had a gun. Where did the gun come from?

"It's better that she passed," Marcus said. "She wasn't ever going to be the same."

Madden felt completely out of place. They were experiencing a deeply personal moment and he was standing there watching it. If not for the gun trained on him, he would have gladly disappeared. He saw that it was an ultra-compact Ruger, the LCP .380, prized for its concealability. In Marcus's hand it looked like a toy.

When they broke their embrace, Madden repeated the speech he gave Cathleen.

"My associate in New York knows exactly where I am," he warned Marcus. "If I don't call him by noon—three o'clock his time—he's going to call the police."

"Thanks for the heads up, Hank," Marcus said. "Now just sit tight for a minute."

He and Cathleen walked toward the kitchen for a quick pow-wow. Marcus kept an eye on Madden the whole time they chatted. While Madden couldn't make out everything they were saying, he did hear enough bits and pieces to get that she was rehashing what she thought Madden knew and what she'd told him.

Madden considered an escape. He saw a sliding glass door that led out to the backyard, but the backyard appeared to be fenced in—and that fence was a good five or six feet tall. There had to be some sort of side gate that led to the front of the house, but he didn't know that for sure. And then there was the dog. Dakota kept coming up to the glass and looking at him, wagging his tail. Would he run after him, thinking he wanted to play, and maybe trip him up?

A younger version of himself might have bolted—or maybe even tried to take Marcus down—but he didn't feel the current, post red-eye version was up to the challenge.

Marcus continued to console Cathleen. Madden sensed an intimacy in their relationship; they were clearly much closer than he'd ever imagined. He heard Marcus assure her that everything would be all right, an opinion Madden didn't quite share.

"Let's take a ride, Hank," Marcus said as he walked back into the living room. "I want to show you something."

Madden didn't like the sound of that. "You know, when you say something like that, I hear a certain ominous connotation in it. Especially since the guy who's saying it has a gun in his hand. No offense, but it seems a little too cute for you."

"It's hers," Marcus said. "But I taught her how to shoot it."

"I didn't realize you guys were so close."

"You didn't realize a lot of things. Come on, let's go. You said we've got 'til noon, right?"

"You mind if I hit the john first? Coffee's run its course."

Marcus considered the request. "Give me your phone," he said.

Madden handed it to him. Marcus told him to lift his pant legs, gave him a quick pat down to check for a weapon, and then he pointed him toward a door off the kitchen.

"Right there," he said. "Keep it open."

Marcus kept an eye on him as he did his business, but didn't watch too closely. He didn't normally stand outside bathrooms and watch men pee, especially older men, and Madden could tell he wasn't enthralled with the task.

Turning on the water to wash his hands, Madden noticed a wad of used tissues at the bottom of the small garbage bin to the left of the sink. That got him thinking. Cathleen had been crying. She must've wiped her eyes or blown her nose into one of those tissues.

He put both hands in the sink, but only put one of them under the stream, keeping his right hand dry. He turned off the water, removed the hand towel from its rack and dropped it on the floor. His back turned toward the door, he reached into the bin, gathered the tissues with his dry hand, then picked up the towel with his wet hand. He quickly stuffed the tissues in his jacket pocket, then took his time using the towel to wipe both hands, turning toward Marcus as he did.

He folded the towel and returned it neatly to its rack.

"Come on," Marcus said impatiently. "Let's go."

Outside, Marcus walked right behind him, which made Madden nervous. He didn't trust Marcus handling that gun. It might be petite, but it was deadly nonetheless.

His car was parked on the street. Madden realized right away that he'd seen it before: It was the white Audi he thought had been following him a few months back. The license plate was the same. Dupuy had someone run it for him then. The car was registered to Jorge Rodriguez of Redwood City. No one saw the connection so they let it drop.

"I've seen this car before," he said to Marcus as he got in. "You were the one following me, weren't you?"

"A little," Marcus said. "In the beginning. Until I realized you weren't a threat."

"Who's Jorge Rodriguez?"

"He used to work for me. Young kid. Did him a favor and bought his car when he went back east to law school in the fall. I gotta get it re-registered."

Madden watched the road as they drove out of town.

"We going far?" he asked.

"You'll see." Marcus held the gun in his left hand, the steering wheel in his right.

"You do understand how things work these days?" Madden said. "They can track me from my cell phone. They'll know I went to Cathleen's house. They'll see exactly where you drove me. And even if you ditch the phone, they'll know I was up here."

"I'm well aware of that," Marcus said. "Just chill out. We'll be there soon enough."

"At least tell me how you killed him. Tell me what happened."

"Play your cards right and I might," Marcus said.

Madden didn't know what that portended—as far as he could tell, he didn't even have a pair in his hand—but he took at it as a positive.

Marcus got on the 101 and headed north. After about fifteen minutes he turned off at the 481B exit, headed east past Sonoma State University and drove up into the hills, where the landscape became decidedly more rural. They drove down a two-lane paved road for a little bit, then Marcus slowed and turned off onto a dirt road marked by a rustic gated entrance. Above the gate was a crested shield with the bold "NF" logo of Never Found Vineyard at its center.

Madden's eyes opened wide when he saw the name, but his mouth stayed shut. Marcus turned right at a fork on the dirt road, up a gently sloping path. Soon, they were pulling into a driveway in front of a farmhouse that was either new or had been recently renovated.

"Here we are," Marcus said as he got out of the car.

"This is yours?" Madden asked, standing beside him.

"And my wife's. But my little hobby."

Marcus motioned for him to start walking. "Go that way," he said, "I want to show you something."

Trailing closely behind, he guided Madden to the back of the farmhouse, where there was a rectangular pool, a lush expanse of green lawn, and a partially covered patio with different seating areas. It was all very tastefully appointed, though not estate fancy—or estate scale. Whoever had remodeled the property had done it well. It blended perfectly with its surroundings and looked expensively sophisticated without being ostentatious.

Marcus guided Madden up a path that led into the vineyards. There were perhaps forty rows of grapevines, many of them with fruit already showing. Most of the vineyards Madden had visited were on flat ground. But this one—at least this part of it—had been planted on the side of a hill.

When they reached the summit, Marcus stood beside Madden and looked out at the view. They were high enough to see into the valley past the gently rolling hills ahead of them. Madden spotted what he suspected was the town of Santa Rosa. It was a beautiful day, the sky an electric shade of Sonoma blue and practically cloudless. If he had to choose a place for it all to come to an end, this might as well be it.

"Not bad, right?" Marcus said.

"Not bad," Madden agreed.

A little further down the hill Madden saw a set of three structures linked together, which he realized must be the winery. Parked outside the buildings he could see a car and two pickup trucks. He didn't see the people the cars belonged to. He assumed they were inside and the building was where the wine was made and stored.

"We're small," Marcus said. "I'm still trying to figure things out. It's been a learning process. This'll be our third harvest. We're getting better each year."

"What are you making?"

"Pinot and Chardonnay. In the hills here we're dealing with various microclimates. Those grapes grow well here."

"It's a long way to go from bartender at a pub to this," Madden said.

Marcus smiled. "It was my dream. I always wanted this. Since I was a little kid. I'm living the dream, man."

Madden looked over at him. The problem with people living the dream was they had a hard time giving it up. He got the feeling that one of them wasn't walking off that hill.

"How did Ross die?" Madden asked. "Did you find him in Vietnam?"

He didn't think that was what actually happened, but he suspected Marcus would be more likely to react to a more specific question.

"I didn't," he said. "But I did bring him there."

"What do you mean?"

"Here's the deal, Hank. I'm going to tell you everything. And when I'm through, I'm going to make you a proposition. And you will either accept my proposition or you won't. OK?"

Madden nodded. He had a pretty good idea what Marcus meant by the choice so he didn't bother asking for clarification. Besides, he was too eager to get answers to worry about that now.

"Ross was always a bully," Marcus began. "Stacey didn't see that quality in him. Not right away. Not until after they got married. They had their little spats but, for the most part, he treated her like a queen. At first. He might've really loved her, in his way. But then he changed. I don't know if he was manic or bipolar or what, but something was off. He became very controlling and paranoid. He told her what she could wear, who she could see. He went nuts if he saw her even look at a guy, stuff like that. But Stacey wasn't one to deal with anyone telling her how she could or couldn't look at anyone. So she started looking at more guys."

"Was this before or after they had Cathleen?" Madden asked.

"A little before."

"So I guess things weren't so bad that they weren't having sex."

"Well, it wasn't always consensual. At least that's what she told me. But don't get me wrong, Stacey had her issues. She was no saint, always sleeping around. Even in high school. I didn't know her well. She was a year ahead of me. But I heard the stories. She probably shouldn't have ever gotten married. But she had these periods in her life—I call them her conformist phases—where she wanted a normal life so she'd walk a straighter line, so to speak. She was in one of those phases when she met Ross. And he kind of swept her off her feet. In some ways, I think they were both pretending they were somebody they weren't. He was the same way."

"And when did he start abusing Cathleen?"

Marcus dropped his head, like he was about to pray or something. Madden had struck a nerve.

"I don't want to get into that," he said after a moment. "But I'll tell you how it happened. After Cathleen was born, things were OK for a while. They were both focused on the baby. They played family. And he actually was a pretty good father. He was."

Marcus paused again, briefly, then switched to the present tense to tell the next part:

"A year or two goes by and he tells Stacey he wants another kid. So they try to have one. But it doesn't happen. She won't get pregnant. So he has her go in for some tests. And they say nothing's wrong with her. And then he goes in for tests. Afterwards, he tells Stacey everything's fine. But actually it isn't. They tell him he's got some issues with his sperm that would make it next to impossible for him to get a woman pregnant naturally. They can do IVF. They can make it happen. But suddenly he looks at Cathleen and realizes she's not actually his kid. He says nothing to Stacey, though. Keeps it to himself. He only tells her he knows later on, toward the end, when Stacey finds out what he's been doing to Cathleen." He paused here, wincing at the memory. "That's when he decides to say something."

"How'd she find out?"

"I told her."

"Excuse me?"

"You know Stacey and I were close. Had been for years. I could see that she was struggling in the marriage. She had to go back to work, get some financial independence. I worked nights and weekends, so I had plenty of free time to help out. I spent a lot of time with Cathleen, always have. Something happened to her when she was around eight. She started acting strange. Withdrawn, sullen. Not her usual self. Everything scared her, especially Ross. Whenever she knew she was going to be alone with him I could see the fear in her eyes. It wasn't normal."

"That's quite an assumption."

"I saw the bruises. On the inside of her thighs. She was wearing these shorts that rode up when she ran or climbed. I asked her what happened and she just clammed up. Disappeared into herself. She refused to say a word about anything. But I knew. I just knew something was up with him. It was textbook behavior, like something from an after school special. I decided to find out for myself."

"Who's kid was she?"

"Mine," Marcus said. "Cathleen is my daughter. And I've always known that."

Madden felt like he was having an out-of-body experience. The whole scene felt surreal. He tried to force himself back to reality, but he didn't know how. He tried to say something, anything, but no words came out of his mouth.

So that was it, he thought. That was the motive. It wasn't money. He was protecting a child. *His child.* His secret.

But what about Ross? What about finding his arm in Vietnam? What did Marcus mean when he said he'd brought him there?

"You said you brought Ross to Vietnam. What'd you mean by that?"

"He never left California," Marcus explained. "It was me. After I killed him, I took his passport and went to Vietnam because I knew we had no extradition treaty with them. And to be perfectly honest, I'd always wanted to go there. I bought a ticket to Ho Chi Minh City and entered the country as Ross Walker. Exiting the country as me was a little trickier. I ended up going through Thailand, had to bribe a few people. This happened in the nineties, before September 11. International travel was a lot easier before 9/11. Everything was easier. Stacey managed to get herself a social security number and a new identity without much of a problem."

"But what about his remains? What about the arm?"

"I went to Vietnam twice," Marcus explained patiently. "The first time as him, the second as me looking for him. For my book. When I went the second time I packed the arm in my suitcase. Well, by that point it wasn't so much an arm as, well, bones."

"A suitcase?" Madden asked, incredulous.

"Not just any suitcase. I had one made with a special lead-lined compartment, just in case some security person looked at an X-ray of the suitcase. I doubt they even looked, though."

"Why? Why only one arm? Why would you do that?"

"Ah, the arm. That's actually an interesting story. A few years after she'd settled in New York, Candace started talking to me about this guy she'd met who trained people to be lucid dreamers. You know, control what happens in their dreams. She was really into that stuff. And the damn psychics. Anyway, she was really impressed with this guy, not just because he was kind of a Svengali, but also because he was handicapped. He only had one arm. He'd lost the other one to a bacterial infection or something like that. She talked about him a lot. Anyway, that's how I came up with the idea. I just thought it would be interesting, that it would really add something to the story, if I went to Vietnam and found Ross's arm. It would make the book. Not a sure thing, I know. I took a huge risk, but it paid off big time. That piece of arm totally made the book. What was the one thing everybody talked about when they talked about my book? The arm."

"What happened to the rest of him?"

"I was living in Woodside, on the property of this wealthy divorced guy I knew from the bar. He made his money in tech but always wanted to be an artist so he converted one of his barns into an art studio. He had the place all set it up to do some painting but then he never painted. He traveled all the time. I buried Ross up there. And then a few years later, I really got rid of him."

"Where is he now?"

Marcus bent down and took some soil from the ground and held it in his hand, showing it to Madden. Then he tossed in the air and it blew away with the wind.

"You might find a trace of him in our 2014," he said.

"You ground him up?"

"His bones," he said. "When I bought this property nine years ago, I mixed him in with some manure I spread on the fields. Ashes to ashes."

"Where'd you kill him?"

"At his house. Drugged him first then asphyxiated him. It was clean. No blood. I didn't want any blood. Then I stuck him in the trunk of his car and drove to Woodside."

"How'd you end up at his house?"

"He came into the bar that same night. He knew I knew Stacey. Knew she came into the bar and that I'd gone to high school with her. He assumed I'd slept with her, but didn't know for sure. And he came in and started asking me questions, like 'I know you know where she is. I know she's hiding out somewhere, you tell me where and I'll make it worth your while.' Stuff like that."

"Where was she?"

"In Woodside. In the other barn. I was hiding her. She was gone girl years before *Gone Girl*. Except she left because she really was afraid he would kill her. He choked her, you know? Almost killed her.

She had to get away from him. She'd been living in that guest cottage on their property and Cathleen was living in the big house, in her room. Right down the hall from his. It was crazy. Stacey kept saying it's alright, they'd come to an understanding, they were going to get divorced, and she was going to work out a deal where she'd get Cathleen and would take less in the divorce in exchange for full custody. She wouldn't press charges, didn't want to put the kid through it. But then he started to change his tune and didn't want to give her any money at all so she threatened to tell the police about what he'd done to Cathleen. That was the night he nearly choked her to death. He followed her, let her know it too. Told her if she went anywhere near the police he'd kill her. He'd threatened her before that, lots of times. And more than a few times she had to stop me from going over there and killing him. I wanted to. The guy in Woodside had shotguns, we'd shoot skeet sometimes. And I was ready to go over there and blow him away. But she convinced me not to. And then I came up with the plan to get her out of there and make it look like he killed her. And she agreed."

"You planned it for a while then?"

"No, not really," Marcus said. "Planning it happened over a few days, but the actual opportunity, him coming to talk to me in the bar, that was pure serendipity. I knew I wouldn't get another opportunity, and I was ready. I hated that guy for what he did to Stacey, but I wanted him dead for what he did to Cathleen. I can't say we fully thought everything out, but we figured it wouldn't take the police too long to dig into his life and realize that lots of people wanted him dead. Because he was a bad guy."

"So you had no plan for Stacey to reappear one day?"

"That was the initial plan, but then the days became weeks and we weren't sure what to do. Everybody thought he had killed her, but they couldn't come up with enough evidence to get a conviction, so they held off arresting him. They had the stuff Stacey planted, but they had no body. And by they, I mean the MPPD. Pastorini and that other guy, Burns, were working the case with Dupuy and the DA. You guys never felt you had enough to get a jury to convict him. One day—it was about a month or so after Stacey's disappearance—I said to myself, 'Hey, what if this guy disappears, too? Everybody will think he took off because he's guilty. It's the perfect murder.' I just had to make it look like he took off. I didn't do anything right away, though. I thought it would be tricky because you guys—the police— were watching out for him. Or at least I thought you might be. I was planning the whole thing. I already had the pills and everything when he came into the bar. So I told him, 'Look I can't talk about this here, but I might know something.' I told him I'd meet him at his house after I got off work. I warned him it would be late. After work I left my car parked on a street near the bar and skateboarded over there. I used to do a lot of longboarding. Always kept a rig and some gear in my trunk."

"So the opportunity presented itself and you acted on it?"

"Exactly. And the amazing thing is everything went pretty much as I'd envisioned it. Some stuff I added along the way. Calling Bronsky, for instance, and pretending to be Ross. It was mean, but I didn't like the guy. I don't know why she ever hooked up with him. I'm sorry about the backyard, though. It was kind of fun to watch you guys dig it up."

That revelation hurt a little. He thought back to Marcus's whole drone presentation. What a charade.

"They found Ross's car at LAX," Madden said. "You drove it there?"

"I did, with some strands of Stacey's hair and traces of her blood in the trunk. I was concerned that someone might recognize the name if I went to SFO and tried to buy a one-way plane ticket to Hanoi through Tokyo. Someone might tip off the police. That said, there wasn't anything preventing Ross from leaving the country. But I was just trying to be cautious."

"How'd you get the time off work?"

"I was actually scheduled to be off for a few days. I worked Wednesday through Saturday. And when I called one of the other bar- tenders from Vietnam and asked him to take my shifts, I'd screwed up my foot longboarding and couldn't stand. I came back the next week. I might have stayed a little longer but I was worried Stacey was running out of food."

Madden thought about Pastorini spending all those Thanksgivings and Christmas Eves staking out Ross's brother's house. Poor guy, he thought. What a waste.

"I was lucky," Marcus said. "But I was also smart."

He seemed energized by finally being able to tell someone about the great coup he'd pulled off. And it was great, Madden thought. It was spectacular.

"Did Cathleen ever see Stacey again?" Madden asked. "After she moved to New York?"

"Sure," Ross said. "I couldn't tell her the truth right away. But then a few years after Stacey's disappearance, after my book came out, I told Cathleen I had a surprise for her. And that's when I took her to see her. We drove up to Mt. Lassen. Stacey met us there. We'd often meet in National Parks. Yellowstone one year, Mt. Rushmore another. The Everglades in Florida. Once she was old enough Cathleen would travel alone to meet her."

"So everybody thought she lost both her parents when in fact she lost neither of them."

Madden was talking more to himself than to Marcus.

"Well, she lost one today," Marcus said. "And she may soon lose another."

Madden looked over at him. A sly smile had formed on Marcus's lips. Madden didn't like the look of it.

"Let me give you the rest of the tour," Marcus said. "Let's keep going a little bit."

He motioned for Madden to follow the path, which curved around to the other side of the hill, a little farther. They walked maybe another twenty-five yards and came to an area that looked like the early phases of a construction site. There was a small backhoe sitting there, with its tail and scoop tucked in, scorpion-like. Someone had been tearing up the hill, then grading and leveling it.

Marcus stopped near the machine and took in the vista in front of them. "This is my favorite spot," he said.

The view was arguably better than the one they had just left. All rolling hills, nature, golden California sun, and more picture-perfect vineyards in the distance. As tense as he was, Madden found himself suddenly at peace.

"Ready to hear my proposition?" Marcus asked, breaking the silence.

"Not really, but go ahead."

"How much is Shelby going to pay you?" he asked.

"What do you mean?"

"For finding Stacey, how much was the bonus, a million, two million?"

Madden hesitated a moment, then told him. "A million for Stacey, a million for Ross, and an extra million if I found both of them."

"I'll match that," Marcus said. "And I'll even throw in another million for good measure."

"Excuse me?"

"By my count that's about three million more than what you'd get from Shelby. The fact is you never found Ross and you never will. You can prove exactly nothing."

"Once they learn that that was Stacey living in Manhattan, that she was actually alive all that time, they're gonna figure it out."

"They can conjecture. But that's very different from actual proof."

"They'll prove it," Madden said. "And they'd certainly be able to figure out that you killed me. I assume that's what happens if I don't accept your proposition."

"Oh, no," Marcus said. "I'm not going to do that." Then he pointed the gun at his own head. "I'm going to kill myself. And Cathleen will, too. We have a pact."

Madden looked at him, alarmed.

"I'm sorry if you thought the backhoe was for you," Marcus went on. "We're carving out a spot for events. Company parties, wedding ceremonies, stuff like that. We're going to put a lawn in. I was hoping to have it ready for the upcoming wedding season, but we're a little behind."

"You're out of your mind. Put the gun down."

"I'm not a killer, Hank. I'm a broker. I don't have to tell you about the pain of sexual abuse. You know about it firsthand. And you have a daughter. If someone had done that to her, what would you have done? You'd have wanted to do exactly what I did. You gotta let this go, man. We can all go on living happily ever after. Or you can destroy more lives. The choice is yours, Hank. What's it going to be? The pile of money behind door number one or the dead bodies and carnage behind door number two? I'll give you five seconds to decide. Then I'm pulling the trigger."

Madden stood there paralyzed, his heart racing. Thoughts, memories and ideas darted through his mind, bashing into one another. Marcus started to count.

"One . . . two . . ."

"Wait," Madden said. "Wait a minute. You have to let me think. I'm not the only one here. It's not solely my decision."

He still had to clear the chaos and didn't quite know what he was saying. He just blurted out the loudest thought in his head.

"You're gonna have to give me my phone," he said. "I need to call someone."

"Who?" Marcus asked.

"My guy in New York. My associate. I have a deal with him. He's the one that found Stacey. He gets half of whatever I get from Shelby. He knows everything. I need to speak to him."

"Who is he?"

"He's a guy. Just a guy who knew Candace."

"He the one from the hospital Cathleen told me about?" Marcus asked.

"Yes. Now give me the fucking phone."

Marcus thought about it a moment, then reached into his pocket and handed Madden his phone. There wasn't much of a signal—it was fluctuating between one dot and two—and Madden paced back and forth as he waited for the call to go through. Fremmer picked up on the fourth ring.

"Hey, Hank," he said somberly. "I've been trying to reach you. You get my message? I'm drained, man. I wasn't prepared for this. I thought she was out of the woods. The media's been emailing, calling. I don't have it in me to respond."

"Listen, Max," Madden said. "And listen very carefully. I'm standing here on top of a hill near Sonoma with a guy pointing a gun at his head. He says he's going to kill himself if I don't take his offer and let this whole thing go."

The line went silent.

"You messing with me?" Fremmer said. "If you're messing with me, it's not funny."

"I'm not messing with you, Max. I found out what happened to Ross, but I'm not sure I can prove to Shelby that he's dead. I'm with the guy who killed him. And he's going to kill himself if I don't accept his deal and let him walk away."

"That's an interesting negotiating tactic," Fremmer said. "I haven't heard that one before. He's really got a gun?"

"Pointed at his head." Madden said. "Right now. Three feet away from me. Listen, Ross isn't Braden."

"You've confirmed that?"

"Ross never left the country. He was buried in Woodside, then ground up later and sprinkled around this vineyard. I can't prove any of that, though. So I don't think Shelby will pay me the extra money. But this guy will. And then some. He's talking about four million dollars to walk away from this and not say anything."

"Ever," Marcus said.

"Ever," Madden repeated.

"Hush money," Fremmer said.

"Yes."

"Is he good for it?" Fremmer asked.

Madden looked directly at Marcus. "My associate wants to know if you're good for the money."

Marcus nodded.

"He's a real-estate guy," Madden explained to Fremmer. "He made a fortune in the boom out here."

"I invested my money well, too," Marcus said. "I got in a couple of early home runs, thanks to my connections."

He went into further detail, listing the IPOs he got "friends and family" shares in.

"He got a chunk of Facebook shares that are worth twelve million," Madden told Fremmer.

Fremmer wasn't totally satisfied. "Is he the type of guy who can put four million in cash into a duffel bag and not have anybody notice?" he asked. "Because I don't know too many of those guys. He's not a drug dealer on the side, is he?"

"He wants to know if you can put four million in a suitcase," Madden said.

Marcus thought about it a moment, then said, "I can't. But I have another solution. Hear me out on this. I've given it some thought."

As Marcus explained his plan, Madden wasn't exactly optimistic.

Not at first. But by the time Marcus finished his pitch, Madden had to admit it did sound kind of enticing.

"He says he can put us on his payroll," Madden reported to Fremmer. "He'll pay us out over a few years. It'll be legit. If Shelby paid us we'd have to pay taxes on it anyway."

Marcus had offered Madden a job as head of security for the vineyard. The job didn't entail much, and, if he wanted it Marcus would give him a role in the business. Madden could come and go as he pleased. Additional perks included an open invitation to stay in the guest cottage on the property; he and his wife could even retire there when their kids went off to college.

Fremmer would be the Director of Marketing for Marcus Industries East. They'd actually been looking to expand their real estate holdings into Manhattan. Fremmer would be grossly overpaid for his dream job, making deals in New York City.

There was one big downside.

"This isn't technically legal," Madden warned Fremmer. "If we get caught we could get prosecuted. And you'd lose your kid. I'd be an ex-cop in prison. It'd be rough, man. Real rough. I have a key to the city. There's a plaque on a wall in my old office back at the station house. Whether or not I deserve it, I'm kind of a big deal in the community."

"I'm not there, Hank. I can't tell you what to do. But tell me you want to do this and I'm in. I'll get something on paper for him to sign. I've got an hour or so before I see Zander. I might be able to draft something quickly."

Madden didn't answer. He was lost in thought.

"You hear me, Hank?" Fremmer said.

Madden still didn't answer. He stood there, pretending to listen, nodding his head. Then he turned to Marcus and said:

"He wants to talk to you."

He went to hand him the phone, but just as it touched Marcus's fingertips, Madden let it slide out of his own hand. Marcus juggled it for a second, instinctively knocking it into the air, but he couldn't quite catch it on the way down. As it touched off his hand and fell to the ground, Madden went for the gun. In one motion he embraced Marcus and pushed the weapon up and to the side, away from both of them, and drove his knee into Marcus's groin. Madden felt him go almost limp in his arms, took a step back and knocked the gun out of his hand. Soon it was in his own hand.

He pointed it at Marcus, who was doubled over, his face twisted in pain.

"Hank, you there?"

Fremmer's voice on the phone. He was shouting but Madden could barely hear him.

"You OK?" Fremmer shouted. "You there, man?"

Madden kneeled down to pick up the phone, keeping the gun trained on Marcus. His heart was pounding.

"Yeah, I'm here," Madden said into the phone a little breathlessly.

"What happened?"

"I got the gun. I got the gun away from him."

"Nice work, Detective."

I've still got it, Madden thought, smiling. But then he watched Marcus straighten up, look at him and wince. He was still in pain, but no longer debilitating pain. And now he was coming at him.

Madden waited 'til the last second. 'Til Marcus was almost upon him. Then he squeezed the trigger.

A click, but nothing. He squeezed again. Another click. And again nothing.

Marcus put his hand over the top of the gun, gently taking it from Madden's hand, which didn't resist.

"Was never loaded," Marcus said, forcing a smile through another grimace. "I told you I'm not a killer. I'm a broker. So, what can I tell the seller? Do we have a deal?"

34/ Fourteen Postcards

Zander Bell lived in a five-story brownstone on West 84th Street. The building was similar to Fremmer's, only nowhere near as well maintained. He pressed the intercom button marked 5B and smiled at the intercom camera. Zander was expecting him. He hiked up the five flights with his backpack on, slowing down for the last two. He was slightly winded by the time he got there, which disappointed him a little. He thought he was in better shape.

Bell greeted him at his door.

"Hello there," he said with a warm smile. "Sorry about the walk up."

"Drew Masters," Fremmer said, shaking his hand.

Zander's appearance shocked Fremmer. The man looked nothing like the guy in the handful of videos Fremmer had found on the Internet. In those he had a round, slightly chubby face and a full head of dark curly hair that he parted on the left. The guy in front of him looked older, his face was narrow. He looked gaunt. Although he was wearing a baseball hat, Fremmer noticed he had no hair above his ears below the border of the cap. His head appeared to be shaved.

Fremmer was also wearing a hat, a knit beanie. It wasn't much of a disguise but he wanted to change his appearance in some way in case Bell recognized him from somewhere. So he shaved, put on a hipster cap and a New York Rangers track jacket. He also wore an LG collar-style wireless headphone with retractable earbuds wrapped around his neck. All he had to do was double-tap the call button to redial the last person he'd called. Deliberately, Chu.

They sat down at a small table in the middle of the small living room. It was a nice day. Bell had the window wide open, a nice breeze blowing in.

"So, are you at all familiar with how this works? Have you been to intuits or psychics before?"

"Now and then," Fremmer said. "I can't call myself a regular, but I've had some trauma in my life recently and wanted to speak to someone. I poked around on the web, saw you were close by and highly rated on Yelp. Your reviews are really good."

Bell thanked him for the compliment. "So what I do is I have my oracle," he said, "which is this stack of cards." He pointed to a shoebox on the table next to him. "I'm a little different from other intuits in that instead of standard Tarot cards I use artwork postcards I've collected from around the world."

"I saw that," Fremmer said.

"Everything can be interpreted in different ways. I read what I see in the cards and intuit how it applies to you and your life. A lot of my impressions are meant to be taken symbolically, but some of it may be taken more literally. It's also important what you see in the cards. I'm here to help you find your way around obstacles, understand the circumstances and relationships you're in, help you make positive decisions that have positive outcomes. I want to be clear, I can tell you what I see in your future but I can't predict exactly what your future will be. I'm here to help you see your life more clearly and recognize your strengths and weaknesses and bring out your talents. Make the most of them."

"That sounds good," Fremmer said.

"OK, then. There's the matter of payment. I don't take cash, only credit cards. I have no money in the apartment."

"Oh," Fremmer said. That was a problem. His credit card said Max Fremmer on it, not Drew Masters. "I only brought cash. I thought all you guys only took cash. You know, for tax reasons."

"No, this is a completely above-board business. I pay taxes."

"Well, how about I give you $200 instead of the usual $175 to make an exception this one time. You can still report it if you want."

Bell thought about it a moment, then agreed. He talked a good game, but he didn't seem like the inflexible type, especially when it came to getting paid. Fremmer handed him the money.

"I flip 14 cards," Bell said after he put the cash in his pocket. "We talk about each card for a short time. After I flip them all, we'll have a longer talk."

"So it's kind of like therapy?" Fremmer asked.

"Very much so," Bell said. "But unlike with a therapist you're free to record our session and take it with you. Most of my clients do."

"I can record this?"

"Sure."

Fantastic, Fremmer thought. When he and Chu talked about this meeting, Fremmer got the sense that Chu was choosing his words carefully and trying to guide Fremmer into making suggestions for Chu to follow. From what he knew of the law, Fremmer gathered that Chu didn't want him to become an agent of the police, which could create appearances of entrapment if not handled correctly.

The cops didn't have enough on Zander to get a warrant for Fremmer to wear a wire. If Chu didn't play it right, a defense attorney like Morton could pick their case apart, argue they had illegally obtained key pieces of evidence.

So Fremmer told Chu exactly what he wanted to hear: He'd go fishing, put whatever he caught on ice, and bring the catch back to the detectives. After the reading with Zander, Fremmer would meet Chu at the Lenwich sandwich shop a block away, on 84th and Amsterdam. Chu was there now, waiting for him. If things got testy, Fremmer said he'd call and alert him. Otherwise he'd meet him there.

Zander's offer to let him record the session just made it a lot easier for Fremmer to report on the meeting. He could simply play the file back for Chu. And there'd be no question whether he was lying or coloring his story.

So Fremmer put his iPhone on the table, opened the Voice Memos app and hit record. Then he asked Zander to state that he was allowing him to record the session.

Zander complied, then started the session.

"So why'd you come to me today, Drew?" he asked. "What's troubling you?"

"Well, about six months ago my fiancée had an accident and is now confined to a wheelchair."

"What kind of accident, do you mind my asking?"

"We were on vacation and we were bodysurfing—I'd encouraged her to come out with me, I pushed her to do it—and she ended up in the curl of the wave and it drove her into the sand. She broke her neck."

"Wow," Bell said. "I'm sorry. That's really tragic. And you feel responsible for the accident?"

"Yes, there's that. And then I'm not sure I want to marry her anymore."

Fremmer left out the part about hating himself for feeling that way. He spoke flatly, not trying to give Bell too many additional hints. Fremmer wanted to see how much of a fraud he was, but he'd probably already told him too much.

"OK," Bell replied confidently. "I understand. Let's flip a card then, shall we, and see what I see."

Bell pulled out a hefty stack of postcards from the shoebox—maybe fifty—and gave them a good shuffle. He was pretty deft at it; he could have been a casino dealer.

He turned over the top postcard. Fremmer found the image arresting: A photo of a man, his eyes looking downward to his right, shot from the chest up. The paper the photo was printed on was damaged and discolored. It had water stains all over it, like it had accidentally become a coaster. Of the several moisture rings left by glasses placed on the photo, two stood out prominently: one over the left side of the guy's face, the other high on his chest circling his heart. The subject of the photo looked like a depressed Hemingway in his early forties. But it wasn't Hemingway.

"Ah, the Rudolph Stingel self portrait," Bell said. "I got that one in Venice. 2013. Palazzo Grassi. During The Biennale."

Fremmer looked more closely at the card. He realized then that it was a painting, not a photograph. He got the sense that the artist had found the photo sitting on a cluttered desk buried amongst other papers and decided it was the perfect subject for a painting. Now that he knew what it was he found it quite striking.

Bell turned his gaze on the card for a few seconds, then lifted his head and stared straight ahead in silence, letting whatever thoughts came into his mind take over. Or at least it looked that way to Fremmer.

"This speaks to your forlornness," he said. "Your head and heart are in conflict. Have you been drinking?"

Fremmer conceded that he had.

"I see you drinking to excess," Bell said. "It's discoloring your thinking. You are no longer sure of who you are and what you stand for. You seek to lower yourself, even destroy yourself, so she will push you away and make the decision for you."

Damn, the guy's pretty good, Fremmer thought. He was starting to like him.

"What should I do?" Fremmer asked.

"For starters, stop drinking."

He flipped card two. Another realistic painting. Equally provocative, of a young woman leaning back in an ornate chair, her dress open at the top to expose her bra. Bell told Fremmer it was by Balthus, a Polish-French modern artist, full name Balthasar Klossowski de Rola.

"You are concerned about the sexual aspects of your relationship. You no longer feel sexually inclined toward her. You don't see her as she once was, a sexual creature."

There was some truth to that, too. But it was more complicated than Bell's simplistic explanation. He'd always found her attractive and always would.

It went on like that for a while. Fremmer began to realize that Bell could read anything he wanted into the cards. Their reverse meaning had meaning. A tiny portion of an artwork could represent a big, overarching theme. It was quite remarkable.

Finally, Fremmer had enough. It was time to do what he came to do, what he'd *told* Chu he was going do. It was time to go fishing.

Before Bell flipped card eight, Fremmer said, "How about I flip the next one?"

"Come again?" Bell said.

"I'm going to flip the next one. And tell you what I think about your current predicament."

Fremmer reached over and did just that.

Card eight was a painting of a human skeleton riding the skeleton of a dog. Fremmer recoiled a little. Bell stared at it, slightly alarmed.

"Another Stingel," he said. "An ominous sign. The same artist rarely comes up twice in one session."

Stingel? The same guy that did the self-portrait? The two paintings looked nothing alike. Fremmer turned the card over and looked at the inscription. Bell was right. It was another Stingel.

"Who are you?" Bell asked.

"You know what I see in this image," Fremmer said. "I see a woman walking her dog into an intersection on Central Park West—"

"She's riding the dog."

"Or maybe the dog is riding her," Fremmer countered. *Two can play this game*, he thought. "Or it's Cerberus. The dog that guards the entrance to Hell. Which is where you're afraid you're going."

Bell stood up. "I'm going to ask you one more time. Who are you?"

"I'm a friend of Candace. She died this morning. Did you know that?"

Bell didn't acknowledge anything. But he also didn't deny it. He just stood there, looking angry. "You need to leave," he said. "You're not welcome here anymore. The session is over."

"I found something interesting online, Zander. It looks like in your spare time you're an actor, aren't you?"

"I used to be," he said. "Many years ago."

"I found your acting reel on Vimeo. The 'Zander Bell Acting Reel' is its title, I believe. Entertaining stuff. You do some really nice character work. Very convincing. Especially that student film where you played a homeless person."

"I was a hobo. There's a difference. And that was close to ten years ago. What's that got to do with anything?"

"You took money from the Lucidity Center. You were working with them to bring people in for workshops from around the country and around the world. You were good at it. Except you were skimming money. Thousands of dollars. They thought Candace took it. But it was really you. And Candace figured it out and told you she knew."

"Get out," Bell said. "I've heard enough of this shit."

"Here's something else. You were arrested four years ago for scamming foreigners looking for short-term rentals in the city."

"That was a misunderstanding."

"A sixty-thousand-dollar misunderstanding? Right. Here's how I'm intuiting it. As part of your plea arrangement, you were put on probation for five years. But your next offense was mandatory prison time. Something tells me you really didn't want to go to prison."

"If you don't get out right now, I'm calling the police. I run a legitimate business. I pay my taxes. I haven't skimmed anything from anybody."

"Go ahead. Call the police. I dare you." Fremmer stood up and picked up the stack of cards from the table—the stack Zander had been flipping from—and threw them in the air. They rained down all over the room.

"Don't touch my cards," Bell said.

"Your precious oracle? I thought you were The Oracle, Zander. Isn't that what you told Ronald? It's over, Zander. The police found you on a surveillance video. You were taking pictures of him. You know they can find those even if you delete them from your phone."

The mention of "phone" reminded Bell that Fremmer's was still recording their conversation. The screen had gone dark but Bell knew enough to know it was still going. He went to snatch it but Fremmer got to it first.

That little battle lost, Bell told him to leave again. He pulled Fremmer's cash from his pocket and handed the bills back to him.

"Here's your money."

Fremmer took the money. Why not?

"I'll go. But not before I have a look around and make sure you aren't still holding on to your homeless person outfit."

Fremmer made for the door that looked like it led to the bedroom. He went into the room and headed straight for the closet. Bell was smart enough to have shed any evidence, so Fremmer didn't expect to find anything; he'd leave that for the police to sort out. His job, like it always had been, was to rile the opposing team.

He began poking around the room.

"What are you doing?" Bell asked. "This is my bedroom. You're not allowed in here."

"It's in the cards, Zander. Isabelle sold you out. She was the one who told me you worked together in the aquarium shop downtown."

That struck a nerve.

"She told you that?"

"And a lot more. The detectives went to see her last night."

"You're lying."

"You knew Candace's whole routine," Fremmer said. "You knew she walked her dog every morning at a certain time. Maybe you even walked the mutt with her a couple of times. You and Candace hooked up. That's what Isabelle said."

"Isabelle didn't know abou—" He caught himself at the last second, but it was too late. Fremmer had given him a tiny length of rope and he just hung himself with it.

"Give me the phone," he said.

From the look on Bell's face Fremmer realized it was time to call mayday. With his right hand he double-clicked the call button on his headset. He looked down at the phone in his left hand and thought it was dialing. But before he could confirm it was, Bell came at him full tilt, smashing him backwards into a set of drawers that had a flat-panel TV on top of it. The middle of Fremmer's back met the top edge of the bureau. His shoulder blades knocked into the TV, toppling it against the wall. It hurt like hell, but he held onto the phone.

Fremmer came right back at Bell and body checked him, sending him sprawling, regrettably, onto the bed, a much more comfortable landing spot than Fremmer had encountered. Soon it was a full on cage match with table lamps and glass shattering, books falling off their shelves, and the shelves themselves falling. Most of the damage was Bell's doing. Fremmer, still guarding the phone, was mainly trying to evade him and delay.

"You came into my apartment and now I'm defending myself from your vicious attack," Bell said to Fremmer, circling him in a wrestler's hunched stance.

"I'm not taping the conversation anymore," Fremmer replied, struggling to get away from him.

"I'm recording it," Bell said. "I record every session."

He suddenly got Fremmer in a chokehold, dragging him toward the front of the living room. He was stronger than Fremmer thought. The dude had moves. He'd trained. He probably wrestled in high school.

Fremmer grabbed onto the table they'd used for the session. The shoebox fell, the postcards scattering onto the carpet. Fremmer thought Bell was trying to get him to the front door. But the window was what he was after.

"Put the knife down," Zander shouted.

Fremmer didn't have a knife. He wished he did. *Come on, Chu*, he thought. *Was he hearing this? What was taking him so long? Could he not get in the building?*

Fremmer suddenly realized he was in a very bad spot. He still had a hold on the table leg but his head was halfway out the window. He'd fit through the window, but the table wouldn't. It was the only thing keeping him inside the apartment.

"You shouldn't have come here," Zander said.

Fremmer hit him with the phone, trying to gouge his eyes with the corners. Finally, Bell wrestled it out of his hand and chucked it out the window. Fremmer heard it land in the street below. He screamed for help.

Just as he was losing his grip on the table leg he heard someone or something slam up against the door. But breaking down a front door in Manhattan was easier said than done. Finally, on the third try, the lock broke. One more slam and Chu was in the apartment, his gun drawn.

Bell took a step toward the door, allowing Fremmer to get his head—and the rest of his body—safely away from the window.

"On your knees," Chu said, gasping for breath.

"I didn't do anything," Bell said. "We were having a session and this man attacked me. I was just trying to defend myself."

"You OK?" Chu said to Fremmer.

"Not really," Fremmer said. "But I'm a lot better than my iPhone lying down in the street. I hope it can be resurrected. I recorded everything."

"What's on it?" Chu asked.

"Enough," Fremmer said.

"Enough for what?"

"Enough to put you on the cover of the *Post* and the *Daily News*, Detective," Fremmer said.

35/ Epilogue

ECEMBER, A LITTLE MORE THAN SEVEN MONTHS AFTER CANDACE had died and Ronald was exonerated, Fremmer was with Denise in the Starbucks on 76th Street and Columbus Avenue. He was working on his laptop when a man in a Yankees hat and glasses approached him. Fremmer didn't recognize him but the man clearly knew him.

"I've been to about every Starbucks on the Upper West Side. I knew I'd find you." He turned to the woman behind him, who was standing there a little shyly. "I told you he'd be in one of them," he said to her.

They were both in their forties. She petite, he very tall. Fremmer knew him from somewhere but couldn't remember where.

"You remember me?" the guy said.

"Yeah," Fremmer said, searching his memory. *Was he from his spinning class? An old client?*

"Brian."

"Hey, good to see you," Fremmer said, his delivery a little too disingenuous. Brian realized Fremmer didn't have a clue who he was.

"Brian Tynan," he said. He took off his hat, revealing his wavy salt-and-pepper hair.

And then it came to Fremmer.

"Brian," he said. "Your wife ran off with your contractor."

"Yeah," Brian said. "I mean no. He was *a* contractor. Not our contractor."

"Oh, yeah," Fremmer said. He stood up and extended a hand. "You look good, man."

"I feel good," Brian said. He pulled his companion closer to the table and introduced her. "This is Sylvia, my fiancée."

Nice dark eyes. Mediterranean complexion. Thin. She was attractive, Fremmer thought, shaking her hand. "Wow, fiancée," he said to Brian. "You got right back on the horse, didn't you, you maniac? I had fiancée once. Tell them about her, Denise."

"She was taller than me," Denise said. "And had a better sense of humor. Nice to meet you both."

"We saw you on TV," Sylvia said to Fremmer. "Brian talks about you all the time and how he was there that day the police came to speak to you."

Fremmer suddenly remembered Brian *was* there, he was the prospect he was speaking to when Chu first approached him.

"That was up the street," Fremmer said. "The 81st and Columbus Starbucks," he said. "You'd come from work. You were in your suit. That's why I didn't recognize you now. Now you're all like hip and cool."

Brian wasn't all that hip and cool. But he was dressed in jeans and a thin ribbed down jacket that were better tailored than his suit.

"That was a pretty amazing story," Sylvia went on.

"You don't know the half of it," Denise said.

"You were the only one who believed that homeless person didn't push her," Sylvia said. "No one else did, did they?"

"Well, no," he said, thinking about it a moment. "I guess not."

"That guy owes you his life," Brian said. "And so do I, frankly."

Fremmer looked at him. The guy seemed quite emotional. *Were those tears welling up in his eyes? What am I missing here*, he thought.

"I sold my book," Brian announced.

Fremmer blinked. "Really?"

"That's wonderful," Denise said.

"I did what you said. I made the main character a woman and I sold it. I gave him a vagina," Brian explained, letting out a laugh. "A few houses wanted it. There was an auction in the end. Closed bids."

Fremmer was so shocked he couldn't say anything. He didn't even remember what his story was about. He vaguely remembered the villain. *Evil Steve Jobs*. That was it.

"They sold the movie rights, too," Brian added. "But it's not big money unless it gets made."

This was getting more absurd by the second, Fremmer thought.

"It totally changed my life," Brian said. "All of a sudden my ex-wife was trying to get back with me. But I'd met Sylvia already, so I wasn't even tempted. We're looking to get married this coming summer, or maybe in the spring if we can nail everything down quickly enough."

"You picked a spot yet?" Fremmer asked.

"We're thinking maybe Maine. It's a second marriage for both of us, so we're probably going to keep it small."

"Oh, no," Fremmer said, glancing over at Denise, who knew exactly where he was going. "You gotta go big. You're doing destination, you gotta do real destination, none of this Maine shit. How 'bout California? We've been working for this guy who has a winery out in Sonoma. He just started doing weddings on the property. We can probably get you a deal. Check this out."

He motioned for the two of them to sit down—there was an extra chair at the small table because Denise wasn't using it—and then he went off in search of a third chair for himself. When he returned and sat down, he turned his laptop toward the couple and pulled up a link from Madden.

Marcus had posted a slick promotional video on the winery's website. The wedding he shot took place a couple of months ago, in late October. Fremmer had never met the bride, a lawyer named Carolyn Dupuy, who married Ted Cogan, a doctor who'd been a suspect in a murder case Madden had worked on several years ago. Fremmer didn't know the full story, nor did he want to, but Madden had arranged an extremely attractive rate for the wedding.

The video was beyond impressive. Almost the entire thing was shot using drones. The opening shot had the bride and groom walking down the aisle with the panoramic views of the hills and valley around. It was magnificent. So, too, were the shots of the guests who'd gathered on the hill.

The reception footage, interspersed with video shot from the ground, was equally compelling. Whoever booked the music was a genius. The first act was a talented Sinatra impersonator. That alone would've been enough for any glorious wedding. But act two was J.J. Carradine performing five songs from a new album that hadn't been released yet.

"Isn't that J.J. Carradine?" Sylvia said when she saw him appear on the small stage. "Oh, my God, it is. I used to love that guy. I always wondered what happened to him. His band had all those hits. And then he disappeared."

"Writer's block," Fremmer explained. "Musicians get it, too."

"That looks beautiful," Brian said, mesmerized by the sweeping closing shot. "But I don't think I can afford it. The book deal wasn't that good."

"Let me see what I can do," Fremmer said. "It doesn't have to be as elaborate as that one."

"You work for the owner?" Sylvia asked.

"They have a small office here. I do real estate marketing and acquisition for him in New York. Denise has been helping me out. They're really a West Coast operation, but they're expanding."

"So you're not a book doctor anymore?" Brian asked.

"Hung up my cleats on that," Fremmer said.

"His fans are still distraught," Denise deadpanned.

"I tried to email you," Brian said. "But I never heard back. Now I know why."

"Sorry about that. I kind of started ignoring emails from that address. And a lot of other things for a little while. But I've got this new gig now. Better pay, less hustle."

"Well, you were good," Brian said. "Your advice paid off for me. I got my advance check last week. Which is why I wanted to find you. I have something for you."

He stood up, reached into his front pocket, pulled out his wallet, opened it, and took out a check. Fremmer thought for a moment he was going to show him his advance. But the check he placed on the table beside Fremmer's laptop was made out to Max Fremmer.

For five thousand dollars.

"I want you to have that," Brian said. "That's what I was supposed to pay you."

Fremmer looked at the check, envisioned it briefly in his own wallet, then decided nah, he couldn't. He picked it up, folded it, then tore it half, not once but three times. He handed the little pieces to Brian.

"You're an honorable man," Fremmer said. "But keep your money. I said the advice was free. And I meant it."

Brian put the pieces in his pocket and shook Fremmer's hand.

"I'll never forget what you said, Mr. Fremmer."

"Max."

"I'll never forget what you said, Max. 'Do whatever you do with conviction. Always.' I say it all the time now."

"Words to live by, my friend," Fremmer said. "Words to live by."

36/ Acknowledgments

WHILE THIS IS A WORK OF FICTION I HAVE A FEW PEOPLE TO THANK for helping me keep it in the realm of reality. As always, I took advantage of the colorful commentary and bits of inspiration Commander Tony Dixon of the Menlo Park Police Department provided me. I also want to mention Jim Simpson, Detective Sergeant (Ret), who graciously chatted with me about some of his old cases a few years back. For legal counsel I have two fellow soccer dads to thank: Don Rollock, former Nassau County ADA turned criminal defense attorney, and Jason Berland, former New York County ADA turned criminal defense attorney. For the medical portions of the book, I turned to the incomparable Sanford Littwin, MD, who gave me his unvarnished opinions with his usual gusto. Special thanks to my agent John Silbersack and esteemed publisher Peter Mayer for putting up with my delays in writing this novel (I do have a day job, guys, though that's not an excuse). Big props to Adrienne Friedberg, who went through a draft of the book, tightened a sentence or two, and got me to the end. My father, Martin, and John Falcone, thank you for reading early drafts and making comments. And editors Chelsea Cutchens and Tracy Carns, thanks for your input and shepherding the book to publication. Last but not least, I couldn't have written this without my wife Lisa, who puts up with my shenanigans, good and bad.